The Billionaire's Shrubbery

POWER COUPLES

DANIKA BLOOM

FIRE LILY PRESS

Published by Fire Lily Press

Library and Archives Canada Cataloguing in Publication

Bloom, Danika, 1966- , author
The Billionaire's Shrubbery / Danika Bloom

Issued in print and electronic formats.
ISBN 978-1-7780384-8-8 (paperback)
ISBN 978-1-7780384-6-4 (ebook)

1. Title

This is a work of fiction. Names, characters, businesses, and events are from the author's imagination. Any resemblance to actual people, living or dead, is coincidental. Funny ... but coincidental.

Cover design: SGA Creative Services

Editor: Jennifer Sommersby, Plumfield Editing

Rescuing a wilting heart may seem a daunting task, but laughter and love are powerful nourishments for the human spirit.

— VIRGINIA BEACH

<h1>1. Virginia</h1>

BONSAI BONANZA

Uber rich people are like the deadly nightshade of gen pop—they might look all pretty and harmless, but they lure you in for a taste of their sweet lives, and then, *gotcha!*, poison your heart and leave you for dead.

I know this in my bones, and still, I torture myself by working for them. But only because they're the people willing to pay what I charge to care for their pretty potted plants. That's my job, wisteria whisperer to the wealthy witches and wolves of West Vancouver.

Don't get me wrong. I love what I do. I just wish I could do it for people who didn't look at me like I was an invasive species out to steal their precious resources. So, when I stumble across a cardboard box on the sidewalk as I'm walking to the bus stop, I hesitate to slow down, but ... there's something green peeking above the open top. I try to look casual, like, "I don't really care what's in your trash. I don't need your rich people's hand-me-downs."

But, whoa! There are four bonsai trees cuddled up inside. I look around, make sure nobody's watching, and take one out. Judging by the circumference of the trunk, I'd guess it's at least a hundred years old. Three others are the same. Then I see the small note with wobbly handwriting:

Free if you promise not to kill them.

I look up at the house beyond the hedge. Leaving plants like these out on the sidewalk, prone to kidnap by any old conifer-killing klutz, makes no sense. I lift the box and carry it up the winding path to the front door. The grass is months past needing to be cut, the garden that edges the long walkway is overrun with weeds. If this was the opening scene of a true crime, re-creation documentary, I'd be the subject who was foolish enough to waltz straight into harm's way.

Despite my unease, I ring the bell.

After a long minute, an elderly man answers.

"Oh, good," he says, nodding at the box in my arms, "you found them before a dog did. I put them out a few minutes ago."

I don't know what I expected him to say, but it wasn't that. "Umm, did you know these trees are precious? And they're quite tricky to care for. You want to make sure the right person takes them home."

"Do you know how to care for them, young lady?"

"I do," I say, "and it's clear you do too. I don't understand. Why are you getting rid of them?"

He looks me right in the eye and scowls with the expertise of a man who's been practicing his stare for seventy years. "They were my wife's trees. Her pride and joy. She gave her goddamned shrubs more attention than she gave me. I don't know how to care for those tiny trees because she wouldn't let me touch them. Told me I'd kill them. So I thought, better to re-home the bloody things than have her *tut-tutting* me from the great beyond."

The tone in his voice suggests congratulations on his wife's death are in order, but the pain in his eyes says otherwise. "I'm so sorry for your loss."

"Well, my loss is your gain. Mabel, my wife, said they were priceless. The pots alone are antiques worth thousands. We bought them in Japan in the 1970s."

"Not that I wouldn't love to care for these, but why not sell them?"

"Bah. Money. Do I look like I need more? I'll be gone long before I can gamble myself into bankruptcy." He gives me a serious look.

I return a questioning one.

"That was a joke." He sighs. "Nobody understands my jokes anymore. At least Mabel did. One thing I miss about her—she knew when to laugh." He taps the edge of the box. "So you like plants and you know how to care for them?"

"I do. I have a graduate degree in botany and own a plant-care business. I was just heading home from a client up the street."

He waves his hand. "Put that on the floor. Come in. I'd like to show you my greenhouse. My *wife's* greenhouse. Haven't got a goddamn clue what I'm doing. I just put water on everything and hope that Mabel and I have separate rooms once I shed this mortal coil, or I'll be spending an eternity hearing about how I murdered her babies. God help me."

"My name is Virginia." I extend a hand.

He tips his chin. "Henry. Henry Bernard."

Mr. Bernard leads me through several rooms to the back of his mansion and into the most gorgeous greenhouse I've ever seen. And I've seen my fair share of greenhouses in mansions. This structure was obviously built with love. But the contents? It looks more like a plant palliative care unit with a side of morgue than a greenhouse.

While Mr. Bernard sits in a cushioned, wingback chair reading a book, I spend ninety minutes looking over hundreds of plants, checking soil moisture, making mental notes of which ones might be saved. Most of the pots contain rare varieties of flowers and small shrubs. If Mrs. Bernard was the green thumb her husband claims, my guess is she must've passed away several months ago, since many of these plants are too far gone. They've definitely missed their spring pruning and fertilizing.

"Good news or bad news first?" I ask, pointing to what I assume is the late Mrs. Bernard's chair beside him.

"Sit," he says. "Just tell me, do I need to start kicking puppies to secure my place in an easier hell than the one I'm expecting?"

"Well, like people, all plants have a life span. We can't expect them to live forever—except maybe a well-cared-for bonsai tree. But what you have here?" I wave around the room. "There are some unfortunate losses, but a lot of these plants can be saved."

"And you can do that? Get me back in Mabel's good graces? We had fifty-five good years together. I'd hate to ruin things now."

"I can certainly do my best. And I'd hope she'd recognize that if you hired me to do this, you're doing *your* best, too, and she'll forgive a few oopsies."

Mr. Bernard grunts. "Would you do that for me?"

I nod. And my stomach twists. After three years, I still hate this part of self-employment—asking for money to do something I'd gladly do for free and most clients could easily pay double my rate for. I steel myself for the grunt that expresses my rate is too high.

But Mr. Bernard doesn't puff when I tell him my rate is fifty dollars an hour. He doesn't wince when I say I need to spend at least twenty hours, preferably within the next few days, to do my best for his plants. And then two hours a week to make sure what we save flourishes.

"Too goddamn much death in my life this past year. That's a small price to pay to keep what Mabel loved alive."

"With all due respect to your wife, Mr. Bernard, I'd love to have you work alongside me so you can experience the joy Mrs. Bernard got from caring for these plants. And you might think I'm crazy, but her plants will appreciate it too."

He scoffs. "You sound just like her. She talked to them like they understood what she was saying. She hated when I cursed in front of them."

"They do understand. They absorb the energy."

Mr. Bernard holds eye contact with me for several long seconds, and I wonder if he's worried his grief has been hurting the plants. I risk it and guess that he's spent hours each day out here in his well-loved chair. "More would've died if you hadn't sat with them. Every time you exhale, it's fuel for them. We'll make Mrs. Bernard proud, I promise."

"I'm paying you forty hours up-front since I don't want to be in your debt if I die between visits. You keep track of your time, and tell me when I owe you more." He pushes himself to standing. "I'll get my checkbook."

I grab an Uber home since I can't carry the four boxes of plants Mr. Bernard insists I take with me—the bonsai trees, plus all the flowers that are likely too dead to save. He doesn't want to look at them anymore. He told me if I can save the plants, I can keep them. And if I can't, I should sell the pots and pocket the money.

A few blocks from home, I text my sister, Georgia, and ask her to come out to carry in a few of my prizes.

She meets me at the curb. "Really, Virginia?"

"Just help me get them inside. I don't want to leave them on the sidewalk for someone to steal."

"Who would steal boxes of dead plants? And these are going in your room."

"Chill out. I'm not holding on to many of them. Not for long."

On the ride home, I'd looked up the pots that the bonsais are planted in. I snapped pictures, and Google Images found their sisters. Mr. Bernard hadn't exaggerated. Each is valued at over a thousand dollars. They're pretty, but really, half a month's rent for one ceramic pot?

Rich people ... I truly will never understand them.

I pull the check from my wallet and dangle it for Georgia to see. She eyes it, then me, like it might be counterfeit. She attempts to steal the flimsy paper from my grip, but I snap it away.

"The rent you owe me?"

"The dead plants will pay you back. I'm using this to attend the Come Into Power seminar next month. Deadline to apply is Friday, and this is exactly what it costs. It's too perfect. Obviously meant to be."

"Virginia," she warns, picking up one box and then another, finding her balance. "Another get-rich-quick scheme?"

"Ha. No." *It's not.* "I'm not an idiot."

Georgia lifts a teasing eyebrow. I'd smack her, but my arms are full as well. "This is an investment—in me, in my future."

"Yes, because you're an *entrepreneur.*" Georgia almost chokes while exaggerating the French pronunciation.

"One day, you'll see."

"I'll see when you've paid me all the back rent." Georgia pushes open our door with her butt, and I follow her inside with Mr. Bernard's check burning a hole in my pocket.

The plants from the four boxes cover our kitchen table and the counter beside the fridge. Aside from the bonsai trees, all the other plants really are too far gone to save. It breaks my heart, but I empty their soil into the compost bin in the backyard. Our ground-floor suite is too small for two people, but the giant yard more than makes up for it. And the landlord lets us pay part of our rent in-kind—which means I make sure the gardens are well cared for in exchange for a hundred-dollar discount on my share.

With the pots soaking in the bathtub, I make dinner while my sister hand-stitches the final touches on a 1950s dress pattern in our living room-slash-studio. *Unsolvable Crimes: Solved* plays in the background. We've seen every episode at least twice and have turned the show into a predinner drinking game we call "Truth or Lie."

To earn a sip of wine, we have to declare whether the criminal is telling the truth or lying, before the narrator's voiceover explains how the investigator was able to tell. I am the reigning champion, able to read body language and tone of voice from the first time we watch an episode. Aside from being a plant whisperer, that's my superpower.

"Instead of wasting two thousand dollars on a weekend listening to a billionaire give you business tips you can learn for free on the internet, I think you should invest in your education—get a certificate in criminology. You could make so much more money than you'll ever make watering plants."

Georgia has said this more than once, and I've considered it more than once. And yet I always come to the same conclusion: one path is filled with lightness and life and oxygen and hope, the other is paved with horror and sadness and the broken lives of victims and their families. There's not enough money in all the world to convince me to take that route. I prefer to keep unsolvable crimes trapped in the frame of our old TV, right where they belong.

Silence is my answer. Georgia redirects the conversation. "Guess who I saw on the mid-day news."

"Good guy or bad guy?"

"Depends ..." she contorts her mouth and wrinkles her nose.

My enthusiasm about the bonsai trees and the giant check in my pocket deflates. I know exactly who she's talking about. "Did he save a bus full of puppies from driving off a cliff?"

Virginia laughs. "Close, actually. He donated his clinic's services to help over a hundred dogs that were in a puppy mill."

I roll my eyes.

"He's still not wearing a wedding ring," my sister sing-songs.

The alleged love of my life—Frank—who I fell for during my sophomore year of university and graduated two years ahead of me. He went on to veterinary school, promising we'd do the long-distance thing, that he'd stay faithful so we could build a real future together after we both finished our respective programs. But he fell for a woman who offered to bankroll his clinic.

I should've known better. If Dad taught me nothing else, it's that men will always level up, given the chance.

2. Will

SLEEPLESS IN SEATTLE ... AND L.A. ...
AND VANCOUVER ...

I kick open the door to my penthouse and leave my carry-on for the housekeeper to deal with in the morning. It's after midnight, and even though my body screams for sleep, my brain is on fire. I turn left from my elevator entrance, down the hall to my bedroom. Dim lights in the ceiling activate a few steps ahead of me.

I hang my suit and pull on a pair of sweat pants. Even though I live alone, walking naked around my condo is not an option. With three brothers who have access to my suite and use it at their leisure, I never know what I'm coming home to after being on the road.

Despite having been away for six weeks, delivering my Come Into Power seminar in fourteen cities across Canada and the US, the odds of finding my place exactly as I left it are about zero, since cleaners don't come in while I'm not here.

I head to my living room to see what they've done this time.

"Hey, bro." My identical twin brother yawns his greeting from the dark corner.

"Horse. What's up?" I can see his shape, but not his face. "Alexa, full lights."

"You bastard," he complains, covering his head with a throw cushion.

"Seriously? Me? Why else would you be up after midnight unless it was to see my face when I saw what you pricks did to my place?"

I scope the room. My giant TV screen is intact, still mounted on the wall. The white patterns in my sixteen-by-sixteen area rug are still white. I don't see any tears in my leather furniture. I sniff the air. Smells like nothing, just the way it should.

Horse drops the pillow. "Alexa, lights at fifty percent. I wasn't sure I'd see you in the morning and I wanted to check in, make sure you're surviving."

"And if I say I'm not?" I collapse into the Herman Miller lounge chair beside him. "You going to offer to trade places with me and deliver the European seminars?"

"And have to cut this glorious hair? Shave my beard? Wear a suit and tie every day? Not a chance."

"When was the last time you needed a security guard at your hotel door to keep the women away? Isn't that worth a razor and having to dress like a grown-ass man for a few days?"

He shakes his head.

"Horse, why are you here?" I'm exhausted and my brother's life of freedom—because he was born twenty-one minutes after me—is pissing me off.

"We had seven requests for refunds from the San Francisco event. And four so far from Seattle."

"Take it out of my salary."

"Not the point. What's going on?"

Nothing new. Nothing I haven't been dealing with for a

decade. "Nothing a few nights in my own bed can't fix. Speaking of—" I stand and wave toward the door. "I've got to be up at five to go over the notes for the day."

Horse punches my arm on his way by. "Dinner. My place tomorrow. We'll all be there."

"Sounds good."

He lets himself out, and I fall into my chair.

"Alexa. Time?"

"It's eleven fifty-one p.m."

"Alexa, call Joe."

"Calling Joe," the invisible voice replies, followed seconds later by the sound of a phone ringing.

"Hey, Will. You home?"

"Yeah, for a minute."

"In bed? Ready?"

"Sadly, not. I'm amped. And I have to be up in five hours."

Joe inhales long and loud, then sighs as he exhales. Being the good Pavlovian dog I am, I mimic him. Then Joe yawns. I open my mouth to copy him, but the trigger doesn't work. "Fuck," I moan.

"Not helping yourself, Will. You at least lying down?"

"Ish. There's no point going to bed. I'll nap in my recliner. Just do this thing, Joe. I am so done with today. Hey, Alexa, lights off."

The room darkens, but it's not pitch-black. City light pollution filters into the space. I close my eyes.

"Alexa, share cameras three and four," Joe says. Tiny blue lights from the infrared cameras on either side of my TV come on so Joe, who's somewhere in Texas, can see me.

I rarely go to bed without his company. He's on call, twenty-four hours a day, seven days a week. He stays with me until he can see I'm properly asleep. Sometimes it takes twenty minutes, sometimes two hours, to talk me into the space I need to be to shut off my brain.

Joe has been my live-albeit-virtual personalized sleep and meditation program for almost three years. I rely on him the same way I rely on one espresso an hour to keep me awake during the day.

"Squeeze your eyes closed," he says, "and open your jaw as wide as you can. Now relax. Deep breath in and hold, two, three, four, five, six, and release."

What Joe does could be recorded, or I could do it myself since it's virtually the same script every night, except I've tried all the apps—even had some developed specifically for me—but they all fail once I hit REM sleep. This is where the real-time, human interaction is critical.

So critical that I pay him a hundred grand a year for his service. He's worth every penny.

Once he decides I'm adequately relaxed, Joe reads from the sports page of a community newspaper in butt-fuck who-knows-where. It doesn't matter. His job is to read until I fall asleep. Sports pages—because sports don't interest me—and teams I know nothing about so I can tune out the details because I don't want my brain filled with useless crap.

Our system works.

I don't know how long he reads, but at some point a dream image replaces his voice. And this is why I pay him what is the equivalent of three hundred dollars an hour. Because unless that dream is redirected, I'll be wide awake again in seconds with no hope of falling back under. The perils of parasomnia, a clinical sleep disorder that has no cure. But as long as I have Joe, I have relief.

The image of my dad dead in his hotel bed blurs and refocuses, this time with Dad lying on a beach blanket beside Mom while my three brothers splash in the ocean as I watch the scene unfold from above. And then Horse calls me, "Will, I need you!" and I join the beach scene, feel the water around my ankles, and the sand between my toes. I catch up to my twin, chasing our youngest brother Aiden, who laughs and hollers and swims toward seaweed, floating on the waves.

Alexa's gentle voice prods, "Will, it's time to wake up," followed by the sound of running water, prompting an immediate need to urinate. The lightening sky tells me I've slept through the night—or at least, the very early morning.

I shower, dress, and down my first of a dozen daily espressos. Then I check messages on my phone before heading to my office to go over the notes for today's Come Into Power seminar. I have a single text. No surprise, since everyone I know other than Joe is still asleep.

JOE
Reminder—our contract expires in 30 days.

He's given me ninety- and sixty-day warnings to inform me he's quitting. Apparently, the middle-of-the-night calls are ruining his marriage. Same negotiating tactic he used last year that resulted in a $25,000 raise. I've already decided to bump him to $120,000.

I delete the message and don't think of it again.

3. *Virginia*

ANGEL WINGS MEET THE DEVIL

It's the last hour of the last day of the Come Into Power weekend, an event I've paid $2000 to attend. Why? Because Will Power, the king of business coaching, is here in my home city, and I need his help to grow my plant whisperer business.

So when he yells out to the audience that he has time for one more hot seat, one more chance to volunteer for live, one-on-one coaching with him, I know I need to stand out like a sunflower in a field of daisies to be noticed in this crowd of a thousand.

"One more lucky entrepreneur is about to have their life changed!" Will Power barks into his invisible mic.

A thousand people yell, "Yeah!"

I cheer as loud as the people around me.

"I want to wrap up this exceptional day of learning with a coaching experience you will never forget." He pumps his fists in the air. "Are you ready?"

"Yeah!" A thousand eager entrepreneurs pump our fists in the air.

"Female entrepreneurs, have I got your attention?"

A much quieter chorus fills the auditorium.

This is good.

"Female entrepreneurs with at least three years of sales, please stand."

This is very good.

The lights come up a little, but not full on. I rise from my seat with confidence and look around. Fewer than a dozen of us are on our feet. The audience is easily ninety percent men, and so far the only woman who Will Power has invited to coach live asked for help to choose between her two businesses. It was fascinating to watch how he figured out which one stood the best chance of becoming successful and what she'd need to make that happen.

But none of it applied to me.

This is my opportunity—my now or never.

In a moment of divine inspiration, I pull my phone from the pocket of my A-line dress, hold my arm high in the air, and shine the flashlight right over my own head. No way he won't see me.

Interrogate me, Mr. Power.

Will Power looks from his left to his right and makes eye contact with me. "You, in the spotlight. Nicely played. Shows courage and drive. Let's get this done."

I inhale a deep breath and walk with my head high, arms loose at my sides like I belong here.

I am a winner. I am making shit happen. Nothing will stop me from success.

I quote the mantra Mr. Power has us chant after each live coaching.

I reach him on the stage. Everything about him is bigger than life, from his height (reportedly, six foot four) to the breadth of his shoulders (twenty-three inches of pure muscle, according to an article in *Inc.* magazine) to the power that radiates from him (nuclear). He reaches out his arm. I do the same, making certain my handshake is as firm as it can be inside his baseball glove–size hand.

A tingle of energy runs through my palm as our hands and eyes meet. I smile, feeling like he's just transferred some of his magical business success genes straight into my body.

"What's your name?"

"Virginia Beach," I say with a smile and a nod.

"Virginia Beach," he repeats. He looks me up and down. "You strike me as more of a Virginia Rainforest." He moves away, waving at my bright green leaf-patterned dress.

Chuckles from the audience.

This is part of being in a hot seat—having to withstand scrutiny and hard questions, hard truths.

Bring it on. I'm ready.

I take a steadying breath and shift my weight toward Mr. Power just a little, projecting unwavering aplomb. I hope.

"Virginia," he says in a most condescending tone, "did you not get the event prep email, the one that said to dress in business casual?" Will Power holds a mic out to me. I take it and tilt my chin, trying to forget about how many eyes are staring at me.

"I did. But given my line of work, I thought business *formal* would be more appropriate."

Mr. Power's eyes widen, and he barks out a laugh, repeating my words, "Business formal. And what business are you in, Virginia?"

"I'm a botanist. I take care of people's houseplants."

I've learned, listening to others on stage all weekend, to be brief so the king of coaching will have more time to impart his wisdom in my ten-minute block.

"Ah. I see. So this getup makes a little more sense."

I smile. "Yes."

"That was sarcasm, Virginia."

More laughs from the darkness.

"Why are you dressed in this ... well, frankly, ridiculous costume? Do you think it makes you more credible as a plant whisperer if you're impersonating a field of ... what kind of plants are those?"

"Caladiums. More commonly known as Angel Wings," I say, trying not to quiver.

"So, is that your logic here? Look like a plant to convince clients you speak their language?" Derision drips from his words. "May god help you."

I drop my arm, the one with the mic, and quietly say, "The plants like it. I dress for them."

"Did everyone hear what Virginia just said?" Power booms, scaring me a step away from him. He grabs my arm and pulls me back.

A chorus of enthusiastic *noes* fills the air.

"Virginia Beach is dressed to impress the plants she waters."

I knew that by coming onstage, I'd risk embarrassment. But humiliation? I've seen him coach nineteen other people during this two-day conference. Sure, he's gotten a few laughs at the expense of the entrepreneur on stage, but I had no idea how different it would feel to be on the receiving end of his ribbing.

I expected him to talk about my business. Ask me about my model, my income, my marketing, the way he has with every other entrepreneur he's coached today. Never in a Giant Sequoia's lifetime did I think the focus would be on my dress. A dress that I love and look damn good in.

After the laughter dies, Power continues.

"Who are your clients, Virginia?"

"People in the top one percent income bracket who want someone to come in once a week to water their plant babies. I have a few who have me visit monthly to make sure all their plants are healthy and happy."

He holds up his hand to stop me from talking. "Healthy *and* happy? To make sure their plants are *happy*?"

I nod.

"She nodded, folks. All right. And what was your gross earning last fiscal year, Virginia, the plant whisperer?"

"Twenty-two thousand." I hold the mic to my mouth so the cynics can hear I actually have a viable business.

"I am deeply impressed," Mr. Power says.

If there's sarcasm in his answer, I choose to ignore it.

"And what is your financial goal?"

"Fifty thousand," I say with more confidence. This is where the humiliation will be worth it, since he'll impart some golden nugget that will help me level up. This is why Will Power brings in a quarter million dollars every time he steps onto a stage. Why, of the thousand people in the room today, one hundred or more will pay another $20,000 to join his executive coaching program, which isn't even led by him; it's led by a team of his staff.

Power tents his fingers in front of his face, looking me up and down, examining me like he's truly considering a strategy for me. But then he shakes his head, inhales deeply, and takes off his black suit jacket.

"Remove your belt," he demands.

I think I mishear him. "My belt?"

What is he planning to do? Screw some sense into me? I mean, that would be something I could imagine he'd say, but actually do? On stage? In front of a thousand people?

I don't move.

"Belt. Off. Now." He hangs his jacket on two fingers and reaches toward me.

I'm paralyzed.

"Oh, for Christ's sake, work with me, Virginia Beach." He grabs the buckle and gives it a twist, and it comes free in his hand. "That wasn't so hard, was it?"

I want to melt into the stage. I try to step away, but for a second time, he holds me in place.

"You paid almost ten percent of your gross income to attend today. You came up here wanting to make the most of that investment. I applaud your courage. Now, stand still and listen. Put on this jacket."

Will Power, the world's most bombastic billionaire motivational speaker, turns me around and helps me into a suit jacket that probably cost more than my rent for an entire year.

It's huge on me. I disappear in it.

"Do up the buttons. Cover that ridiculous dress. And buckle your belt over top."

I do as he commands. He steps back, looks me up and down again. "Right arm." He takes it before I can move and rolls up the sleeve so my hand is visible. Then he does the left.

He waves to the darkness offstage. "Savannah, get out here. I need your hair elastic."

His stage assistant walks toward us, pulling her glossy black hair out of its bun. It falls in a sophisticated tumble around her shoulders, but she smiles and hands her boss the elastic.

"That Bozo the Clown look is not helping your business. Do you know how to use one of these things?"

I glare at his chest, too embarrassed to make eye contact,

and gather my shoulder-length hair into a ponytail. With a couple of twists, I wrangle the wild curls into a messy bun.

"Better. Now, face the audience."

I turn, certain my cheeks are as red as my curls.

"If you want to double your income, you need to dress like an entrepreneur, not a circus performer to the sick and leafy. The plants do not hire you. People with healthy cash flows do. I am certain there's a healthy market in this city that has the income to spend on non-necessities. But this," —he lifts the hem of his jacket to show my skirt—"is why you're not earning your full potential. Dress to impress the *people* who put checks in your hand. I guarantee your business will grow." He nods to Savannah.

She rejoins us onstage, as she does after each coaching session. Her hair is sleek and perfect again. Savannah takes the mic and my elbow and whisks me out of the spotlight.

"Let her keep the jacket," Power calls as I walk away. "A reminder of the day Will Power changed. Her. Life."

The crowd goes wild.

Savannah leads me down a hallway to a door that opens into the lobby.

"You can go back to your seat," she says with a warm smile.

I don't stay for the wrap-up. I know it will be the sales pitch for his executive coaching program. Sure, there are drinks and networking after the event, and these people are my perfect clients. At least a few among them have the resources to hire someone like me if they're plant lovers. That was one reason I'd been able to justify paying $2,000 to attend. I even had professional business cards made and perfected my ten-second introduction.

But now? The last thing I want is to have any more strangers looking and laughing at me.

I hurry to the coatroom and collect my purse and jacket, leaving my notebook behind at my seat.

"It was horrible!" I tell Georgia. "He didn't focus on the way any of the men were dressed. He's a sexist asshole. I can't believe I threw away all that money."

Georgia is six years older than me and shares my normally positive disposition. "One day, when you're rich and famous, this will be a great story in your memoir."

"You'd think!" I stand, anger even stronger now. "But no, because we all had to sign nondisclosure agreements before being allowed in. We're not allowed to talk about what happened inside that auditorium in any public forum."

"If you do?"

"Total annihilation."

"Shit."

"Yeah, shit."

"Well, the jacket's worth a pretty peony." She makes a goofy face. The one she uses to cheer me up. We love puns, but that one has been used to death. "If you can prove it was owned by the High and Mighty Will Power, I bet you could make your money back." She waves for me to give it to her. "Let me try it on. It will be as close as I ever get to touching a billionaire."

I lift the jacket from the kitchen chair.

"Ooh, shivers," she jokes. Georgia does up the buttons. "So, do I look like a million bucks? Maybe instead of selling it, we should rent it out."

"Or maybe ... you should tailor it so it actually fits me, and I should wear it to some hoity-toity event, get myself photographed, and make sure Mr. 'Pill' Power sees me in it. I'd be interviewed, and the only quote I'd give the paparazzi would be, 'This jacket changed. My. Life.' Then I'd roll my eyes."

Georgia pulls off the Power suit and smooths it on her cutting table. She flips it over, turns it inside out, puts it the right way again. "I could totally tailor this for you. Want me to?"

"Why the hell not? I imagine there's something in the NDA fine print that would have me arrested if I tried to sell or rent it using his name. But he did gift it to me in front of a thousand people, so it's not like he could sue if I made it fit me. Right?"

Georgia shrugs. "Damn it, Virginia, I'm a seamstress, not a lawyer," Georgia says in her best impression of Dr. McCoy from *Star Trek*.

"But you can tailor it?"

"Not so much tailoring. I'll take it apart and start fresh with the pieces. It's so big, I won't have any problem." Georgia continues to fuss with the jacket while I make dinner.

"Hey, check this out." She waves a small gold-colored card at me. "It was in a pocket like I've never seen before in a man's suit jacket, just big enough to hold one business card."

I take it from her.

"Oh. My. Goddess." The air leaves my lungs. "It's his golden ticket."

4. Virginia

A MOCK MARIGOLD

Georgia grabs the card from my hand and flips it over four times.

"Explain."

"I can't even believe this." I grab the card back. "OK, so you know in *American Idol* how the panel can push that button and it automatically sends the competitor to the final round?"

My sister nods.

"This is the Will Power version of that. If he gives you one of these, it gets you one-on-one coaching time with a person trained by him for his Power Broker Program. It's worth at least $20,000 because that's what it costs to get in. But this is even better. He basically says that one of these cards is his personal guarantee that you'll hit your business targets. Like, not just a money-back guarantee since, well, it was free, but—" I am hyperventilating.

Georgia is wide-eyed.

"And he gave it to you?"

"No! No, no, no. He *despised* me. He was so condescending. He gave one to a guy who had some tech idea, of course.

This,"—I snatch the golden ticket—"is an accident. I wasn't supposed to get this. He must've forgotten it was in his pocket."

"But you did get it! Oh my goddess, call the number. Call the number!" She pushes my phone across the table with so much force, it flies right off, onto the floor, and under the stove.

I sit across from my overexcited sister and grasp her arms to stop her from waving them in my face like a psycho Muppet.

"Yes. I know. I will. But I need a plan. I can't just waltz in and say, 'Hey, I accidentally got one of Mr. Power's golden tickets' and expect them to give me anything other than a personal escort out of the building. Right?"

Georgia scowls.

"Right?" I repeat.

She snatches the card from my fingers. "If you're not going to call, I will. I could use some thousand-dollar-an-hour coaching for *my* business."

I pluck it back and stuff it into my bra. "Chill, Venus Fly Trap. I will call. But can we take a breather here? Also … phone … under stove … gross … you can dig it out for me."

Over the next two months, I water the seed of an idea about how I'll finagle my way into the Power Broker Program. I know it's a long shot, but as Georgia keeps reminding me, since I've already been publicly humiliated by Will Power, I have nothing to lose. Comparatively, how embarrassing will it be to be turned away at the door in front of a security guard?

Georgia, of course, helps me prepare. She uses the fabric of Mr. Power's jacket to make a Power suit-like dress for me with the same collar style, the same pockets, the same every-thing—with two key differences. The first—it fits me like I hired a high-end London tailor to make it. The other differ-ence—instead of lining my Power dress with the original dull gray fabric of Will Power's suit, Georgia uses a silk with the exact pattern as the dress I wore the day of the Come Into Power seminar.

It's our little *screw you* to the boring world of conserva-tive billionaires. It helps me feel like me, even if I am the only one who knows the secrets my dress holds.

And to top it off, my brilliant sister has made the dress reversible so I'll be able to wear it to more than just the intake interview I've scheduled with a man named Mr. Liu —the coach who will either help me double my business income or kick my green ass to the curb.

I cover my frizzy hair with product to smooth it and pull it into a tight knot. I have Georgia do my makeup, since she's way better at the whole "dressing for success" thing, which includes masking my freckles. I'm not a country bumpkin, but the circles I work in care more about soil moisture than skin moisturizer. At least that's what I've always told myself.

I hail a cab—because that's what successful people who don't own cars do when going to important meetings—and arrive fifteen minutes early. It's a warm May day, so I don't need a jacket over my dress, a relief, given my limited busi-ness-friendly options. I enter the high-rise in downtown Vancouver and pause a few steps into the massive lobby with the giant nest hanging overhead. It's supposed to be some nod at showing that the company is female-business friendly. I scoff out loud, then pretend to cough when two people turn to look at me.

A visitor slash security desk sits to my right, but I'm not ready to get my badge yet.

Poster-sized photographs line the wall across from the desk, from black-and-white to crisp digital images. It's the succession of the Power leadership.

Of course, I've read everything I could find online about the company to prepare for this meeting. But I haven't seen these pictures or their associated captions.

Will Power is the fourth of his name, and each of his predecessors was also a motivational speaker who captivated audiences and grew the Power empire to its multibillion-dollar valuation. But the current Mr. Power is the first to refer to himself as Will. His father was William; his grandfather went by Bill. And according to the info card under the photo taken in 1933, the OG Mr. Power was known as Stretch, due to his height—six foot four at a time when a man was considered tall if he was anything over five eight.

You can see the progression of arrogance from one generation to the next in the way they've branded the company. The current motivational guru was bold enough to legally change the name from William Power and Sons to Will Power & Bros. I used to think that the "Bros." was the standard corporate abbreviation for "Brothers" since there are four of them. But now I know the truth—it really means that fratty, masculinity of bro culture. I discreetly stick my tongue out at his smug and admittedly drop-your-panties gorgeous face.

As I turn to sign in and get my badge, a woman smiles and points at my dress.

"Stunning. Absolutely gorgeous. Brand?"

"Um, it's not?"

"Don't be coy. It won't look the same on me as it does

on you. Where did you buy it?" She sniffs the air close to my shoulder, as if she can smell the store I bought it from.

"I didn't. My sister is a seamstress. She made it for me."

"Card." She shoves her hand three inches from my nose.

I step back. "I don't have one."

She reaches down and grabs the hem of my dress. Runs her fingers along it. Flips it up to catch a glimpse of the green lining. "Exquisite work. Reversible?"

"Yeah. She's very good." I smile, trying to walk away.

The woman catches my arm. What is it with rich people thinking my arm is some kind of pull toy?

"Here,"—she shoves her phone in my face—"name and number. What did it cost?"

What did it cost? I had to make dinner for a week. I had to listen to every single episode of *The Will Power Hour* podcast with Georgia over the last two weeks, so I talk the way they talk in the program.

She taps the phone again. I take it and type in Georgia's name, business name and number, then hand it back.

"My sister said if I'd had it made on Savile Row in London, it would've cost me four thousand."

"Dollars or pounds?"

"Pounds," I say, only because I know that's way more than Canadian dollars, and if this woman is seriously going to hire Georgia, my sister deserves PITA pay.

"A steal," she says, turning on her heel toward the elevator bank.

"You're welcome," I call, loud enough for her to hear. "You giant hogweed," I whisper to myself.

I sign in with security and am told that someone will be down shortly to take me to my meeting.

"That's OK. I can find it," I say with a bright smile.

Aksita—according to the name on the guard's gold badge—looks over his glasses at me. "That's cute. Guests don't travel unaccompanied inside the Power & Bros. building. Have a seat." He points to a row of custom-made armchairs in corporate colors—gold and Duke blue, the literal brand color of Duke University. Georgia and I were surprised the company didn't create its own named color: Power Blue. She's decided to pitch the marketing department on the idea because ... well, because Georgia is brave like that.

I sit. I wait. I watch.

Megarich people, and those who serve them, are a different breed. It's not just their clothes and briefcases and jewelry. They hold themselves differently from the people I ride transit with. Even naked, their privilege would be obvious. I know that even cleaned-up and sent to the barber or hairdresser, that in a police line-up of seven naked normal people and one rich person, I'd be able to identify the one who had over a million dollars in their bank account.

The next time the elevator door opens, a young woman who looks my age approaches. "You must be Virginia," she says, extending her hand. "I'm Amanda, Mr. Liu's executive assistant. I'll take you to your meeting."

She punches a code into the elevator panel, not a floor number. The doors close, and we whoosh upward.

"Congratulations. It's quite an honor to be chosen by Mr. Power to receive this coaching. What business are you in?"

I've prepared for this moment. *Ignore the assumptions, answer the questions.*

"I'm a ..." My heart rate spikes, breaking every one of its promises to stay calm. I feel my face flush—a dead giveaway that I am a fraud. I clear my throat. "I'm a plant whisperer," I say, voice still too quiet.

"A what?" she asks, tilting her ear toward my mouth.

"I take care of plants and flowers. I'm a professional plantswoman, a floraphile, if you will."

"Huh! Learn something new every day. A floraphile ... flower lover ... interesting."

I nod. The elevator reaches the floor and I'm regretting every life decision I've ever made. "I'm sorry to ask, but is there a powder room on this floor? I just need a quick—"

"This way. Don't be nervous, though. Mr. Liu is lovely. You got one of the gentler coaches. Some of them,"—she raises her eyebrows and widens her eyes, a small whistle slipping from glossy lips—"some of them scare even me."

She leaves me to do a few calming breaths in the privacy of a bathroom so beautiful, it only reinforces that I don't belong here. My palms sweat, and I kick myself for not tucking paper towels into my pockets, something to pat my hands dry if they decide to leak again while I'm talking to Mr. Liu. Nothing screams *fraud* faster than sweaty palms when shaking the hand of a person with authority. I smooth a square of toilet paper into each pocket.

Amanda is waiting right outside the door and gives me an encouraging smile. "You've got this. I have faith in you. What is it that Mr. Power says?"

We repeat it together as she leads me to the office: "I am a winner. I am making shit happen. Nothing will stop me from success."

"Yeah, you are." She knocks once on a massive wooden door, then pushes it open. "Virginia Beach is here, Mr. Liu."

5. Will

GOLDEN HANDCUFFS

I rest my head against the plush seat of my Gulfstream G650 and close my eyes. I'm so ready for this speaking season to be over. Just one more stop. One more stage. One thousand more wantrepreneurs to inspire.

"Your tonic, Mr. Power," my flight attendant says.

I nod but don't open my eyes. "Thanks, Trish."

The jet bounces, and my hand knows exactly where the glass will be to stabilize it. How many million miles have I traveled in the past decade? I am tired. Sick and tired of being Will Power, motivation fucking guru to the wannabe rich and famous business stars.

I wonder at what point in his career Mick Jagger started to hate touring, singing the same goddamn songs over and over. He had to hate them. God, I'm tired of my spiel.

I raise my arm and wave, eyes still closed since even the sight of this jet bores me. "Savi," I bark. Yeah, I bark at her, not to be a dick, but to be heard over the thrum of the engines and the white noise in the jet.

"Hey, Will. What do you need?" My executive assistant, stagehand, and right arm sits in the seat across the aisle.

"I need you to check Horse, I mean, Colt's schedule. If he's not busy this weekend and next week, get a jet lined up and fly him to Paris. Book him a suite at Le Caprice and extend my stay for an additional seven days."

Savannah stares at me like I'm speaking freaking Greek.

"Problem?" I ask.

"Um, I have plans next week. I booked the time off, remember?"

"And?"

"And ... I can't stay in Paris for an extra week."

"Aaannnddd, I'm not asking you to. I'm asking you to find out if my fucking brother can make time in his fucking schedule to spend a week doing fucking company strategy in fucking Paris."

"Sorry, I thought—"

"You're not paid to think, Savi. You're paid to do." I close my eyes so I won't see her flip me off. I know she will and am waiting for the day she finally says what she's actually thinking when I'm being an asshole.

I sip my tonic slowly and focus on the effervescence.

I should apologize.

I turn my head, but Savi is busy texting, no doubt telling her husband that she cannot wait to be done with me. And I am too damn tired to get up, so I text Brian, one of my two younger brothers, the money guy and chief financial officer of our family empire.

ME
Give Savannah a $10,000 bonus.

BRIAN
What did you say now?

> **ME**
> Nothing that Legal will care about. I'm
> just crankier than normal. And she's
> done a great job this tour. Can you make
> it happen?

After a two-minute pause, I receive Brian's reply.

> **BRIAN**
> 10K deposited in Savannah's account.

> **ME**
> Staying an extra week in Paris.

> **BRIAN**
> If you're not home for Mom's bday, I will
> have you killed in your sleep.

> **ME**
> First I'd have to sleep. I'll be there.

I click off my phone and wish my body and brain had an off button.

This gig was so much easier in my twenties, being on the road for months at a time. Changing cities every other night after spending all day onstage, full focus, high energy. It was exhilarating back then. I'd get as amped as the crowd.

But the last four years? It's been exhausting. I dread speaking season.

Unfortunately, these months of my pain pay for a year of Will Power & Bros.' operations and make my family one of the top hundred richest families in the world—and the wealthiest in Canada. That's what $30 billion in assets gets you these days.

But a good night's sleep? I'd pay a billion for a solid month of non-medicated shut-eye. And medicated sleep? You couldn't pay me enough to take sleeping pills. I know better than anyone the damage they did to Dad—and then to Mother—when a bad combination of booze and pills killed him at forty-two, a year younger than his dad, and the same damn age as his grandfather.

The thought of one more year of this lifestyle is equal parts relief and terror. One more year until I can sleep like the dead.

I raise my empty glass, and like magic, it's filled again.

Plain tonic water. I close my eyes and think about Paris.

One of the easier international seminars, since I parlez-vous like a pro. But Germany, Spain, Italy, Holland ... I know enough to make a connection when I walk onstage, and I've memorized my trademark Power mantras in twenty different languages. But all those events hire translators for the non-English speakers. And for me, of course.

Maintaining the fervor while I wait to understand what the aspiring tycoon du jour is saying is no small feat—and no one pulls it off the way I can. Not just no one in my family, no one in the goddamn world.

That's why I need Horse, my identical twin and CEO and chair of the Power & Bros.' family board of directors—a.k.a., my boss. I need him to see what this job is doing to me and work with me to make a change before it kills me.

I run through ideas and scenarios for the remainder of the eighty-minute flight between Frankfurt and Paris.

"**M**r. Power. Crew. We're about to start our descent to Charles de Gaulle Airport. Please make sure your seat belt is fastened," Dave, my personal on-call pilot, announces.

Dave—Uncle Dave when we were kids—has been with the company since before I was born. Mother and Dad always treated him like family. Since Dad died, Dave has spent a great deal of time flying Mother wherever her heart desires during my off-seminar season. We kids have long speculated they have a thing, but Mother denies it. Too bad. He's good for her. And we trust him.

It's not easy being widowed or single with a net worth higher than the GDP of most countries. Hard to have faith in people's true intentions. As a result, not one Power son is anywhere close to giving Mother a grandchild, something she complains about every time there's a family gathering.

Like her birthday.

We taxi to Arrivals and Dave opens the cockpit door.

"Thanks for the comfortable ride." I extend my hand.

"Pleasure, Will. See you in two days?"

"About that." I turn toward Savannah. She nods.

"Dave, take the next seven days off. I'll text you my departure details after I talk to Colt."

"Of course, sir." Dave nods.

"Oh, and don't forget it's Mother's birthday on the twenty-fourth. I hope you can make it."

"I wouldn't miss it, sir."

It's the last client of the Parisian seminar. My wild card. The one thing that makes the two-day event interesting for me.

The other nineteen people invited onstage were all plants. Of course, they paid the registration fee like everyone else, and *they* didn't know they were plants, but I did.

Before we'll take a person's money to attend a Come Into Power seminar, they have to complete a mini business plan. This serves two important purposes. One, it makes the events look exclusive since individuals "apply" and are "invited" to two glorious days basking in my brilliance. The truth is, if your credit card is good, you meet the attendance qualifications. But they don't know that, which makes acceptance a confidence boost before they even arrive. And confident entrepreneurs are more likely to drop $20K on our Power Broker Program.

The other is that my team pores over every application and pulls nineteen people for me to bring onto the stage. They prepare one-pagers about each person, detailing facts about their business and recommendations to grow or recover or whatever they're looking for. It makes me appear to be supernaturally fast on my feet, but every one of those nineteen have already won at least an hour of my company's coaching time.

These seminar participants are the entrepreneurs my team deem the most likely to succeed because *their* success drives *my* success. Word-of-mouth marketing accounts for eighty percent of the asses in chairs. It is a brilliant business model, thought of by my most humble brother, Aiden.

All I do is memorize a few key points about each business, make sure Savannah seats our secret VIPs in designated spots that seem random but are the same in every goddamn city, then turn on my big fucking personality when they walk onstage.

Except for person number twenty. That woman is truly the wild card. And I always choose a woman since they are grossly underrepresented at my events, and I see it as an opportunity to level the entrepreneurial playing field, even if it's by just one starfish. Selfishly, one starfish that will feed the Power empire.

In choosing my wild card, I look for three things as I sweep across the room. She has to meet my eyes and hold my gaze. She needs to have enough self-confidence that it will project to the thousand people in the auditorium. Typically, half the women standing are eliminated when they blink or look at their feet as soon as our eyes meet.

Then I focus on the way she's dressed. I want to see personality in her attire, a splash of color, something that communicates she's comfortable being herself. The majority in most cities, but not all, interpret business casual to mean blend in, be invisible. I am not interested in them. Authenticity projects confidence.

And with the few who remain as possibilities, I always point to the most physically attractive woman because people are assholes and are more inclined to aspire to be like someone they'd expect to see as an anchor on the evening news. A pretty woman is good for business.

Ever since the Vancouver seminar, whenever I've looked into the auditorium to find my last coaching mentee, I've hoped to see her again ... Virginia Beach. In all the years I've been doing this and all the people I've called onstage, only one has ever stuck with me: that fiery redhead.

Her firm handshake told me, given a chance to spend more time together, I'd like this woman. The way she said her name without apology—a name I knew from my own experience people laughed at. Her dress was clearly custom made; it was too perfect, from the pattern that matched her personality so well, to the fit that emphasized all the right curves.

In that three seconds when our hands clasped and our eyes focused on each other, I flashed on a feeling of utter relaxation. I envisioned lying in the sun, being myself with a woman who is being herself. Just ... being.

And then I got angry because that is not a viable future

for Will Power. I hated that she reminded me of a life that is inaccessible to me.

So I punished her. Publicly. Unapologetically. For having what I can never have.

And since that day, I've regretted it. Not only because it was off-brand for the company, because if I were Horse or Brian or Aiden, I'd have asked her out to dinner. I would've brought her home, given Joe a night off, and kept her up until I'd explored every inch of her.

But I wasn't born with the luxury of the life my brothers inherited. I am Will Goddamned Power and that means I have no possible future with Virginia Beach—or any woman—since I am not going to put another wife through the hell of losing her husband in his prime or of kids having to attend their dad's funeral before they're old enough to vote.

"This card is from ..." Mr. Liu punches a number into his laptop and looks at me with confusion. "New York City three years ago. What took you so long to reach out?"

"I, um, I mean, my *business*, wasn't ready for this level of focus until now." Truth.

I can see him running questions through his mind. But he doesn't press further, thank goodness. I'd already decided I wouldn't outright lie, but if a question allowed me to be honest but not necessarily clear, that would be OK.

"Your business plan is well done. It helped me understand a lot about you."

"About my business, you mean?"

"Yes, your business, of course. But where I'd like to start our coaching is not on your actual business, but on you." Mr. Liu tents his index fingers and taps them on his lips.

"On me?" I discreetly pull a square of toilet paper from my pocket and place it on my lap where he can't see to absorb the moisture from my palms.

"I find it fascinating that you've been given an opportunity to set a business income goal that, at a minimum, could be $1 million."

My eyes betray my surprise. I didn't see that small print in the info I found online.

Mr. Liu catches my expression. "Mr. Power would not have given you that card otherwise. The gold card is not just symbolic, Ms. Beach. He has confidence in your business reaching that target—not in one year, of course, but in five to seven. So, knowing you would have a coach who would be compelled to work with you until you met that gold standard target, you set an income projection of just $50,000 in Year One.

"So yes, I'd like to start with some personal coaching, since this financial goal is a waste of my expertise and the time I could be spending working with an entrepreneur who is actually going to make shit happen, as Mr. Power would say."

Since he didn't ask a question, I continue to listen and watch. He doesn't appear annoyed that he'd been given my file, despite saying my business is a waste of his time. He's smiling and nodding. I can tell he's looking for nonverbal cues from me.

I tilt my head just a little as he speaks, silently communicating that I am comfortable with this information, even though if he asked to shake my hand at this moment, it would tell a different story.

"At first," he continues, "I assumed you'd simply made a mistake in stating your annual income target was $50,000. Look ..." He turns my business plan toward me and points to where he's crossed out the word 'year' and replaced it with 'month.' "You see? I read your plan and in my mind, I could easily visualize you earning $50,000 a month. But the rest of your budget made your true intentions clear."

He stops speaking. For several long seconds, he and I hold eye contact. I do not fidget, but I do move. I lean forward and place my forearms on his desk. It's a bold move, but one I feel I need to make to gain his confidence and not have this be a one-and-done meeting.

"Would you like to know what I believe your biggest barrier to success is, Ms. Beach?"

I lean forward even more, but just my neck and head, keeping my shoulders back, chest open. "I would," I say.

He sits back in his chair, smiles as if he, and he alone, knows a big secret. "You, Virginia Beach, are afraid of success."

Whoosh.

My jaw drops enough for even a baby detective to notice my panic. My arms jump from the desk and cross in front of my body. I hug myself, then berate myself for the tell.

I will not rock. I will not rock. I will not ...

Damn it, I'm rocking. Subtle, but I feel it, and if Mr. Liu is as astute an observer as I figure he is, he can see it.

"Bingo!" His laugh is filled with so much joy. If anyone were to walk into this office to see and hear this exact moment, they'd likely assume Mr. Liu had just won a jackpot or solved the "Did Carole Baskin feed her husband to tigers?" case.

He pours water from a carafe into a glass and places it in front of me. Without words, I accept and drink.

"Here's the offer," he continues. "If you would like to grow your business to one that grosses, or even nets, $50K a year, let's shake hands, and you can leave today knowing that I have full confidence you'll get there within twenty-four months without ever having to speak to me again. But"—he levels a stare at me—"if you're willing to do what it takes to build a million-dollar business, I would be delighted to take you under my wing and mentor you."

I gulp more water since my mouth has gone dry in the time it's taken him to say that last sentence. Is this a joke?

"A million dollars? A year?"

He nods. His smile is mirthful.

"To water plants?"

Mr. Liu holds up his index finger. "Ah, you see, once we address your fear of success, you'll realize how naïve a question that is. But the short answer is no. Yes, watering plants will be at the core of your business, but it will be the ancillary products and activities that will make you a millionaire."

I nod, even though I'm not totally sure what he means.

"You're feeling unsettled. Off-balance. And that's fine. I expected this. All I need to know right now is, are you willing to let go of whatever is holding you back, or are you happy playing small? There's no wrong answer—except a lie."

"A million dollars a year," I repeat to make it feel more real. "Minus expenses and taxes. What kind of annual net do you think the business you've imagined would give me?"

He claps his hands, then gives me a double thumbs-up. "Excellent. That question tells me you're ready. You are going to love this process. I am going to push your boundaries and buttons the way they've never been pushed and then ... I can't wait to share this with Mr. Power. I can see why he gave you that card. He's brilliant. Just brilliant." Mr. Liu nods, and all I can do is mimic.

Nod and smile. Nod and smile. Throw up later.

. . .

I leave my first coaching meeting with Mr. Liu with a list of action items to complete before our next meeting in two weeks. The hardest is that I have to replace myself with all my existing clients since I cannot run a million-dollar business and spend thirty hours a week going from house to house for fifteen-minute watering appointments.

When I said I wasn't willing to give up all my time with plants for the sake of becoming stupidly rich, he told me not to worry. He agreed that I will need to maintain my connection to the core of the business, but that there are more efficient ways to do so. When I said I don't want to buy a car, assuming he meant reducing travel time between jobs, he asked me if I am willing to trust him and be open to ideas that my current way of being doesn't allow me to imagine. I said yes ...

So that's what I'm doing in the next two weeks. Taking a business that has brought me great joy but not enough income to truly support myself, and giving it all away so I can start something that will give me everything I've never dreamed of.

When I push open the apartment door, Georgia screams and runs at me like a lovesick teenager who's just scored concert tickets to Rihanna. She pulls me into a tight hug, bouncing against my frozen form.

"OK ... too much coffee today ..."

"You gave my name to a woman at that Power palace."

"Oh, right. Yeah, she was—"

"She is the executive assistant to one of the brothers at the company. And ..." Georgia jumps from foot to foot.

"And she hired you to make a dress just like this one?" I finish.

"Yeah! And you know how much she's willing to pay?"

"Whatever four thousand pounds sterling is in dollars?"

"Yes! Seven thousand dollars. Plus material costs. For *one* dress!"

"It's a pretty nice dress." I laugh and smooth down the front of mine.

"Did your meeting go as well for you as your time hanging out in the lobby went for me?"

"You better sit down."

The common area in our microscopic two-bedroom apartment has a kitchenette, a kitchen table with two chairs, a relatively comfy armchair, a decidedly uncomfortable armchair, and Georgia's giant-ass cutting table and ironing board, which are always set up.

Normally, we joke argue over who gets the better chair, but tonight, she sits in the one we should've trashed years ago and waves for me to sit in what we call The Throne.

"So ... I'm glad you're excited about that custom job and how much you're going to be paid. Really happy."

My sister's face drops. "Oh no. It didn't go well ..."

"Depends how you define 'well,' I think."

"Okay," she drawls. "Define it for me."

Since the moment Mr. Liu said the number *one million*, I've been tossing over the best way to tell Georgia. Ripping off the Band-Aid quickly is best.

"If I follow the plan that Mr. Liu—he's my business mentor—has for The Other Side of the Fence, it can be making us quite a bit more than just $50,000 a year."

"Like, sixty? Seventy?"

I shake my head.

"A hundred thousand a year?" Georgia's eyes widen.

"A million. A million dollars. A year."

R-i-i-i-p!

I watch my sister's body language to anticipate her reaction and prepare my response. Like mine was, hers is a combination of stunned silence and small self-soothing actions. She brushes her legs with her hands, touches her face, runs a fingertip across her lips.

I give her space to process. I want her to be the next person to speak.

"You said, '*If* I follow the plan.' Does that mean you haven't decided yet?"

My eye twitches.

"You already said yes."

"Damn those true crime shows," I joke, trying to lighten the mood.

Georgia fake smiles. "OK, then." She picks up a scrap of fabric from the floor and mindlessly frays an edge. "You'll be able to afford your own place."

"And furniture that's not dragged in from the sidewalk."

"My little sister, a millionaire business woman. You won't need me anymore." She seems to be talking to herself.

"Georgia, look at me. Of course I'll still need you. Having money won't change that."

She raises her eyebrows and frowns.

"Want to know what I think?" I say, breaking the silence. "I bet you make your first million before I do."

Georgia scoffs.

"Think about it. Your business is so much easier to scale. And while I can't charge more than a hundred an hour for my expertise, you can charge five times that much. And you can hire seamstresses who charge one-tenth your rate to do the sewing. Easy money once you get the clients."

Georgia rolls her eyes but laughs. "Look at you, all Power Brokered up after just one meeting." Then her expression changes. "I'm worried about how being rich will change us."

"Yeah, Mr. Liu mentioned that I have a serious case of fear of success. I didn't give him details about why. But you know, we're not Dad. I promise on ... all the bonsai in the world that I won't ditch you once I can afford my own place."

"This kind of change and this much money will definitely change things. I'm kind of freaking out," she admits.

"The rocking and wide eyes weren't a giveaway at all. I actually had the same reaction in front of Mr. Liu. That was fun."

Georgia laughs. "Do you think he noticed?"

"Oh, he noticed! He clapped his hands in joy because I'd proved his assumption right."

We sit in silence for many minutes. "We'll be fine, Georgia. We will. And anyway, after taxes and expenses and everything, a million is really like half that much, and that still means having a mortgage, if we decide to buy something, so it's not like we'll be swimming in pools of champagne. But maybe we'll at least be able to afford a place with a pool. And AC. And an actual full kitchen with a fridge that's big enough to hold a bottle of bubbly."

"I'm scared," Georgia admits.

"Me too. But I've got you, and you've got me, and together ..."

"Hmm," she mumbles.

"And together?" I repeat.

Georgia shakes her head.

"Georgia Muthafuckin Beach ... And together?"

She glares at me but says, "And together ..."

In unison, we finish the mantra we've been using since we legally changed our last name about a year after Mom died, so if Dad ever did come looking for us, we'd be harder to find. Fuck him, that's what we said.

"Beach sisters are all that and a muthafuckin bag of sweet-and-spicy chips!" Corny, but the old sentiment does the job.

"Damn right we are." I stand and wrap myself around my big sister. "We won't let success or money tear us apart. Deal?"

"Deal."

7. Will

SLEEP IS SECONDARY TO SUCCESS

Horse and I spend a productive week in Paris.

In some respects, we didn't do anything we couldn't have done back home in Vancouver, but in other ways, I don't believe we would've come up with what we did while sitting in the hallowed halls of the family business. There is a weight, invisible yet oppressive, in this building that Dad built. It feels like he and Granddad are still here, casting their imposing shadows over any new or fresh ideas. I always feel stifled in their ghostly presence.

It doesn't seem to affect Aiden or Brian. Horse admits he feels it a little, but not to the degree I do.

"You only feel it so strongly because you're spawn of the Devil. The doctor should've called in a priest when you were born, what with that pentagram birthmark on your ass cheek."

Only Horse could, or would, ever say that to me without being on the receiving end of my wrath. Benefit of being an identical twin. There have been more times than I can count when I've wished his leg had been the first one the OB-GYN grabbed hold of. Then he'd be William Power the Fourth, and I'd just be another asshole billionaire Power brother who gets to choose my career path based on what I'm good at and what I enjoy.

Sure, I am a rock star with the motivational speechifying. Do I love it? Not anymore, if I ever did. But retire at forty-two? That will never fly, so I need a pivot. A giant fucking pivot. That's what Horse and I strategized in the penthouse suite of Le Caprice in the heart of the City of Light, the center of ideas during the Age of Enlightenment. And damn, did I need some enlightenment.

It's good to be home. To have insomnia in my own bed and walk around my own penthouse at three in the morning, instead of up and down hotel hallways. I spend the weekend locked in my suite, trying to avoid family since they're the only people with access to my space —but they all seem to feel like I need to know I've been missed, am appreciated, yada yada.

On Monday morning, I take a quick trip down to the lobby to say hello to the security staff. It's a small gesture that, according to research my brother Brian believes, improves the odds of having them actually care about my safety. Not that I've ever worried about external threats to my life.

"Mr. Power, great to have you back." Aksita stands and comes around the front of the security desk to shake my hand.

"Glad you're still here. Any gossip I should know about? Shit my brothers won't tell me?" I gently punch his arm.

"You mean, like the brouhaha that took place when Mr.

Aiden *accidentally*," he makes air quotes, "rolled the stairs away from the giant nest while Mr. Brian was showing it to a woman he may or may not be seeing? Nope. I can't think of anything worth reporting."

"That doesn't sound at all like Aiden," I say with an eye roll.

"Quite right, sir. Good to have you home."

"Glad to be back. Thanks for all you do."

Since it's too confusing having four Mr. Powers in the building, staff call my brothers by their first names. I am the only Mr. Power, which is weird since Horse is the CEO, the head honcho, the guy who deserves to be called *mister*. But since I am the public figure and my role demands that level of esteem, Horse is Mr. Colt to staff, Horse to me.

And although we're identical twins, we do everything we can to look nothing alike. From the way we dress—I always wear a black suit, and Horse wears whatever the hell he feels like, as long as it isn't a black suit—to our hair. I look like a billionaire—hair meticulously maintained, cut every two weeks, and a beard I trim daily to make it look like two days' growth. Horse? He looks more like a ski bum with his wavy, jet-black, shoulder-length hair and a beard that swallows the lower half of his face and neck.

My first meeting of the day is to personally welcome all the new Power Broker Program members who received a gold business card at one of my recent events. I handed out fifty in total. The cost to the company in staff coaching time is significant—approximately one hundred hours per client at one hundred dollars an hour of salary for my team—half a million dollars.

But Brian figured out that every success costs us ten grand in real money but generates over $80,000 in the three years that follow their participation in the program from leveraging their successes and their word-of-mouth marketing. There is no investment that gives us better returns or that provides as much control over who we have promoting our brand.

With our headquarters in Vancouver, BC, the majority of coaching is done via video conference, and this morning's welcome will be exactly that: me alone in my office with a giant wall of faces from all over the world looking back at me. Each client will have his or her mentor on as well.

Given time zones, about half our clients will be at this morning's meeting and the other half at the end of the day, so nobody will have to drag themselves out of bed at two a.m. to participate. Some might have to work late or start early, but that's the cost of doing business. Sleep is secondary to success.

I'm at my desk when Savi arrives. "Good morning, Will." She greets me with her always cheerful smile.

"Did you miss me?" I ask, looking up from my laptop.

"Nope. I set my alarm to go off and yell orders at me at random times during the day while I was on my holiday."

I look at my keyboard and mumble, "Gotta keep that middle finger in shape." I then look up in time to see her expression of shock return to a smile.

"Everything's set up and ready to go for the top of the hour."

"You're the best."

My desktop has only one document open, a spreadsheet containing all I need to know for this meeting, to make every participant feel like I am personally invested in their business. The first column lists names written phonetically. The second, their business name. Third, what the business sells or offers. The fourth has the most content—one sentence that describes their key business target for the next quarter. And finally, I have one question to ask each person, something to encourage their meaningful engagement.

My team provides me with all this info—truth is, I know nothing about any of these entrepreneurs. But this quarterly touch-base with *the* Will Power translates into big money.

To keep things easy, the tech team moves the participant I'm meant to talk to into the video frame directly to my right on the screen. It allows me to keep the appearance of eye contact since they're directly below my camera. They are pulled up in the same order as my cheat sheet, which covers all the faces in the row below the one person I'm talking with.

Another of Aiden's brilliant ideas, this system makes me look personally invested in every single mentee's success and has made our family business stand head and shoulders above every other motivational coaching outfit on the market, bar none.

My preparation is simple: scan the list and make edits as I see fit so the words sound like me. I skip the first three columns—no need to memorize names—and go right to the targets and questions.

Hire staff ... optimize online presence ... reduce over-head ... diversify offerings ... blah blah blah. Nothing jumps out as interesting or challenging, so I minimize the window and open my email program to send Horse a note:

Free for lunch, boss?

· · ·

The group Power Broker call is humming along. Scheduled to last ninety minutes, we are right where we're supposed to be, with fifteen minutes and four participants remaining. As I read the next name on the list, the words are out of my mouth before my brain registers what I'm saying. I pull my eyes away from the camera to look directly at the face to my right. Red hair pulled back in a tight bun. The name on the bottom of the screen matches the name on my spreadsheet.

Holy shit.

I stumble, repeating her name, trying to regain my footing.

"Virginia Beach."

"As I live and breathe, Mr. Power." Her smile fills my screen.

Get your shit together, Power. How did she get here?

This makes no sense. But I can't figure it out now. I cannot pull my eyes away to look at my cheat sheet. Not that I need to. I know who she is. What she does.

"Plant whisperer," I say. But *ball buster* is what I think.

"Yes, sir, one of the many areas my business will be focused on in the coming year as I scale up."

My thoughts spin. Why is she here? I slide my eyes to my cheat sheet and read the target that has been prepared for me:

"You have an ambitious goal of reducing greenhouse gas emissions from your business by thirty percent."

Virginia's expression changes to one of confusion as she looks away from her camera to her right. A voice offscreen says, "Just go with it." She looks back and smiles. "Yes, quite ambitious, but with Mr. Liu's guidance, I'm confident I'll reach it."

Shit. I realize my mistake when I look back at the spreadsheet. I've read the next person's target, and Virginia handled my error like a pro. And since the question John prepared for her was too easy, too boring, I wing it.

"Ms. Beach, I'm having trouble keeping a plant in my office healthy. It's called Angel Wings. Any idea what I might be doing wrong?"

"Without actually seeing the plant, sir, I can't say for sure, but if I was to wager a guess, based on what I know about you from your Power Hour podcast and the seminar I attended? I'd say you're not leaving enough oxygen in the room for it to breathe."

She is so earnest in her delivery. My chest tightens and I'm certain I scowl. And then she smiles again. Bites her bottom lip and wrinkles her forehead. "Sorry. I'm just kidding. I really would have to see it to have anything of value to offer."

My anger melts back and I force a smile. "Then consider this an open invitation to whisper sweet nothings to my unhappy plants, Ms. Beach. Up next we have Robert Ma—"

I click the Leave Meeting button as I'm saying the next entrepreneur's name and storm from my office to Savi's desk.

"Contact Robert Mari's mentor and tell him I'm having internet connectivity issues. Reschedule the last three participants. And put a copy of Virginia Beach's business overview from John Liu's files on my desk."

I don't wait for her reply. I stride to the elevators and get into the wrong one. Force of habit since I rarely visit staff floors. When the doors reopen, Savannah is looking at me with a goddamn smirk, pointing to the right.

"Liu's floor?" I demand.

"Twenty-six."

As the doors close, I hear her yell, "You're welcome."

Why the fuck is Virginia Rainforest Beach in our program?

I don't slow down to acknowledge John's assistant Amanda on my way to his office, rap twice, then push open the door, only to barrel smack into a smiling, freckled face topped with fiery red hair.

My arm shoots out and I catch her before she tumbles backward, but the momentum pulls Virginia tight against me into a stiff, one-armed hug. I release her almost immediately, but not before my body registers the transfer of an energy that goes straight to my core and whispers, "Relaaaaax."

I take a calming breath as I stare down at her. She's holding her ground, staring right back at me with an authentic and confident smile.

"How?" It's the most complete sentence I can pull together.

8. *Virginia*

WILLY WONKA FOR ENTREPRENEURS

I knew that participating in the call would be a gamble, but I also figured Will Power would likely have no memory of our brief encounter and how he'd humiliated me onstage. And really, there was no credible way for me to avoid the group meet-and-greet without telling Mr. Liu the full truth, which I didn't want to do since I've learned so much from him in the two meetings we've had so far.

I stand my ground, arms akimbo, projecting the energy that I belong here as Mr. Power stares down at me, and I look up at him, not quite defiant but in the same stare family. I've practiced the look for hours with Georgia, the one that says, "That's right! I'm here, and there's nothing you can do about it!"

"How?" he asks.

I wait for him to complete the question, but silence hangs between us.

Does he mean, "*How do you do?*" Seems a little formal, given how frantic he was when he burst into the office.

Or maybe *"How are you doing? It's so good to see you again."* Ha! That makes me smile. Not bloody likely.

"How are you enjoying the program? Is John mentoring you well?" I like that one and am about to answer, but Mr. Liu comes around from behind his desk, hand outstretched.

"Welcome home, Mr. Power. Exceptional talent in the program this year. Well chosen." Mr. Liu drops Mr. Power's hand and moves his to my shoulder, patting in a fatherly way. "And this young filly? Your talent identifying dark horses never ceases to amaze me."

Mr. Liu extends his arms, palms up and open, in a silent invitation for him to speak.

Mr. Power's eyes move between Mr. Liu and me three times. I hold my smile; Mr. Liu drops his hands. Then finally, finally, Mr. Power snaps to life, grabs my elbow, and pulls me beside him.

"Thank you, John. I'd like a private word with the surprising and talented Ms. Beach."

This is it. My inevitable, undignified escort from the building. In my mind, I'd pictured the security guard at the front desk as the person called on to humiliate me. Never did I imagine I'd have to endure a repeat performance of that day onstage. Will he lock me in the giant nest that hangs in the lobby and have people point and laugh until I have a lawyer in shining armor arrive to rescue me?

"Thank you for everything, Mr. Liu," I call over my shoulder before the door closes behind me. I stumble to keep up with Mr. Power's long strides, his hand still firmly around my arm. "Bye, Amanda. Nice meeting you. Thanks for being you," I call in the direction of her desk.

"Stop yelling," Mr. Power growls.

"I can see myself out, thank you very much." I twist my elbow free and wave my building access pass so he can see it.

He grunts. "That pass does not give access to where I'm taking you."

I stop dead in my tracks. "I didn't do anything illegal," I say, no louder than a whisper, not wanting Amanda to overhear. "You can't arrest me." *I hope.* "I mean, you did give me a golden ticket, even if you didn't intend to. And what kind of entrepreneur would I be if I didn't seize every opportunity? Those are your words. I simply followed your coaching. Can't arrest me for that." *Boom!*

"Stop. Talking. Get in the elevator. I'm taking you to my office. Your Guest Pass doesn't give you access to my floor." He closes his eyes and sighs. When he opens them again, he tries to smile, but it looks pained. "I'm not having you arrested. I just want to talk."

The ride to his floor, whatever floor it is—the stupid elevator doesn't have normal buttons, so unless you know the code, you aren't going anywhere—is quick. And silent. And smells nice. He smells nice. A fresh, floral scent. Unexpected. I tilt my chin up and sniff the air near his neck.

"What are you doing?" he asks, stepping away from me.

"I like your cologne. I'm trying to get a better smell. I assume you put it on with the intention of people smelling it."

"Are you always so direct? It's off-putting. Dial it back."

The elevator doors slide open, and Mr. Power motions for me to leave before him. I step into a brightly lit foyer on what appears to be one of the building's top floors by the fact that not a single other building blocks my view of the North Shore mountains.

I clear my throat so he's sure to hear me and deepen my

voice. "If what you're doing makes people uncomfortable, keep doing it. It means they're paying attention. That's the first step of success: getting people's attention."

Mr. Power spins on his heel. "Are you quoting me to me —as a challenge? Is that supposed to be *my* voice?"

I smile because the look on his face makes me want to laugh out loud, but that might be a bit rude.

He shakes his head, but his lip tips up enough for me to notice. "The Tragedy of Lord William. I believe that's the cologne I put on this morning."

"I like it," I say, stating the obvious after being caught inhaling as deep as my lungs would allow.

"It's my favorite too," a woman's voice says. I hadn't noticed her sitting behind a desk to the side of an office door twice the size of Mr. Liu's.

Compensating for something? I think.

Mr. Power grunts, then opens the massive door, which suddenly makes sense given the size of the office. It's twice as big and ten times nicer than my entire apartment with Georgia.

Mr. Power walks to the wall at the end opposite his giant desk. It appears to be a wet bar—a sink, fridge, espresso machine, and other chrome gadgets sit on a counter that looks like polished maple wood.

I wait ten seconds for him to ask me to sit, but he seems to be making himself a coffee, totally ignoring me.

"Mr. Power."

He turns to face me.

"May I?" I point to the wall where a dozen or more plants are arranged, from a giant African milk bush whose pot is on the floor and reaches inches from the ceiling to a chrome-and-glass table covered in a variety of leafy green gorgeousness.

He waves. "Be my guest. Espressos will be a minute or two."

"Babies, look at you. Oh my goodness, aren't you beautiful." I take a broad leaf of the croton and run it between my fingers. It doesn't feel supple enough. I poke at the soil. It has a hard crust on top. Not good. I run my fingers across the leaves of several plants, barely touching them, making note of their colors and letting them know I see them. I notice a gap in the coverage and push some leaves aside to find a small pot with a hibiscus struggling for sun and air.

"Oh no, what's happened to you, Hibbi? Someone forgot you down there. Don't worry, we'll get you sorted out. You'll be OK. I see you now."

I hold the struggling plant up to the window and pinch its browning leaves.

"Ahem?" A voice from across the room draws my focus away from the plants. Mr. Power has moved to his desk. Two small espresso cups sit in front of him.

"Oh! Sorry. I forgot you were there ... I get kind of ... yeah." I take the sickly plant to Mr. Power's desk. "She needs space, light, air, and attention. She'll do better here, but she really needs some direct sun, which she can't get in this office. None of your plants—"

"That dress." He interrupts, pointing to my body and spinning his finger.

I wait, but it appears that's all he's going to say.

"Mr. Power, if I may say, you make it extremely difficult to follow your advice when having a conversation with you."

"Which is?"

"Oh, thank goodness! I thought you were testing me." I realize I've just said what I should've only thought. And then I reinforce my goof-up with a grimace. So I do a pirouette to reset and start over. "Which is ... to only speak when answering questions. You say, and I quote, 'Leaders do not fill the air with mindless babble.' So, when you point at me and state a fact, I'm not sure what to say or do."

"Have you memorized *all* of my pithy pull-quotes, Ms. Beach?"

"Maybe. That *would* require a test to find out."

He actually smiles. "Your dress is quite something. Am I correct in believing you have taken the jacket I wrapped around the"—he smacks his lips—"*outstanding* costume you wore to my seminar and had it tailored into this?"

Although I want to argue that my beloved dress is not a costume, I simply say, "You are." I want to say more. To tell him I was afraid he'd sue me if I tried to sell his jacket. To let him know this dress resulted in a copycat commission for my sister. More than anything, I want him to know I am a trainable vine and he should therefore allow me to stay in the Power Broker Program, so I keep my answer short.

He motions for me to take the chair across from his desk and pushes one of the tiny cups toward me.

"Why did you turn my tailored jacket into a dress, Ms. Beach? Was it not clear that I was simply making a point, that the *normal* thing to have done would have been to return it?"

My stomach twists. I've screwed up, but I'm not going to let him know that. I mirror the position of his head, tilted just a little toward his shoulder, and say with the cockiest confidence I can conjure, "I did not return the jacket because that's not what a smart businessperson would do. You told me that I needed to dress for success, and then you handed me the tools to do so—a Power suit, so to speak, so I embraced what you gave me."

I smile.

He scowls.

I cringe, realizing I've irritated him with the play on his name. I understand, having spent the last dozen years enduring jokes about what area of myself I most recommend for a memorable dining experience and what time the family-friendly activities make way for the adult-only experiences on Virginia Beach.

"I apologize. Poor choice of words." And damn it, I feel myself blush. A dead giveaway that he's in control.

"Did you tailor it yourself?"

"No. My sister did."

"Talented family." He sips his coffee.

I smile to acknowledge the compliment and mirror his action, raising my cup for a drink.

"Ms. Beach, how did you get into the Power Broker Program?"

"With a golden ticket."

His nostrils flare. "Number one, I am not Willy Wonka. You didn't win a golden ticket to a magical candy factory. And number two, I distinctly remember having given my *gold business card*," he emphasizes the words, "to a software developer at the Vancouver event."

I nod my agreement.

"Really, Virginia? We're playing twenty questions?"

Someone who doesn't understand body language might interpret Will Power leaning forward on his desk as aggressive, but my addiction to true crime shows has made me an expert in nonverbal communication. Mr. Power is not angry, he's engaged.

So even though most people would back away from Will Power, I push my chin forward a fraction of an inch, enough to tell his subconscious mind I am not walking away from his game.

"I'll play for as long as you'll have me."

He stands and walks around the desk to sit on the corner beside my chair. I'm sure he thinks he's intimidating me, but I imagine him as a puppy, taunting a bigger dog by getting up in her face. Yup, he is a handsome, muscular, powerful German shepherd with the darkest eyes I've ever stared down.

He crosses his arms and frowns, but the crinkles around his eyes tell me he's trying to look serious. And he is failing so hard.

"How did you get one of my gold business cards?"

"Do you remember an unusual little pocket in the lining of your jacket?"

He shakes his head, and I debate showing him. Georgia included an identical tiny pocket on the fun side of my dress since it seemed an important part of its origin story.

"The card was from your New York seminar three years ago. That's what Mr. Liu told me. And I'd be happy to show you the pocket, but it's kind of on the inside of the dress, and since it's a dress and not a jacket anymore, well, I'm not wearing anything else ..."

His Adam's apple bobs. His jaw clenches and he swallows twice. He doesn't turn away, which means he perhaps, maybe, finds me more attractive than appalling.

To test my theory, I continue, "I mean, of course, I'm wearing *underwear*, but you know what I mean."

Will Power does not take his eyes off the buttons on my dress when he growls.

Damn it. I've miscalculated. With that one sound, I am now the puppy, and he is the master. I have a sudden desire to please him, to lick him, to roll over for him. And that means I need something powerful to keep me from letting my attraction to his smell and his body and his eyes and the way he smiled when he was trying not to, suck me in.

I close my eyes and picture my father. In the time it takes for one deep breath, I see—or more accurately, my body remembers—all the confusion and fear from the days and months after he abandoned Mom and us.

None of it made sense to a ten-year-old, but what I learned from Georgia was that Dad left after becoming uber-rich since he thought the way we looked and dressed and behaved wasn't good enough in his new world.

I blow out a hard breath to interrupt the panic that accompanies remembering what happened after he disappeared with all his money and then Mom died. From normal little girl to welfare kid to orphan in under three years.

I push my chair away from the billionaire and walk back to his plant table, speaking with my back to him.

"These are not healthy nor happy plants. If you don't take action, Mr. Power, they will all die. It's already happening. They're slowly suffocating." I turn to face him.

"But you can save them?"

I don't know if it's a lack of oxygen in his hermetically sealed office tower or a result of my increased pulse rate when I'm near him, but something in Mr. Power's energy overrides the words in my head which are, "There's nothing I can do." Instead, I say, "Not a problem."

Damn it.

9. Will

A SCREAMING PLANT WHISPERER

The plants aren't the only thing suffocating at this moment. I loosen my tie and clear my throat. I can't decide whether it's worse to have her face me or to be staring at her ass and calves. And that madness of copper hair she has tied up, that I want her to let loose so I can tangle my hands in it while I pull her smart-ass mouth to my—*stop it!*

I stand and move quickly back to my chair and the safety of several hundred pounds of wood desk between us. I can't remember the last time I wanted a woman in this way. But Virginia Beach is a lawsuit just waiting to be launched. I can see the headlines: *"Will Power Made Me Scream," Claims Plant Whisperer.*

Not helping, brain.

I clasp my hands together and press—hard—hoping to redirect the blood that thinks it needs to be elsewhere in my body.

"Ms. Beach, we have people who care for all the plants in the building. And they look fine to me."

She nods but doesn't respond. Is she seriously going to

wait for a question before speaking to me? I manage to keep my eyes from dropping below her mouth, held in a comfortable smile. Her lips part as if she's going to say something, but she simply inhales a long, chest-expanding breath. God dammit.

I flinch first, picking up the sheet of paper that sits on top of the small pile in front of me—the one-sheet of Liu's analysis of Virginia Beach's business potential.

I hold it up to block my view of Virginia and read it twice to confirm that what I've read is accurate: John's confidence in her success is high, based on her drive, her willingness to adapt and learn, her fearlessness, and the space in the market for a person with her expertise. She might have scammed her way in to the program, but according to John, she belongs.

I hear the fabric of her dress rustle and look up, watching her back as she fusses with the plants. She's whispering to them. I can't make out what she's saying, and it's distracting as hell.

"I can hear you whispering, you know. If you must talk to them, use your normal voice. It will be less distracting than trying to filter out the 'pss, pss, pss' sounds of you trying to be quiet."

She faces me.

"Am I clear?"

"Actually, I'm not really talking to them. I'm just breathing on them. The air in here is too still. To thrive, plants need CO2 to know they're alive and to photosynthesize. And since we can't open a window, this is the best I can do. If you want them to live, the people you have *taking care of them*"—she air quotes—"need to be told that. Even better than that, if you're having conversations on your cell, you can really help them if you stand over here and talk while you face them."

Virginia "Plant Crusader" Beach, steps toward me with her hands held in front of her like she's presenting an offering. "And even better than that? When you come into your office in the morning and before you leave at the end of the day, blow a slow, warmed breath over them all."

This woman must have plus-sized lungs. When she inhales, her upper body expands like a freaking puffer fish plush toy. She purses her lips and blows slowly toward me while making gentle wind sounds that end with a faint moan. I realize, after I've made the same sound myself, that I'm mimicking her. She might not be spiky like a puffer fish, but this woman is just as dangerous.

"I am not going to breathe on my plants, Ms. Beach. If you have suggestions for the team that is paid to care for them, please make a note and give it to my assistant, Savannah."

She nods and looks around my office. I follow her eyes to the wet bar.

"The hibiscus is dry. May I give it water?"

"Knock yourself out."

She fills a glass half full and brings it to my desk.

"I know you say you have people for this, but since this plant has been ignored for so long, it's going to need more than once-a-week attention, or however often you have them coming. So, may I please show you how to bring this one back to good health, Mr. Power?"

I shake my head no, but say, "Fine."

She picks up the pot and places it right in front of me.

"Poke the soil."

I look from the plant to my fingers, sitting tented before me.

Virginia leans across the desk, giving me a highly inappropriate close-up of her cleavage. New headline: *"Virginia Beach: Will Power's Pick for Favorite Vacation Destination."*

She points at my hands and when I don't move, she pushes her own finger into the soil. "See?" She pulls a dry, clean digit from the pot. "It's *bone* dry. It needs to be *moist*, but not dripping wet. It would be good for you, for the hibiscus, I mean, to be able to *feel* how much moisture this container needs to bring it to life."

Is she seriously using words like *bone* and *moist* while asking me to poke my finger in her container?

"Ms. Beach," I warn, "get that pot off my desk. If it needs so much goddamn attention, give it to Savi to deal with. Or take it home and fix it yourself." I wave for her to back the fuck away from my desk and my boner. "Are you done with the whole first-responder schtick with whatever this plant is?"

"If that's what you prefer, then yes." She takes the glass of water and the almost-dead green thing back to the wet bar and messes about for a minute or two, humming the whole time. She washes her hands and dries them on a paper towel, which she puts in the compost bucket under the sink. She looks like she feels totally at ease in a space designed to make people like her feel the opposite.

People like her. I let the thought bounce around in my head, trying to decipher what it means.

Most people, even the ones who work here, are intimidated by my office and the power it communicates. Not Virginia Beach. If anything, I suspect she sees weakness since she's so intently focused on what's dying in here, not what I've built and am sustaining. I'm curious now.

"Ms. Beach." I point again at the chair in front of my

desk. She sits. "You committed fraud by taking advantage of that gold business card. That's a $20,000 crime. I don't know what the exact penalty for that level of theft is, but one of the several dozen lawyers Will Power & Bros. has on staff will be able to tell me before your feet hit the sidewalk outside this building."

She presses herself into her chair, her arms wrapped around her front, her head tipped so I can't see her face. For the first time since she walked into my office, I am in control. I count to thirty in my head, expecting her to state her case, to give me a reason why I shouldn't charge her with whatever the fuck Legal tells me I can. Maybe I'll even see some tears.

But true to form, she doesn't say a word.

"Ms. Beach, what did you think would happen when I found out about you sneaking into the Power Broker Program?"

"Honestly? I gambled that you probably wouldn't even remember me." She looks up. "I figured that since you have forty people onstage with you every week and that you've delivered at least a dozen more seminars since Vancouver, that your interaction with me would be like, I don't know, buying a coffee from a random barista, just one of the people who exist in the background."

"But you're in my premium coaching program. You didn't think I'd notice that?"

She shakes her head. "From all I read about the program, and what I learned in my first conversation with Mr. Liu, you don't do any direct work with the entrepreneurs enrolled. So yes, I guess I expected to get away with it."

"Did you consider what might happen in the off-chance I did remember you? If we found ourselves in the situation we're in now?"

"I figured you'd kick me out. I didn't think the company would want the publicity of having me sent to jail, but that you'd sue me and I'd have to give you all the money in my bank account—which is nothing, since I'm in debt. And that I'd have to declare bankruptcy, which, quite honestly, would make zero difference in my life since, before I met Mr. Liu, I was never going to be able to afford to buy a place, anyway, so my credit rating is irrelevant."

She looks at me with defiance in her eyes. "I live with my sister. The lease is in her name. Basically, sir, there's not much you can do to make my life any less financially stable, so it seemed stupid not to follow your advice, grab the opportunities life drops in my path, and say thank you." She pushes herself to standing and extends a hand. "So, thank you."

Huh. Not at all what I expected. No teary eyes. No plea for leniency. Not even an apology. This woman is unbelievable.

"Sit." I command.

Unbelievable, but compliant. As well as confident and creative. I could work with that. And for god knows what reason, I want to.

"Back up a little here for me. You said my suit jacket had a hidden pocket."

She nods.

"For Christ's sake, Ms. Beach, if you don't want to be escorted from the building, give up the whole 'don't speak unless asked a question' bullshit, all right? It's a guideline, not a goddamn edict carved in stone."

She pats her left rib. "Inside the inner breast pocket is a

smaller one, just large enough for a business card. I assumed you had it tailored specifically for your golden card."

"Gold. Not golden." I sigh.

"If you let me use your bathroom, I can show you. This dress is reversible, and my sister kept the suit jacket's inside pocket, so it's an outside pocket on this dress, if I wear it with the lining side out."

I point to a door behind her, beside the wet bar. "I'd like to see that."

After she closes the bathroom door, I slide my hand into the inside pocket of the jacket I'm wearing. Since all my suits are made by the same tailor, it should have the same hidden pocket. And by god, it does.

The door clicks open, and there she stands in what appears to be a more fitted version of the same damned dress she wore to the seminar. The one I'd mocked. The dress I've dreamed about taking off her body for the last two months.

10. Virginia

PRETTY PLUMBAGO

As soon as he sees me, Mr. Power closes his eyes and rubs his forehead. It appears that the very sight of my dress has given him an instantaneous headache.

"Should I turn it back to its business side?"

He nods, still not looking at me, and says, "No. It's fine." He opens his eyes and tracks me as I walk back to his desk. "It suits you. It's better than the black side."

"I'm not sure that's a compliment, since you said it was ridiculous. Does that mean you think I'm as ridiculous as the pattern on the dress?"

"No. It means I owe you an apology for how I treated you at the seminar. In fact, I've thought of you several times and the terrible way I tried to humiliate you. To be honest, I half expected you to file a complaint or at the very least, ask for your money back."

"People do that?"

"It happens," he says.

"Do you want to see the pocket?"

He holds up his hand. "I checked my own jacket while

you were changing. I have the same one. I had no idea. I guess it was something we tried and I forgot. Savannah, my assistant, handles the cards. Always has—at least, since I hired her." Then he laughs, deep from his belly. He presses a button on his desk phone. "Savi, do you have a minute to come in?"

Seconds later, a knock accompanies the door as it opens. The woman from the desk outside his office walks toward us. I stand to greet her.

"I thought I recognized your hair!" she says. "You're the woman Will made me give my elastic to at the Vancouver event."

"Virginia," I say, extending my hand. "I'm sorry I didn't recognize you. I was kind of ..."

"Blinded by the assholery of this man's behavior toward you? It's all good. I hope he's apologized." She glares at her boss.

"I have apologized, thank you very much. But I didn't call you in to berate me in front of one of our Power Broker Program participants."

Savannah doesn't hide her surprise.

"Do you remember which event you lost the Gold Business Card at?"

"You mean my first seminar? The one where nobody actually gave me the card? You all just assumed I had it? Of course, it was New York City."

"Well, Ms. Beach found the card." He nods at me. "Show her."

I tell Savannah the jacket pocket story. Aside from the one time she glances at the spot I point to on my dress, Savannah glares at Will Power for the entire minute I speak.

"Well, this is a day we're going to mark in the corporate history books. The day Mr. Perfect apologized—twice."

"Savannah, I am sorry I've ever doubted your efficiency and ingenuity."

Savannah reaches for my hand and shakes it with great enthusiasm. "If you ever need anything—anything at all— just ask. I will move heaven and earth to help you. Thank you for finally clearing this up and proving that the almighty Will Power has made a mistake in his life."

"Enough bonding. You can go now, Savi."

"Ha! Wait until I tell Reshma!"

"Savi, wait." Will Power stands. Savannah stops dead in her tracks. "You cannot tell a soul about this. If you do, John Liu will be humiliated, and he'll be forced to remove Ms. Beach from the program. You have to keep this to yourself."

The joy on Savannah's face melts away. "Of course. Not a word."

"I'm sorry you don't get to gloat. I'll make it up to you."

I sit again and try to make sense of what he's just said. It sounds like he isn't going to sue me or have me removed from the program.

After Savannah leaves, I release all the questions tumbling around in my head in one word: "Why?"

"I don't know." He meets my eye and then says, "Actually, I do know. But I'm not yet convinced that my logic is right, so for now, let's just say that John has confidence you'll reflect well on the Will Power & Bros. brand, and that's reason enough not to mess with what he's working with you to create."

I'm disappointed by his answer and I know exactly why. For the first time in longer than I care to consider, I am reminded that, like all the plants I care for, my own body also needs loving attention. Something in the way Will

Power looks at me tells me he's a man who brings his workaholic perfectionism to bed.

And I want a taste of that.

I want him to tell me the reason he's not kicking me out is because he wants to see me again. I don't want to have to choose between cake and cookies. I want both—success *and* sex with this man who makes my skin tingle when he touches me.

"When are you meeting with Mr. Liu again?" he asks.

"A week from today."

"Will my shrubberies survive another week without your expert attention?"

I smile. "Your shrubberies will survive. They won't thrive, but ..." I do my best fake British accent, "They're not dead yet."

"A Monty Python fan." He nods and smiles.

"Not sure I'd call myself a fan, but I have a thing for quotes, and they have some memorable one-liners."

He stares at me without speaking again. If eyes could have sex, I'm certain mine are dry-humping his long, thick lashes. I blink and look away, letting him win that round.

"Twenty thousand dollars. How many plant care consulting hours is that in your current business model?" he asks.

"Current as of this morning? That would be two hundred hours."

"Two hundred weeks. That's four years of once-a-week visits. That math won't work." Will Power pulls his phone from his pocket and opens the calculator app. I watch as he taps the screen in silence. "How many client hours do you currently work in a week?"

"Twenty, but—"

"So, you have twenty hours free for more clients."

"No, because I'm reworking the business model and have until next week to find a replacement for all but one of my residential clients. And then, following Mr. Lui's advice, I'm to find one or two corporate clients."

"Perfect. Has he suggested you approach Will Power & Bros. for a contract?"

I shake my head.

"Then I will." He picks up his desk phone. "Savi, find out what business has the contract to care for the plants in this building. Have Legal send me a copy, please." He hangs up. "I don't know what kind of commitment we have with whoever's doing the job now, but I hear from a reliable source that they're doing a crap job of it."

My heart swells. He doesn't know it, but that endorsement is worth more to me than a hundred apologies for the public humiliation.

"This building has thirty-two floors of offices. I'm sure they all have plants somewhere on them. What do you have scheduled right now?"

I check my phone for the time. "Nothing until one p.m. when I have to be in the British Properties."

"Cancel."

"I can't."

"Can't or won't?" he counters.

"Won't. He's an elderly man, and I'm helping him win back his dead wife's love."

Will Power raises his eyebrows and opens his mouth, but I wave and interrupt before he can speak.

"It's a long story, but he's the one client I'll never cancel on, nor will I stop seeing personally."

"Strange, but I respect the commitment. Here's what I need from you—a detailed proposal for how many hours a week you'd need to properly care for all the plants in this building."

"I'd need to see—"

"How many plants there are. I realize. Which is why I'd like you to cancel your appointments tomorrow, come back, and visit all the floors and offices so you know what's needed. And then, I want the specific amount of time it will take for you to earn $18,000 working at your new rate."

"Eighteen?"

"You really should've asked for your money back after how I spoke to you onstage."

"I figured the jacket was worth two thousand." I shrug a shoulder and smile.

"Fair." He nods. "Since I assume you still need to pay bills and eat and such, I'd like you to figure out how long it would take you to work off an $18,000 debt at your old rate."

"So basically, your company will pay me at my old rate until I earn $18,000?"

"No. Wrong on two counts. First, I'm not hiring you. I don't have that authority. I'm asking you to prepare a proposal, which I will personally recommend to the department that does hire external contractors.

"And second, if my company hires your company, it will be at your current rate, with a fifty percent discount until your debt of $18,000 is paid off, so you'll be billing today's hourly rate and discounting the difference as your debt repayment. Does that make sense?"

I stand and lean forward, far enough to reach just halfway across Mr. Power's desk to shake his hand. He stands as well, but ignores my outstretched arm, walking around to my side. He moves directly in front of me and places his hands on my shoulders. I look up at him and feel myself leaning up on tiptoes. I fight the urge to kiss him—just a little thank-you kiss on the cheek. Or the lips. A professional kiss on the lips. People do that, right?

"Virginia ..." He pulls me from my fantasy. "May I call you Virginia?"

I nod and twist out from under his hold before he's able to read my thoughts.

"Sorry," he says. "In my family, hands on shoulders means, 'Pay attention, I'll only say this once.'"

"I'm listening."

"Get Savi's number on your way out. Call her in one week to find out if WPB will be your first corporate client. If that doesn't work out, I still want you to make an appointment to have a look at my plants each time you meet with Mr. Liu."

"OK."

"I'm not done. From now on, call me Will. And for the love of common sense and sanity, when we speak, say what's on your mind—do not wait for questions to answer. I'm dead serious. I may not have the power to hire people, but I can fire them, and that will be a fireable offense. Understood?"

"Mm, hmm." I nod. I pause. And then say exactly what's on my mind. "I have about a hundred curses I have to reverse. You're not the plumbago I thought you were."

"Plumbago?"

"It's a really pretty ground flower that's toxic to touch. It causes terrible blisters." I squint my eyes closed. "I should not have said that out loud."

"Plumbago." Will Power actually chuckles. "*One hundred* curses? I hope you get the contract. I'd like the chance to hear what those curses are—or *were*—one day."

11. Will

IF FOOD BE THE MUSIC OF LOVE

This is Virginia's fourth day coming to my office to breathe my plants back to health. Honestly, I thought it was bullshit. Or at least partially bullshit. Not being a shrub expert, what did I know, but this sighing into the leaves across the office, while I'm trying to focus on talking points for my podcast, is making it hard to get anything done. Unfortunately, that isn't the only thing she makes hard.

I do my best to ignore her, and for her part, she truly seems to forget I'm in the room. Today she's wearing another of her sister's custom-made dresses—this one is shades of red and pink with flowers on it. I watch her skirt sway under her hips, moving as though she's dancing in place to a song in her head. Maybe I'm staring.

"The fuck, Virginia?" I storm toward her before my brain realizes what my body is doing.

She turns with a look of surprise. "Sorry. Was I humming? I hum when I'm focused."

I point at her skirt. "I thought this was another plant-themed pattern, but it's fucking vulvas."

Her eyes widen, and then she laughs out loud. "It *is* flowers. Flowers with style. It's from a Georgia O'Keeffe painting."

Her joy. Her energy. Those provocative vulvas all over her curves. I walk back to the safe side of my office to keep from acting on what every cell in my body is demanding.

"Virginia, if I was to wear a tie covered in cocks, I am certain HR would be up my ass warning about sexual harassment lawsuits. What makes this dress any different?"

She lifts the hem of her skirt just enough to show her knees and looks at it like the answer could be found in the goddamn folds. My mind wanders up and under her skirt, imagining what her hidden folds might look like.

"I mean, it really is a pattern based on a painting, so it's art as clothing. And art is open to interpretation, right?"

"There is nothing open to interpretation about that pattern. When I look at you, *all* I see is a giant vulva." I drop my head, realizing too late what I've just said.

When I look up, Virginia's eyes meet mine and I breathe a sigh of relief. Her silence isn't rage. She's covered her mouth and is trying not to laugh. This woman. She has no idea how much power her authenticity gives her.

"I'm sorry," I say. "That came out wrong."

"Like Freud said, 'Sometimes a cigar is just a cigar.' And sometimes a flower is just a flower. But if it upsets you, I won't wear it again. Would you like me to leave and come on your lunch break?"

I would very much like you to come on my lunch break, you and that fucking vulva dress.

I nod. "Arrange it with Savi."

"Of course." She stops at the door. "See you later. I mean, tomorrow? Or would you rather I always come when you're not here?"

For the love of god, stop saying come.

"I'll see you tomorrow morning. In workplace-appropriate attire, please."

As soon as my door clicks closed, I call Horse.

"You free for lunch?"

"Your office or mine?"

"Yours. Definitely yours."

I look back at my laptop and the work I've been trying to do. In the ten minutes that Virginia's been in my space, I've managed to type all of one question when normally I'd have bashed out a full page. I stare at the topic, "Episode 723: How to manage time with the wrong people, with guest Artemis Hagel."

The Power Hour podcast is my contribution to the business bottom line when I'm not delivering seminars. It's easier, that's for sure, but boring as shit, which makes it an enormous energy suck. I have to appear to be interested in the stories from these medium-success businesses, all of which at one time or another have participated in the Come Into Power weekend.

From a Will Power & Bros. business perspective, it's a brilliant strategy since the only way to get on my show is to have first paid $2000 to be in my seminar audience. Entrepreneurs that have joined the Power Broker Program are guaranteed a spot. The rest are by application, which gives the team several upsell opportunities. It is a time-intensive undertaking that requires a dozen staff people, but according to Brian (the financial brains of the Power brotherhood), the podcast contributes substantially to our bottom line.

And so, I do my part—ask deep questions, make astute observations, and offer detailed analyses of our guests' businesses. I smile and nod, hating every minute of it.

I stare mid office at the chrome-and-glass table covered in green, a small burst of life in an otherwise sterile space. It's only been a week, and just for fifteen minutes a day, but I miss Virginia's energy, distracting as it is. She obviously loves how she makes her living. And paltry as her income is, she appears happy—happier getting up to come to work than I am, that's for sure. Though knowing she'll be arriving at nine makes dragging my ass down the two floors from my condo to my office significantly more appealing.

I stare at the empty space in front of the plant table and imagine her quietly, but not silently, dancing to music I can't hear, breathing out life that I can't feel, and I am envious of her freedom. It's the same feeling that drove me to humiliate her onstage. But now, knowing her, even as little as I do, I wonder what I might learn from her and the way she approaches her business.

How did she discover her aptitude with plants?

What made her think she could have a career as a plant whisperer?

What did John Liu see in her and her business that made him believe it could be a million-dollar enterprise?

I start typing questions as quickly as they come to mind, not worrying about the typos since my fingers can't keep up with my brain.

Once I have a page, I create a new file, upload it to the shared drive, then send a message to John Liu and Catherine, the company's new Power Hour Podcast producer. I ask John to prep Virginia and to let me and Catherine know when she's ready for her sixty minutes of fame-by-association.

It may be a little premature for Virginia to be a guest since she doesn't have a book to hype, a product to pitch or a franchise to promote. What she has to offer is a personality that will appeal to a new-to-us audience that will benefit Will Power & Bros. more than The Other Side of the Fence, but it certainly won't hurt her business.

Imagining her across the mic from me gives me an idea. I message my other two brothers and ask if they can meet in Horse's office for lunch.

Three hours later, just before noon, I step out of my suite. Savi and Virginia are seated in the giant armchairs in my waiting area, drinking what look like lattes, laughing.

"Hey, Will," Savannah greets me with a smile. She's always smiling, which I take to mean she enjoys her job. "Virginia was just telling me about some of her more memorable fashion faux pas."

"The vulva dress made the list, I assume." I wink at Virginia.

She squeezes her eyes shut, shaking her head. "Top position."

I look at my shoes but still don't avoid imagining Virginia in the top position.

"I think it's a gorgeous dress, and if someone sees more than flowers, it simply means they need to get laid."

My shock at Savannah's comment comes out as a cough, quickly followed by anger. "Too far, Ms. Cook," I warn.

Savannah grimaces. "I am so sorry, Mr. Power. That was entirely inappropriate."

"I'll be back in thirty minutes. Please be finished in my office by then, Ms. Beach." I leave the ladies sitting in silence and head toward the elevator bank to get to Horse's office on the other side of the building. We all have basically identical office suites on the same floor, each taking a corner. Our private elevator only stops at five floors: ground level, these offices, and three floors of living suites. The four of us each have half a floor to call home. The penthouse, Mother's, is the full 9,000 square feet.

The elevator doors open on two sides. Exit to the left for mine and Brian's offices, to the right for Horse and Aiden. On the living floors, one side opens to my suite, the other to Horse's. If he wants to drop in to see me, he just has to walk through the elevator and he'll be in my personal space.

Other than cleaning staff, my brothers, and Mother, Savi is the only other person who's been in my suite in years —and only to drop off files or dry cleaning. That she assumes it's been a while since I've been laid, as she so graciously put it, is based on the intimacy we've developed traveling the world together over the last three years. It's a professional friendship that in no way threatens her husband, since it's clear to everyone who sees us interact in public that I am her boss. And inside our building, she's like a meddling little sister. It's a role I'm fine with when performed in front of family.

But that comment in front of Virginia? That was out of line.

Horse's executive assistant's desk is empty, so I let myself into his office. Aiden and Brian are already here.

"Staging a coup without me?" I ask.

"Reshma should be back in a minute with lunch," Horse says.

"We were actually wondering the same thing—but with Mother as the ousted party. Impromptu board meeting without her? What's going on, Will?" Aiden asks.

"Not at all. Though ..." I raise my eyebrows, as if considering.

"I know, right?" Brian says.

"I just wanted to see you guys. Give you a laugh at my idiocy. And toss a creative business idea by you."

A knock on the door lets us know lunch has arrived. Reshma is far more formal than Savannah in all ways, shapes, and forms. She's been working for Horse for several months but still calls us all Mr. Power, which is amusing in situations like this. She rolls in the bussing cart which carries our food. Lunch is made by our in-house chef, so we rarely order anything specific, instead letting her do what she's best at—preparing Michelin Star–worthy meals.

Today is a hot roast beef sandwich with coleslaw and fries. And each portion is twice as big as it needs to be.

"Which one of you is going to share with me? I only need half of this," I say.

"I'll go half with you," Brian says.

I hand my covered plate back to Reshma. "If you'd like half of this, it's all yours. And can you ask Savi to come and get the other half and offer it to the contractor working on my plants, please?"

"Of course, Mr. Power."

Horse gives me a look but waits until Reshma is gone before saying, "If food be the music of love, play on."

"That's not the way it goes, dumbass," Aiden says.

"Oh, but it is. Will's love language is food. You've got it bad for this plant lady. Why are you with us if she's in your office right now?" Horse asks.

I tell them about Virginia's dress. And my inappropriate declaration. And how I can't focus when she's around but that I enjoy the distraction of her. And that Savi said I need to get laid. The bastards laugh, and every one of them sides with my assistant, encouraging me to ask Virginia Beach out on a proper date.

Although I wasn't going to admit it, that's exactly what I needed to hear.

Since my every move in public has the potential to ruin our family name, I want to make sure my brothers are fine with me leaving the safety and reputational security of the building. My entire world, when I'm not traveling, is contained within the top five stories of the Power luxury high-rise.

"Thanks for the unsolicited relationship advice, but that's not why I wanted to see you. I have an idea for a new product line that should appeal to a demographic we've been struggling to engage."

It's been three weeks since I started caring for the plants in the Power tower, and I adore everything about the job. I'm getting to know people who share my love of all things green and growing, and I think I'm even making friends. But the person I am most happy to see every day?

Will.

He's changed my schedule, so I go to the executive floor —and his office—at the end of each day. He says it's too distracting having me in his space during his productive morning hours, but that he enjoys our banter so he doesn't want me doing my work over his lunch break.

I love finishing my day with him since I don't have to rush out. I guess he doesn't have anywhere to be either since we've taken to sitting on his couch and gabbing after I finish tending what he always refers to as his "shrubberies." The way he says *shrubberies*, like an uppity, British blue blood, always makes me laugh.

"Big Friday night plans?" Will asks, setting a cup of

herbal dragon chai on the coffee table for me, my signal to wrap up what I'm doing.

"Huge," I answer, dropping into the seat beside him. "I'll be rehearsing for this podcast I'm scheduled to be on. I'm a big deal, in case you weren't aware."

"I am quite aware of how substantial your deal is, Ms. Beach." He smiles, then shakes his head. "Really? No date?"

It feels like Will Power and I are becoming friends, but we're most definitely not the kind of friends who share relationship stories. So I will not be telling him that the idea of dating brings on nothing but discomfort since he's the only man I've thought about since our first non-public meeting. I know he finds me attractive and appreciates my company, but it's also clear that he has no interest in crossing a line from friends to ... more than friends.

"I'm surprised that you're surprised. I mean, what about you? It's more surprising that a man of your,"—I pause for effect and lick my lips—"a man *with* such an incredible ass, er, assets, isn't out wining and dining Hollywood North starlets."

Will rolls his eyes.

"Seriously, though," I say, "how did Virginia Rainforest Beach manage to win the boss lottery?"

"You rigged the game and printed your own golden ticket." Will pokes me in the side, so I grab his hand. Instead of withdrawing, he weaves his fingers with mine. "Stay for dinner?"

A thousand leafy pothos sway in my gut, cheering their support. I stare at our hands and all I can think is that Will has nicer cuticles and nails than I do, and that I really should wear gloves when I dig in soil, but then I wouldn't be able to feel it and without that direct contact, I won't know how healthy it is.

"Earth to Virginia." Will breaks my trance. I pull my hand into my lap.

"Sorry. I was just noticing ... never mind. Dinner? Um, uh—"

"Do you have other plans?"

I shake my head.

"Then it's settled. I'll have our in-house-chef prepare an extra meal. Is there anything you can't eat? Any allergies or anything you don't like?"

I shake my head again and Will picks up his phone.

"Hello, Marcy. Can you add a second meal to my delivery, please?" He smiles at me and nods. "What is it we're having tonight?" He winks while he listens. "Sounds delightful. Thank you, Marcy." Will slides his phone onto the coffee table and says, "You're in luck. It's pub night, Power style. Bison burgers on house-made sour dough buns, onion rings, twice cooked fries, a green salad with avocado and apple slices, and chocolate milkshakes for dessert."

Until this moment, I've never felt uncomfortable with Will. I've acknowledged my feelings for him—lots of them —but never anything like this. This is more than an employer giving his broke contractor half of his giant sandwich. It's like ...

"Will, am I about to have a dinner date with the most eligible bachelor in the Western Hemisphere? Because if I am, I think I need a moment to process this." I try to sound light and jokey, but inside my spirea bushes are uprooting themselves, jumping with joy.

"Most eligible bachelor in the Western Hemisphere?" He laughs from deep in his belly. "I have three single brothers who would challenge that assertion. And I wouldn't argue. Of the four of us, I am, without a doubt, the least desirable Power brother."

I raise an eyebrow and open my mouth to challenge him, but he presses a remarkably soft index finger to my lips and says, "I'm an unapologetic workaholic. I'm on the road twice a year for at least two months. My sleep schedule would be impossible to live with. And,"—his playful energy nosedives—"I'll be dead before I'm old enough to know the answer to life, the universe, and everything. So, no, not a date, simply dinner with a woman who reminds me that there's more to life than being Will Power."

My inner daffodils wilt. I'm not sure if I am sadder that Will doesn't consider this a date or that he seems to truly believe he is undatable.

"I'll stay for dinner on one condition—that we take our milkshakes outside and drink them in the park."

Will crosses his arms and leans back. I can't read whether he's self-soothing, blocking, or considering. I've noticed over the last ten days that my ability to read him has muddied, that I've been overlaying his cues with my emotions, expectations, and hopes.

"You want fresh air? What if we go to the rooftop deck? Very fresh up there."

"No, I want to walk in the grass. When was the last time you walked barefoot on actual earth? Do you know how important it is to connect to the earth, not through thirty stories of steel and concrete, but to actually touch the ground with your bare feet and connect to the energy of life?"

He scowls.

"You don't believe me."

"It's not that I don't believe you. I'm sure there's some

study out there to support that idea. It's just that ... it's not worth it for me to leave the building—"

"What are you talking about? Not worth it? Your physical health. Not worth it? Your mental health. Not worth it? Your—"

"It's pseudoscience—"

"It's *science* science, you dummy." I gently punch his thigh and he grabs my hand again. "You've told me you don't sleep well. You said since May Day you haven't slept through the night. Will, that's over two months. Do this one thing for me. Take a walk in the park with me after dinner, and then tell me if you sleep better tonight. If you don't, I'll accept that the great Will Power is above science. But if you *do* sleep better, promise you'll go for a walk outside in the real world with me after work at least three days a week until my contract ends. Deal?"

He's still holding my fist in his hand, but he loosens his grip and directs my palm to the same spot on his thigh I tapped. My fingers rest far too close to his zipper to not make me think about what would happen if I were to reach out and touch it.

The damned windstorm spins anew in my belly. Thankfully, we're interrupted by a knock on the door. Will calls, "Come in," but doesn't move my hand. A young man pushes in a trolly, and the smell of burgers and fried food fills the air. I inhale deeply, and Will tightens his grip. I pull my eyes from the food and see he's staring at my breasts. When my gaze drops back to my hand, I notice the distance between my fingers and Will's zipper has decreased by half. Oh, dear.

"Thanks, Pete. Have a good weekend," he says, sounding entirely normal. How can he speak? I know if I try to say anything, I'll manage only a squeak.

"You, too, Mr. Power," the young man says, closing the door behind him.

"How do you know I'll tell you the truth, that I won't say it made no difference, even if I happen to sleep better tonight than normal?" Will asks, releasing my hand and reaching for a burger, as if nothing just happened between us.

I don't answer right away, even though I don't believe he'd lie to me. But I need to catch my breath, so I reach for the bottle of carbonated water on the trolly and pour us each a glass. I swallow a long drink, and then, when I trust my vocal chords to cooperate, I say, "Because you have integrity, and I trust you. Also, if it works, why wouldn't you agree to do it again? It just makes sense."

"I'll take a walk in the park for you, Virginia." Will grabs his phone and dials. "I need security to have a man ready in about thirty minutes. I'll be taking a walk in the park ... that's right." Will hangs up and returns his phone to the table. "Most eligible bachelors don't need babysitters when they play in the park."

D inner is delicious.

"Is this unicorn meat or something? It's the most magical burger I've ever eaten."

"I've noticed you bring a bagged lunch. The restaurant downstairs uses the same recipes, same cooks. And staff get a discount. Next week, ask Savi to set you up with an account."

Conversation over dinner is comfortable. Our shared moment of sexual tension dissipates as quickly as it came on, and I wonder if I imagined it or made it up. In some ways, I hope I did, since I don't want to lose this job or risk ruining this unexpected, budding friendship with Will.

Once the burgers and onion rings are nothing but greasy stains on our plates, Will pulls two insulated cups from a thermos bag and hands me one. "Ready for dessert?"

"Ready to dig your toes in the dirt?"

"No, but now that I've pulled some poor guy from what I'm certain he expected would be a quiet Friday night, I guess we have to go."

13. Will

TWEEZER TEETH

I debate asking Virginia to wait in my office while I go upstairs to change into something a little more casual, but instead decide to let her ride to the penultimate floor with me.

"We're going up?"

"Just for a minute. If I'm really going to be taking off my shoes and walking around barefoot like some pot-smoking, flower-loving hippie, I don't think a suit and Berlutis fit the moment."

Virginia looks up and smiles with her whole face. "Flower-loving hippies aren't so bad, you know."

"So I'm learning." The elevator door opens, and I lead Virginia into my living room. "Give me five minutes. Make yourself at home."

She walks to the wall of windows and stares out over the city, muttering single words, "Wow," "Amazing," and "Unreal," to herself.

I shower quickly—something I do as soon as I take off my suit each day to draw a line between work and non-work hours—then dress in jeans, a T-shirt, and a baseball cap, and

I quietly return to the living room. I watch her from the hall as she runs her fingers along the spines of my books, humming and moving in that way she does to music she says she feels more than she hears. I want to wrap my arms around her, experience her ease and relaxation. I want to hold her and absorb her into me.

Instead, I say, "All set. Am I the perfect representation of a man who's eager to connect with Mother Earth?"

"Don't make fun of me until you've done it," she warns, smiling. "The ball cap suits you."

"Don't forget your milkshake." I point to the coffee table where she set her cup down.

"We should've ordered an extra for the security guy. I bet he'll be sad he doesn't get one."

"If you're willing to share, we can give him mine." I picture Virginia sucking in the drink, licking her lips, passing her cup to me, and me tasting her on the straw. Dear god, it has been far too long since I've tasted a woman.

We ride down in silence and meet my security detail for the evening in the lobby.

"Nice to see you, Mr. Power. My name is Bruce. Where are you headed tonight?"

"Apparently, just up the street to the park where we'll be enjoying a chocolate milkshake. I brought one for you, if you'd like."

"No, thank you, sir."

I am disappointed not to be forced to share with Virginia, so I hand my milkshake to the doorman. "This is for you. Chocolate milkshake. If you don't want it, that's fine. But I hope you enjoy it."

Having my hands free while walking beside Virginia "Can't Stop Imagining Her Naked" Beach is torture. She holds her milkshake in the hand closest to me and when she takes her first sip, she moans.

Kill me now.

"That is ... seriously, what does your chef put in this food? How is it possible that a chocolate milkshake can taste so good? I mean, it's milk and chocolate ice cream. Why do I have the sensation I'm drinking liquid happiness?"

"Hey, give me that." I reach for her hand and hold it under mine a few seconds longer than necessary before taking the cup from her and putting the straw to my lips. I close my eyes, take a long pull, and swirl the drink so it coats my tongue before I swallow. She's not wrong. "I'd like to tell you it's my company that makes this so good, but the truth is, it's the mix of house-made vanilla ice cream, chocolate ganache, and a pinch of cinnamon and chili powder."

"Oh my god, must have more." Virginia reaches to grab the cup, but I hold it high over her head. "Give it back. Get your own. I made a mistake and don't want to share."

"Too late."

She sighs. "Fine."

I lower the cup and rest it on top of her head, within her reach. She wraps her hand over mine and we walk like this, hand-in-hand, for several yards before I'm willing to give up the connection.

Virginia thanks me with a hint of a smile before she wraps her lips around the that fucking lucky straw again.

The tree-lined, gravel path that snakes through a park covers about four square blocks—not huge, but big enough that the sounds of the city are muffled by the trees and distance from the street.

"Do you have a particular destination in mind?"

"Mm-hmm." Her mouth is full and she moans again.

Note to self: No more milkshakes with Virginia. Or burgers. Or onion rings. Does she moan her delight with all the food she eats? I debate whether I actually want to put myself through the torture of finding out.

"Mmm, so, so good."

I decide I not only want to know if she moans when she eats steak and salad, but also what noises she makes with other kinds of pleasure.

"There's a bench just across the way, over there." She points. "The ground is soft. It's a perfect place to take off our shoes and wiggle our toes in the dirt."

"You're serious about bare feet?"

"Mm-hmm." Her mouth is full again. She hands the milkshake to me. "No more. This is better than sex." She gasps as soon as she says the word.

I would like to prove you wrong.

I check behind us. Bruce is at a comfortable distance, not able to overhear our conversation, but close enough to be at my side within two seconds. I don't expect him to be needed; security is an unwelcome but required precaution for a high-profile billionaire. Sadly.

And even though Vancouver isn't known for its paparazzi, they're here, hiding in plain sight, just like any city that is home to the rich and famous. Given my face is as recognizable as most A-list actors, I prefer to avoid any chance of being photographed. So it's a big deal, going out in the daylight with a woman wearing a dress that screams, "Hey, look over here!" yet in the humblest way.

We reach the bench and sit. Virginia immediately undoes her sandals and runs her feet over the grass. "It feels so good. What are you waiting for? Do you need me to take your runners off for you?" She stands and starts to kneel in front of me.

Bad idea. I pull off my hat and drop it into my lap.

"Get up, you brat." I shake my head and direct her back to the bench beside me. I undo my Nikes, pull off my socks, and place my bare feet on the ground.

Then, I wiggle my toes. The dirt, sand, earth, whatever it is, gives a little.

"It's not terrible," I admit.

"Come on! Let's walk in the grass." She takes my hand and leads me back to the park we've just walked through. "Doesn't it feel amazing? Grounding?"

Her enthusiasm amuses me. "Sure."

"Stop," she says. "I need you to experience this. Close your eyes."

I stare at her, doing the opposite of what she's just asked.

"Seriously, Will, close your eyes." Virginia places her fingers over my eyelids which flutter open as soon as she moves her hands.

"No, stay closed." It's a gentle command, but it is a command.

I obey. Then she presses her palm over my heart. "Just listen. Not to the distant traffic sounds or people talking, but to the energy coming from the ground, into your feet, and up your legs. Can you hear it? It's the energy of the earth. It's so calming. If you pay attention, it can reset your entire nervous system."

She stops talking but doesn't move her hand from my chest. I sneak a peek, and her eyes are closed, a giant smile on her lips. She has her other hand over her own heart. I want mine there, so I place my palm over hers. Without any hesitation, she pulls her hand out and presses it on top of mine. The fabric I'm touching is warm and soft.

"Focus on the earth energy," she reminds me.

And boy, do I need reminding since my focus has moved to the energy that is rising and falling under her sundress.

"Will! Just *feel* my heartbeat." Virginia's hand squeezes mine. "You don't need to pump my heart for me!"

I realize I've begun kneading the side of her breast. "Sorry." I try to pull away, but she holds me.

"Focus on your feet." She giggles.

I don't know whether it's being barefoot or having her hand on my chest or mine on hers, but she's right. Once I relax, I do feel more grounded than I have in as long as I can remember.

I open my eyes. "You may be onto something with this hippie stuff."

"Right?" she says. "And now for the 'stop and smell the flowers' portion of our walk." Virginia removes my hand from over her heart and pulls me toward the rose bushes several yards away. She swings our arms like a kid, her joy strangely infectious.

"Did you know that the roses people buy in flower shops are scentless? They're almost all hybrids that have been bred to live longer after they've been cut, but at a cost —no fragrance."

I didn't know this, and a week ago if you'd asked me if I cared, I'd have said no. But tonight, I'd love nothing more than to hear about the history of roses.

Virginia keeps talking. "These pinky-orange ones smell like pears and grapes. They're called Lady Emma Hamilton. To me, they're the prettiest roses. Lean in and take a deep breath."

I do and nod my agreement.

"And these red-wine colored ones,"—she pulls me a few steps to the right—"are called Munstead Wood. Take a deep breath in. Blackberries, right? They're my favorite fragrance."

I lean in and inhale a deep breath. "Nice. What about these?" I step away from Virginia to a bush covered in bright pink flowers that don't look like the others.

I put my bare foot down and lean in to take a whiff. "Fuck!" A burning spike impales my sole.

Before I can hop away, Bruce is on one side of me, Virginia on the other.

"It's nothing. I think I stepped on a thorn. Surprised me. That's all." I try to laugh it off. "So much for the energy of the earth being so calming."

Virginia looks like she might cry. "I am so, so sorry. Those have the worst prickles."

"Let me help you back to the bench, sir. We can pull it out when you're sitting."

Turns out that's easier said than done, given none of our fingernails are long enough to grab the small bit of thorn still poking out from the ball of my right foot.

"Will ..." Virginia kneels in front of me, pain in her eyes. "I am so sorry. I feel terrible."

"I'd like to renegotiate this whole 'walk barefoot in the wild' deal."

"Sir, I suggest Virginia go back to the building to get tweezers. Unless you'd like me to call one of the other security members to bring them."

"I can get it out," Virginia says with full confidence, even though she, too, has tried and failed.

"Are there tweezers hidden in your sundress?"

"Better. In my mouth."

"In your what?"

Instead of answering, she sits on the bench beside me

and pulls my leg into her lap, forcing my body to twist in her direction.

"Lean back and relax. Give me your foot." Virginia looks up over my shoulder at my security detail. "Bruce, I think there's a small flask in my backpack purse. Will you please take it out and hand it to me?"

Bruce doesn't answer.

Virginia's expression changes—she seems to be scowling at him. She speaks slowly. "I need you to take the flask from my purse." She rests her palm over her heart and taps a couple of times, which seems odd.

I'm not down with this. "Whatever it is you're considering, just stop. If you need to be drunk to take this thorn out, I'd rather wait—"

She interrupts me. "So I can disinfect Mr. Power's foot."

She looks over my shoulder, but Bruce doesn't move. What the hell is going on? I look up at him and he gives me a tentative smile.

"Bruce." Virginia draws my attention back to her.

My security guy does as she asks, taking a flask from the purse on her back and handing it to her.

She takes a swig, swishes it around in her mouth, then spits the booze onto the ground.

"This might sting." Virginia pours alcohol on the ball of my foot, then tries to hand me the flask.

"I'll take that, sir." Bruce grabs the flask from Virginia's hand, but I see the artwork on it—the word *BIG* with a drawing of a rooster—before he pockets it.

Before I can process why Virginia has a flask that says "big cock," she pulls my attention back to my foot. She's palpated the pads on either side of the spot where the thorn pulses like it's trying to become one with my soul. And then she leans forward and bares her teeth as she pulls my foot to her mouth.

"What the actual fuck are you doing?" I pull my leg from her grip.

"Relax." She laughs and makes a show of slowly inhaling and exhaling. Just like Joe used to do. Joe, the bastard, who made good on his threat and left me in the lurch two months ago.

"Will," Virginia snaps.

I watch and follow her breath until my leg relaxes.

Virginia runs her tongue along the edge of her top teeth. "I've pulled dozens, maybe hundreds, of thorns and spiky plant bits from my hands with my teeth. I can do this."

"You are *not* sucking on my foot."

"Will Power, chill. I'm not going to suck your foot. And I'm not going back to the building to get tweezers when I can do this with my teeth. So sit back and shut up."

"Sir, would you like me to call—"

"No, he would not. Would you two just relax? My god, it's as if you've never interacted with the real world." She grabs my calf and yanks it back into her lap. I could fight, but I know I won't win, so I give in and let Virginia press her lips against the ball of my foot.

Talk about hearing a feeling ... when her tongue touches my sole, I swear to Christ I hear angels sing as the air leaves my lungs. I don't know what she's doing or why, but holy shit, it's an unexpected turn-on to have her mouth on the least sexy part of any human body.

After several seconds of performing the most intimate act I've ever experienced in public, her teeth find an edge. She exhales warm air and says, "Don't move," against my foot. I tense my leg, not only to make sure I don't kick her in the mouth, but because I'm suddenly sporting what will become, in about two seconds, a very obvious boner.

I pull the ball cap from my head and drop it on my lap.

She tugs. A sharp pain follows, then the relief as the thorn leaves my flesh. Virginia takes the spike between her fingers, leans forward again, and kisses my foot.

"Ta-da!"

"That was …," I release a long breath, squeeze my eyes closed, and make fists to focus. "Unexpected."

Bruce raises his eyebrows. I can tell he wants to laugh, but one look at the spot where he put the flask wipes the smirk from his face. I've figured out that it must be his. How Virginia knew it was there is beyond me, but drinking on the job is an offense justifying termination.

Virginia pulls my attention back to her. "It shouldn't hurt to walk now. Do you have hydrogen peroxide back at your place? You need to clean this wound. It's highly unlikely you'll get an infection—I never have—but better safe than sorry."

I stare at the chaos of red curls that haloes the smile I desperately need to kiss. The sensation of her tongue probing the ball of my foot echoes against my skin. I want that feeling on other parts of my body. My mouth opens, but I don't know what to say.

"What?" Virginia laughs. "Have you got hydrogen peroxide in your palace or should I get some for you and drop it off at the front desk?"

"Yes, I have hydrogen peroxide. And since you put my life at risk of infection, I expect you to come up and make sure this wound is properly cleaned."

It's dark out by the time I finish cleaning the puncture in Will's foot. I spend far longer making sure I did a good job than I would have if it had been my own flesh. And then there's the bonus foot massage I give him, because how often does a woman like me find herself with model-perfect feet attached to a stunningly handsome man, stretched out on a couch, lying in her lap?

I close my eyes so I can't see the bazillion-dollar condo I'm in and allow myself to imagine that Will and I could have a connection—a relationship-type connection. Over the last four weeks, working for Will Power & Bros., it has become clear that in another world, where Will was a normal human or where I had the right character, personality, and looks to fit in with the über elite, that we could've been more than after-hours friends.

The spark that tingled up my arm when I shook his hand on stage is now a pulse that fills my entire body whenever he's in the room. And from the way he relaxes while I pulsate pressure points on the soles of his feet, I can tell he feels something too. I flash back to the flippant comment

Savannah made about him needing to get laid. How is it possible that a man this wealthy, handsome, smart, and interesting can't have any woman he wants at any time?

In a different life, I'd be throwing myself at Will's feet.

I chuckle, realizing that's exactly what I've done, in my own Virginia way.

"What's so amusing?" he asks, tapping my thigh with his free foot.

"I was just thinking about how unlikely the odds were that I'd find myself doing reflexology on *the* Will Power."

"Interesting. I was just thinking about how unlikely the odds were that I'd ever let anyone into my home to do ..."— he points and spins his finger toward my hands—"whatever it is you're doing. Reflexology?"

"Reflexology lite, really. I'm hitting pressure points to help you relax. There are dozens of spots on our feet connected to our organs and body systems."

Will cocks his head and furrows his brow. Does he realize how obvious he is when he doesn't believe or understand something I tell him?

"You need proof?" I press my thumb deep into the outside edge of the arch of his right foot, just above his heel. I hold constant pressure for a silent count of thirty. "You should register something soon."

"The only thing I'm registering is a need to urinate," he says, wiggling his foot free.

"Point proven!" I cheer, my arms in the air.

"Proves nothing other than I've been sitting here drinking tea with you for an hour and now my bladder is full."

While Will is in the bathroom, I open two diagrams of foot reflexology pressure points on my phone, one with labels and one without. Also, realizing it's after nine, I figure I should be leaving, so I slide into my sandals and wait in the chair by the elevator door for Will to reappear.

"What are you doing?" he asks, looking confused. "I'm sorry. I didn't mean to offend you."

"You didn't offend me. I figured it was time for me to go. Your foot is fine, and apparently, you also have a healthy bladder and kidneys." I hand him my phone with the unlabeled image. "Where was I just putting pressure on your foot?"

"Here." He points to the spot.

"Swipe left," I say. He does, and the labeled image replaces the first. "I applied pressure to your bladder, and *magically*, you had to pee." I reach for my phone, but he steps away with it. "Um, my phone?"

"I want to look at this."

I follow Will back into his living room.

"Sit. Give me your foot," he orders.

I shake my head. I've given foot massages and done reflexology for every man I've ever slept with. No one has ever offered to rub my feet. And here's Will, demanding to give me what I've always wanted.

"Virginia. Sit."

"I really should go."

"I know you don't have other plans," he says.

I stare into Will's eyes, and my stomach twists so hard, I involuntarily press my hands to my belly to ease the discomfort. "No," I admit.

Will's expression communicates confusion with a touch of amusement.

If I stay, it won't take a crime scene investigator to figure out that my feelings for Will crossed the line from fawning fan girl to a full-fledged flame of fiery affection. I swipe my phone from his hand and head toward the elevator.

"I really shouldn't stay," I say over my shoulder.

Unfortunately, I have no idea how to open the elevator without Will's thumb. There's no button to push. So I stand facing the door with my eyes closed, willing it to open on its own.

He silently appears behind me. When Will puts his hand on my shoulder, my heart does a double beat. He tenderly turns me to face him.

"Virginia, you're not afraid of me, are you?"

My emotions are an earthquake, shaking me to my core.

"Not the pepper spray kind of afraid," I say.

We lock eyes and for several seconds I fall deep into his silent invitation to come inside, look around, and see his heart. My breath shutters. "It's not you. It's me." I force a laugh. "I'm sorry."

Will sighs. He reaches around my side without touching me and presses his thumb to the black pad on the wall. The elevator door opens. "Nothing to apologize for." He motions for me to step into the elevator and joins me. "I have to ride down to the lobby with you. It's a security requirement in our private elevator. Nothing personal."

Will enters a code and the doors close. I glance up at his reflection in the mirrored walls. His shoulders are slumped and he's frowning.

"I really am sorry," I whisper.

He shakes his head. "Hey, look at me." Will turns and places his hands on my shoulders. "It's all good. Thank you for the walk and the foot massage and the company. I hope we can do it again. But maybe without the thorn sucking experience." He grimaces, then laughs.

When the elevator doors open, he motions for me to step out, waves to the man at the security desk in the lobby, and says, "I'll see you at work on Monday. I had a great time tonight."

There's so much I want to say, but I don't know where or how to start. I gaze down at my feet to gather my thoughts, and when I look up, the doors are closing.

"Will, I—"

He's gone.

I watch as the number on the wall increases until it stops at his floor. I don't move. I imagine him going back to his living room. Will he put the teacups and teapot in the kitchen, or leave it for the cleaning staff to take care of? Will he move to his desk and work? Watch a movie? What will he watch? A documentary? Science fiction? A rom-com? I picture him putting on a true crime show and envision myself apparating beside him.

"Excuse me, miss." Instead of Will, the security guard appears beside me. "If you'd like to follow me out."

I move toward the three-story wall of glass but stop mid lobby, under the giant nest. With my contractor card, I have access to every office that has plants to tend, including Will's.

"I'm sorry. I left something in one of the offices." I pull my lanyard from my purse, show him, then ride the elevator to the twenty-ninth floor and pass Savannah's desk, not sure what I am going to do, only certain that I don't want to leave yet.

UNSOLVED CRIMES: SOLVED

"Mr. Power, the woman you escorted down to the lobby five minutes ago is in your office. Would you like me to have her removed from the building?"

I hold the phone to my ear but question what I've just heard. "Virginia is in my office? What is she doing?"

"It appears she's talking to your plants, sir. Oh, and now, um, she seems to be dancing."

I laugh out loud. "No, don't send anyone. She's fine. But can you remind me how I access my office camera from my laptop?"

I watch Virginia as she lifts each plant, one by one, from my table and moves in that way she does when she's lost in her own world. Though I cannot hear her humming, she appears to be more hypnotized than dancing. Her hips, shoulders, and head sway. She looks as much like leaves waving in a breeze as the plants that she holds in her hands.

This woman is singular. Never have I met anyone who comes close to her quirk and confidence. The way she ordered me and Bruce to back off when she decided to suck the thorn from my foot—nobody has given me such a direct order since my father died. Nobody would dare. Nobody but Virginia "Tenacious" Beach.

How could I possibly scare her? Fuck, the woman terrifies me. When she grabbed my hand in the park, I know she didn't intend it like lovers holding hands, that it was an action born of enthusiasm, like a child grabbing a friend's hand to race to the swings, but damn if I didn't wish otherwise.

After she puts the last plant back on the table, she picks up her purse and heads toward my office door. I'm not ready for her to go. I jump up and into my elevator to intercept her before she leaves the building. Muscle memory punches in the code to my office floor. When I get there, the doors to the lift she's in are just closing. In my rush to key in the lobby code, I miss by one number and go up instead of down.

By the time I make it to the ground floor, I see her dress swishing by the lobby windows. I run to the front door and out onto the pavement in my bare feet.

"Virginia," I call to her back.

She halts but doesn't turn around.

I jog the ten feet to her. When I try to stand in front of her, she turns away. *Why won't she look at me?* I think quickly. Keep it professional.

"How did you know my security detail had a flask? Did you see him drink from it?"

Her head shakes back and forth. She sniffles, then inhales a shaky breath. Damn it, she's crying. Did I do this? I forget about professionalism and gently spin her to face me. She stiffens.

"No, I didn't see Bruce drink. I could tell by the way his jacket hung a little lopsided that he had something in his breast pocket. It was a guess since he keeps his phone in his hand, and I could tell he had his wallet in his front pants pocket."

"That's ... amazing. That you see all that. I pride myself on being observant, but you take it to a whole other level."

She shrugs.

"Please come back up and tell me how you developed such a keen sense of observation."

Virginia draws in a long, slow breath.

"I freaked you out with the offer of a foot massage, so I'm taking that offer off the table. You could not pay me to touch your feet." I grimace, and she sputters a small laugh. "Will you please come up?"

"I don't know. It's late. You probably have better things to do than drink tea with me."

"In fact, I do."

Virginia hangs her head and nods. I take her chin in my hand so she's forced to look at me. "The better thing I have to do is have the kitchen make us some sweet-and-salty popcorn and then watch an episode or two of that series you've mentioned a few times ... the true crime one ..."

"*Unsolvable Crimes: Solved.*"

Without thinking, I take my hands from her shoulders and point. "That's the one," I say and immediately feel the loss of our connection.

"Why?"

"Because I enjoy your company. You make me laugh. I learn things from you. You're a lot nicer to look at than my brothers. And I don't know, because it's been far too fucking long since I've had a friend I feel I can be myself with."

"I'm not sure you'll still want me around if I show you my true self."

I don't like what I'm hearing. It doesn't sound like the Virginia I've been spending an hour or more with a day. "Can we please take this conversation upstairs? Have it with popcorn and ... do you like ginger beer?"

"Love," she says with zero enthusiasm.

I wrap one arm around her shoulders and head back to the elevators.

The kitchen makes and delivers fresh popcorn and four bottles of homemade ginger beer, which we eat and drink while watching *Unsolvable Crimes: Solved*, side by side on my couch.

Normally, when someone interrupts a show or movie to ask if I saw something, I want to strangle them, but having Virginia tap my thigh with excitement and then pause the video stream to show me what she sees in the criminal's answers, the clues to his guilt, is fascinating. Her powers of observation and deduction are like no one else I've ever met.

"Did you study criminology? You could be a police interrogator."

"No. It's just always been an interest of mine."

"Always, like, while other little girls were playing house with Barbies, you were playing *Murder, She Wrote* with yours?"

Virginia's normal confident and joyful energy has returned. "It is positively *shocking* how many serial killers live in Barbie's world."

"Seriously, how did you get so good at this?" With the screen now off, I want to face her, so I push myself back against the arm of the couch and stretch my legs toward her. Without hesitating, Virginia twists sideways, grabs my calves, and again massages them. Jesus, I could get used to this.

"If I tell you a story that I never share, will you promise not to tell anyone? Not even Colt? Is it even possible for you to keep secrets from him?"

My gut twists. Yes, it's possible. I nod. "And maybe one day, I'll tell you a secret that not even Colt knows."

"My parents didn't name me Virginia Beach. I mean, they called me Virginia, but my sister chose my last name and had it legally changed when I was fourteen. Hers too."

"So the teasing didn't start until high school?"

"I didn't go to high school. Georgia homeschooled me."

"How much older is she?"

"Just six years. But she adopted me when I was thirteen, after our mom died." She looks at her hands and even though her head is tilted down, I can see by the wrinkles in her forehead that she's sorting through what to say next.

I tense my calf muscle, which draws her eyes upward.

"You don't have to talk about this. I don't need to know."

"I want to tell you. It's just, I've never told anyone, so I'm not sure what's important and what's just"—she shrugs —"gory details, I guess."

"Virginia, I'm sorry I asked. I expected a funny story. I don't want to dredge up bad memories." God knows I don't want to have to revisit my own, and yet, I've been doing exactly that for the last nine weeks since Joe ended our nightly sessions.

"Whether I talk about it or not, the memories are still there." She takes a deep breath and plasters on a big smile. "Please hold all questions until the end." Then her expression grows serious. "Do you remember about twenty-three, twenty-four years ago—you probably don't—but there was this case where a man, a relatively new multimillionaire, disappeared without a trace, leaving his wife and two daughters behind?"

I shake my head.

"Well, I guess it was a big thing on the news for months. I was only twelve, so I wasn't actually paying attention to news, but I heard things at school since kids talk, and I guess their parents were watching and making guesses. The missing man was my dad."

"I am so sorry."

She waves away my comment. "Whatever. He was an asshole, it turns out. Like Class A prick material. He was the founder and CEO of a small tech company. When I was nine, he got lucky and sold the business for an obscene amount of money. We moved from a small house in East Van to a mansion in the British Properties. We had a pool and a gorgeous yard with so many flowers and trees and beautiful skylights in our bedrooms. God, I loved that house."

Virginia stares into the distance for a long minute, and I imagine she's remembering details about her old home. I don't move or speak.

"After two years, I was in grade six. One day, out of the blue as far as I could tell, dear old Dad just kicks us out. Like, literally, he had all our things packed up and put in a moving van. He said we didn't fit with his new life, that we weren't polished enough. Mom freaked out and threatened all kinds of stuff, but Dad had figured out how to hide the money, I guess, since Mom got nothing from him.

"Georgia had just turned eighteen, so she got a job and got her own place, and Mom and I moved into a tiny one-bedroom, back in East Van. And things were OK. I never went without food, but it was hard since Mom was obviously depressed and she was angry all the time."

"Fuck, Virginia, I am so sorry." I have no idea what else to say.

"We lived on our own for, I don't know, not even a full year, like a school semester and a bit, and then Dad disappeared. Off the face of the earth. His new girlfriend accused Mom of killing him, assuming he'd be leaving money for Georgia and me."

The penny drops, and I do remember this story. It was big news in our family's social circles. It was before Dad died, and I remember him and Mom talking about what they thought happened. I recall they assumed he'd gotten himself a fake identity and moved to the other side of the world, where he could disappear. I don't remember why they thought that, but that's what I remember.

"Since Mom had been threatening him"—she looks up and gives me a pointed stare—"not as if she would *ever* have done anything. All that talk was to make the point of how angry and hurt she was that he left us after he got rich. But she was arrested, and I was put into foster care."

"She was charged, right?"

"No, it never made it to court. She killed herself in jail."

I want to puke.

"Long story short, that's when I developed a deep obsession with true crime shows and how to read a person's body language and facial expressions to figure out if they're guilty or innocent. For the record, Mom was one hundred percent innocent."

"And your deadbeat dad is still out there living the high life," I add, as if it needs to be stated.

"Maybe. Maybe his girlfriend killed him and took the money. Who knows? And at this point, I honestly don't care if he's dead or alive. As soon as Georgia turned nineteen, she legally adopted me and changed our last name to Beach. She thought it was funny. And after what we'd been through, Georgia wanted our names to make us feel good, not have people look at us the way you're looking at me right now.

I squeeze my eyes shut and grimace. "I'm sorry."

"It's normal. And you're reacting to hearing the story. Imagine though, if every time you said your name, people would look at you like that." Virginia sighs. "It also has the benefit of making it harder for Dad to find us if he decides he wants to. Neither of us wants to ever see him again."

I don't have words. I stand and take Virginia's hand, pulling her up and into a long, tight hug. Before I release her, I'm not sure if the hug is for her or myself.

"Spend the night," I say. It's a selfish demand.

"I shouldn't."

We lock eyes for several seconds. I feel like she can see right through me. She's right, of course. If she thinks she might get attached, she should run in the other direction because her story will end just like her mother's. Well, not with jail and suicide, but with me dropping out of the picture without warning, just like her dad did. Or more accurately, just like my dad did.

"You're probably right."

I follow her to the hall and the elevator door.

16. *Virginia*

SCARIER THAN THE SHINING

I'm a mess and my emotions are ping-ponging because, as I'm putting my sandals on, I'm disappointed that Will didn't argue for me to stay.

"You do realize that a man who tells me I'm right makes himself even more attractive? So you agreeing that I should leave makes me inclined to change my mind and stay ... I'm on to your Jedi mind tricks, Will. Or should I call you Luke?"

I'm trying to keep it light since the heaviness in my heart is a clear warning to step away from the man with the million-dollar smile and the heart of gold under those fine, tailored layers.

Will chuckles but says, "No trick. I promise that once I tell you my family secret, you'll be punching the elevator call button faster than Shelley Duvall trying to get out of that hotel in *The Shining*." He rapidly taps the spot beside the door several times and makes a terrified face.

I shudder and step away from the elevator. "All that blood."

"You don't really want to get in there, do you?"

"You're right. I don't," I admit.

"Stay? Just for an hour longer. You showed me yours ... it's only fair that I show you mine," Will says. The longing in his eyes betrays the truth behind the joke. "Fresh cup of tea? How about a spicy red dragon chai?"

"If I'm going to go through all the effort to take these sandals off, I think I'll need something a little stronger."

Will's eyebrows rise.

"Even though you think I'm a weird hippie, I'm not a teetotaler, you know."

"Oh, I know."

"Really?"

"I'm observant, too. I can tell by the way you swished that alcohol from the security detail's flask. It was obvious that you really wanted to swallow it."

"It was a very smooth scotch. Such a waste to spit out."

Will pulls his phone from his pocket and mumbles the time. "Ten eighteen." He holds his finger up, then mimes for me to stand back before he punches a code into the elevator keypad. "Wine or whisky?"

"Wine," I say.

"Red or white?"

"Red?"

"I'll be right back."

I watch as he opens the door on the side of the car and walks into a foyer that looks identical to his. The door closes. I get comfortable on Will's couch and text Georgia to let her know I'll be home late.

Will's place is so stark, all chrome, black, gray, and white. Nothing homey or warm in his living room. He doesn't have a single plant. I decide I'll remedy that. He has a perfect windowed wall for some of the plants on the lower floors that aren't getting enough light. They'll do well here, and he'd do well having some life in this space with him.

He appears silently, holding three bottles.

"Colt says I'm an idiot since red is not a wine." Will holds up the single bottle in his right hand. "A pinot noir from Burgundy, France." He places it on the coffee table and moves one of the two bottles in his left hand to his right. "A merlot from the Napa Valley, and a Shiraz from Australia. Any of these sound good to you?"

"All of them?" I laugh.

"Need a glass, or ... you happy to swig right from the bottle?"

I know he's joking, but my stomach tenses. That's just the kind of thing my asshole dad would say to my mother. I stand.

"You know, maybe it's best I leave."

Will's face falls. He looks confused. It's clear he hadn't meant to insult me.

I close my eyes, take a deep breath for a count of five, hold for five, release slowly, and repeat the truism, *Fear is excitement without the breath.*

I sit again and say, "Glass, please."

Will disappears and returns with a corkscrew and one lovely, stemless tumbler.

"We sharing?" I ask.

He shakes his head and nods toward the three bottles. I point at the Shiraz. He opens it, pours, and hands me the glass. I inhale the fruity, spicy scent, then let the first sip sit on my tongue for several seconds. I moan as I swallow.

"That is the best wine I have ever tasted." I try to offer the glass to Will.

He waves it off. "I have no doubt."

"It's only wafer thin," I say in a terrible French accent.

"More Monty Python. And yet"—he fixes me with a stare—"you claim to not be a fan."

"Seriously? You're making me drink alone?" I push the glass toward Will again.

He blocks the offer and presses my arm toward my body. "I'm not making you do anything, Virginia."

The energy between us flips.

"And I'm back to thinking I should be going." I take a full mouth swig of the Shiraz, finishing the glass, and move to stand. Will puts his hand on my shoulder and urges me back to the couch as he sits beside me.

"I stopped drinking the night my father died. I don't mind you drinking. Obviously," he says, nodding at the table with the three bottles. "Colt drinks, and that doesn't bother me at all. My choice is personal, and if you'd just sit still and stop threatening to leave every five minutes, I'll tell you a secret few people outside my family know. I think it'll help us keep clear on what we're doing here since I'm ridiculously attracted to you, and I believe you might find me not too distasteful ..."

"Not so bad, you know, for ... well ... a god among men."

"Settle down." Will laughs. He refills my goblet and hands it to me. "I'm actually kind of relieved you're drinking since you are very smart. And observant. And I'm hoping that with a little wine in you, you'll—I don't know, not pay such close attention?"

Will leans his back against the couch, sitting the same way I am. I can't see his face without turning my head, so I push a pillow against the arm and turn square to him, my legs curled under me.

"Give me one of those, please." Will grips my knee and

coaxes my right leg onto his lap and turns his body toward mine. "That's better. Nice to have something for my hands to do." He tickles my foot, and I try to pull away, but his hand is stronger than my leg.

"Resistance is futile," he says in a robotic voice. "The Borg. *Star Trek: Next Generation*."

"Resistance is attachment to an unachievable outcome," I counter. "Will Power. Podcast episode ... 138 ... or something."

Will grimaces. "I hate it when you quote me to me. It's weird and off-putting."

I shrug. "Nothing from my Monty Python repertoire fits. And quoting anything from *Unsolved Crimes: Solved* would have been too creepy, even for me."

Will massages my foot the same way I kneaded his earlier.

"If this is how you prove to me that I'm right to not spend the night, your methods need a little work."

"Just helping make your feet more comfortable for when you walk away, after I tell you what you need to know about me."

"Ooh, I love a game of who's got the scariest back story," I joke.

Will presses his thumb into the hollow above where the bones of my big and second toes meet—the great surge pressure point. I melt into the couch and allow my leg to relax into his palm.

"You are dramatically failing at convincing me to leave."

"How about this, then?" Will's hands stop pulsing and he pins me with a dead serious look. "I am predestined to be dead in less than three years."

I scoff.

He scowls.

"Sorry," I half-laugh, "but what, you have a witch's curse that says you're going to die on a specific day?"

"In essence, yes." He's not joking. "My father and grandfather died at forty-two. My great-grandfather at forty-four. I'm forty-one. The math is easy."

"Oh, come on, Will. That's ridiculous."

"Is it? It's not like they were random, different deaths, like great granddad was hit by a runaway tram or my grandfather was struck by lightning or Dad choked on a cherry pit. They all died of stress-related diseases. And frankly, the stress of being Will Power in this decade is far higher than it was for any of them since they only traveled in three times zones. I'm in ten time zones twice a year delivering the Come Into Power seminars."

"And it's killing you," I state.

"Basically, yes."

"So stop. Quit."

"I can't just stop, Virginia."

I pull my foot from him and stand with my hands on my hips, looking down at him, thinking.

"So, everyone in your family—your mother, Colt, your other brothers, they all *know* you've only got three years left to live, and ... what? What's the plan for the seminars, then? Are you recording video to create holographs? This is crazy."

"No, they don't believe I'm going to die young. But ..." He stands and faces me. "They also don't know that I have parasomnia. They're night terrors. I haven't slept for more than an hour at a time in over two months, and I believe it is literally killing me. Please sit back down."

Will explains that he used to have a person who would

wake him just enough to stop his recurrent nightmare when it started, but after three years, the guy quit. He says there's no point trying to find anyone else, so he's been adapting to what he calls "waffle sleep."

"How did he know when to wake you?" I ask.

"I have cameras in the bedroom and up there, over the fireplace. See, on either side of the television?"

I nod.

"Hey Alexa, activate cameras three and four."

Two small blue lights come on. It's uncomfortable knowing I'm being recorded, so I say, "Hey, Alexa, turn off cameras three and four." The blue lights go out. "OK, so this Joe guy saw you, but how did he know when you were on the edge of a nightmare? And is it the same nightmare every night? I've never heard of parasomnia before."

"Different situations in the dreams, but they always end with me dying. As for how did Joe know when to grab me from the nightmare? It took him a while to recognize the tell, but once he did, he'd save me from at least nine out of ten imminent deaths."

"And then you'd sleep through the night? Eight hours' sleep?"

"Four or five—which is a hell of a lot more restful than waking up with my heart pounding every hour."

"Five hours isn't enough to heal your body, Will. There's so much science about how important sleep is to health and longevity ..." I stop mid-sentence, realizing that Will might have a point about predicting his premature death. And it makes me mad.

"Will, why the hell aren't you dealing with this? You have all the money in the world. Use it to fix this." My anger morphs into sadness. "This is stupid."

"It's complicated."

"Geopolitics are complicated. Reversing climate change is complicated. Figuring out how to get enough sleep? That's just a puzzle. A puzzle that has an answer, but you have to be willing to look for it." I grab him by the shoulders so I can watch his micro-expressions. "Will, why have you given up trying to fix this?"

17. *Will*

HUMAN-SHAPED TRANQUILIZER

Virginia is doing that thing where she looks at me with so much intention, it's like she's looking straight through my skin at how my cells vibrate inside my body. Where I can read a room, this woman can read an expression. Where I can see the forest, she sees the goddamn mites on the underside of a leaf of a plant ten yards away.

Not that I want to lie to her, but I don't know the answer and don't feel like being psychoanalyzed, so I lean forward and pull her into my arms with her head against my heart, hoping she can hear an answer I don't have words for.

I rub her back, and after some time, her breathing and mine are in a slow, calm, deep synchronicity. She pulls away first, but my hand tracks her arm and grasps her fingers before she entirely disconnects. I'm not ready for her to leave.

She points. "Bedroom down that hall?"

"Yes?"

"Will you let me help you sleep tonight?"

I pause and a dozen images of Virginia in my bed click

through my mind. None of them have either of us sleeping. And to prove my suspicion that Virginia "Psychic" Beach is, in fact, a witch, she says, "I'm not going to have sex with you. I just want to help you sleep without a nightmare. A few hours. Show me what Joe did. I'll do that. In person."

This woman, with her directness and self-confidence, with her fitted floral dresses and her out-of-control hair, her quirky quotes and astute observations ... She's going to be my undoing. The opposite of the death of me. And that is the scariest thought of all since I've never considered life beyond forty-four, but since meeting Virginia, I've wished for that option every single day.

"No," I say.

The shock in her eyes makes me laugh.

"Will, I might be able to help you. Let me try."

"Virginia, if you come into my bedroom, I will not sleep. I can promise you that. I'll be so amped, focused on keeping myself from doing what I've imagined I'd do to you if you ever made the mistake of—"

"Will, stop. I get it. Just stop talking. Let me think."

She shakes her hand from mine and walks to the bank of windows overlooking the city. As she stands with her back to me, her upper body starts to sway, the way she does when she's talking to my plants, as if she's listening and moving to music. I desperately want to hear what she hears, to be able to move in such a relaxed way, without feeling self-conscious.

Every move I make is scripted, recorded, analyzed, and corrected to the point that I'm not sure how to walk or stand or breathe if it's just me and no audience, no image to uphold. At this moment, I want nothing more than the freedom Virginia is expressing simply by looking out my window.

She turns. The anger, sadness, and confusion she shared earlier have been replaced by the same look of determination I saw when I first pulled her into my office. She has a plan, and I know it will be flawless.

"OK, so number one, you're going to give me access to your suite as part of my professional duties. I'm bringing plants to this room and to your bedroom. I need to see the bedroom to know what kinds will do well, but not until daylight." She pauses. I sit.

"Agreed?" she asks.

"Fine," I say.

"Good. Number two, you're going to tell me *exactly* what Joe did to help you crush the nightmares and sleep." Again, she pauses. Again I wait, this time trying not to smile. She's using my own negotiating tactics on me.

After at least a minute of silence and piercing eye contact, Virginia gives in.

"Agreed?" she asks.

"No," I say.

"Good. Number—wait. No? Why no?"

"Because I am not hiring you to put me to sleep every night."

Virginia scowls. "Of course you're not. I have zero interest in becoming your human-shaped tranquilizer, but if you let me get to number three, you'll hear the rest of my plan."

"Which is?"

"Number three, I'll watch you for one week. Seven nights. We'll record it so I can go back and try to find patterns I might miss when I'm focused on what you call 'the tell.' I'll look for other clues, signs. Something that Joe might have missed."

"Virginia, Joe spent over a thousand nights watching

me fall asleep and then sleep ... I don't think there's anything you'll see in one week that he didn't over all those years."

"Well, has Joe watched and rewatched every episode of *Unsolvable Crimes: Solved*, and learned what actual investigators look for when interviewing suspects?"

"Umm ..."

"I guarantee he has not. And that if you give me one week, there's a fifty-fifty chance I'll catch something he didn't."

"I'm not a criminal, Virginia, covering some lie I've told." I've flipped from amused to a little pissed off.

She walks to the couch and eases to the floor, crossed-legged facing me.

"I know that, silly. Your subconscious mind probably has the secret, since it's driving the bus when you're sleeping." She tugs on my leg so I'll angle myself toward her. "Will, you know this. You've talked about it on your podcast."

"That's entirely different."

"I disagree. I may be wrong about there being another way to wake you up that doesn't require a live nightmare interrupter, but what if there is something else that will help? What have you got to lose?"

My dignity. Your respect.

"Let me ask you," I say, "what do you gain by doing this?"

"Are you kidding me?" Virginia punches my leg. "Prestige. Power. A great story to tell at parties," she says.

"Seriously."

"Seriously? Will I hate knowing you suffer like this." Virginia fists her hands and growls. "And that you seem to believe you're going to be dead within two years. That breaks my heart. You say you've tried everything, but that's just not true. Today is a perfect example of something that's proven to help people sleep that you've never done—walking on grass in your bare feet."

"My problem isn't falling asleep." OK, that's not quite true.

"You didn't answer my question. What have you got to lose? Give me one week. I'll sign whatever confidentiality contract you need. I won't tell a soul. Just give me a chance to try to help. Please."

"You believe that in one week you can figure out how to solve a condition I've had for four years?"

"Uh-huh." Virginia nods and a few red curls tumble in front of her face.

I reach to push her hair behind an ear, something I've dreamed about doing since she first stood on my stage.

"Fine. Give me your phone. I'll load the app you need to access my cameras."

"Did you see that? His left fingers twitched." My own finger shoots toward our new high-definition television. "Did you see it?"

"Calm down, Super Observer. I did not see it," Georgia says from the comfort of her brand-new, custom upholstered recliner, which is identical to mine. Splurges she's made with the second dress commission she landed from Will Power & Bros.' staff.

"I'll rewind—"

"Please don't. I trust you. And I thought you wanted to get through this episode before bed."

I check the time on my phone: 9:36. "Darn. OK, no more rewinding."

It's my fifth day of trying to help Will sleep through his nightmares, and it's a good thing he's not paying me since I haven't succeeded. At least, not in stopping the bad dreams. I've had a couple of other small wins, though. Getting Will to agree to be in bed at ten o'clock was huge, since his normal bedtime is usually after one a.m.

He wouldn't agree based on all the science that says

"early to bed" is healthier. He only agreed after I argued I couldn't stay awake that late *and* still be able to do my job the next day. Given it takes up to thirty minutes for him to fall asleep, and then I watch for signs of the bad dream, which starts when he hits REM sleep up to an hour later, I'm not falling asleep until midnight.

Every night for the last four, at ten on the nose, I log in to his PowerSleep app on my laptop, and within a minute, he turns on the two cameras in his bedroom so I can see that he is, in fact, in bed.

The app also allows me to hear all the sounds from Will's room, but thankfully, he can't see me. He can only hear the "dulcet tones" of my voice, as he calls my reading.

"Did you and Georgia have a good evening?" he asks as soon as the feed pops up.

"We did. We're watching a new documentary series called *The Body Language of Body Snatchers*. It's fascinating."

"I don't understand why *you* don't have nightmares."

"Knowledge is power." I pause. "I'm surprised you haven't trademarked some educational product with that word combination."

"Don't be such a Beach about the clever names of our company's assets," he counters.

"Do you think if your family name had been, I don't know, Wobblebottom, that your businesses would have become so successful? Will Wobblebottom ..." I let the name roll around in my head while Will shakes his. "I mean, it does evoke a pretty amusing—or should I say—unsteady image ... Will Wobblebottom & Bros. ... Get Wobbly with Wobblebottom ... The Will Wobblebottom Hour ... and the most popular asset in the family company, Wobblebottom Sleep!"

"Funny lady. You should do standup."

"I'm only half kidding. There's loads of research that proves a person's name can have a direct impact on their health, well-being, and success. For instance, this PhD student in engineering named Candace something-or-other applied to jobs that she was perfectly qualified for. She submitted identical cover letters, résumés, and references to four hundred employers. But on half the applications, she used the name Candy, and on the other half, Candace. Do you know what she discovered?"

"That she loved applying for jobs and that instead of becoming an engineer, she started her own business as a résumé writer?"

"Ha-ha. Candace was offered interviews by twenty-seven of the two hundred companies she applied for. And Candy?"

"None, I'm guessing."

"Not one single interview. That's the power of a name. No pun intended."

Will sighs. "If anyone understands the power of a name, it's the son who inherited the job of being the face of a billion-dollar business ... If I could go back in time and shove Colt out of Mom's womb ahead of me, I would not hesitate for a second.

"OK, sleep whisperer, you going to lull me into never-never-land with some gentle waves on the shore or what?"

"Better. Tonight I've got a coma-inducing short story about a train ride through the prairies. I expect you'll be out within ten minutes ... heck, I may put myself to sleep rereading this one."

Will nods, closes his eyes, and inhales deeply. "Ready when you are," he says on the exhale.

I snuggle under my duvet and begin. My screen is split,

so the images from two cameras are stacked on two-thirds of my monitor and the book is on the remaining third. That way, I can see Will's movements while I read. Not that it's helped so far, but I won't be beaten. For the first ten to twenty minutes, he lies on his back, fidgets a little, enough for me to know he's still awake. But then he rolls to his side and releases a long sigh. His breathing becomes regular and I know he's asleep.

I read for another ten or fifteen minutes, then stop and pay closer attention to the video feed, watching for signs that he's moving into nightmare territory. But so far the only sign I've caught is a pretty dramatic one of Will twitching, then rolling to his back with pronounced arm swinging.

After another thirty minutes or so, I've failed again. Zero for five.

"Will," I sing in what I hope his still-sleeping brain hears as a friendly voice. "Will, wake up," I say a little louder. "It's Virginia. I'm here. Can you talk to me?"

His eyes pop open, and he looks around the darkened room, which I can see due to the infrared lenses on the cameras.

"Hey, Virginia," he says. He never sounds upset or disappointed that I've failed.

"Do you remember what the dream was?"

I've been researching and have learned that sometimes journaling dreams can help release whatever secret they're sharing in the dead of night. But Will refuses to journal, so he talks and I take notes. So far, he's woken after a mangy cougar breaks into his house and eats a baby lying on his bed, just as a car he's a passenger in crashes into oncoming traffic, as a plane he's piloting crashes into a mountain, and when he's teaching a seminar and is suddenly being eaten alive by ants.

I can't link any of his nightmares to a symbol that provides clues.

"It was a *Children of the Corn* kind of scene. This time, I wasn't about to die. I was one of the murderous kids about to hack off my father's head with a machete."

"I wish I was with you right now," I mumble, not actually intending for Will to hear me.

"I'll send a car."

"No."

"Why not?"

"Because that won't help you."

"How are you so sure? Having you beside me might be exactly what I need to get a good night's sleep." Will pats the blanket to his left and wiggles his eyebrows.

My insides squirm. "I worry we won't actually get much sleep." I realize that I don't want to fuel his expressed desire to get naked with me. "You know, because I talk so much."

"Speaking of, I forgot to whisper sweet nothings to the plants in my suite today. I think you should come over and make up for my lack of care and attention."

"Will ..."

"Virginia ..." Will looks directly at the camera to the left of his bed, in effect, making eye contact with me. "I wish I could see you. Come over. You're not working tomorrow, so even if you don't sleep, does it matter? Make up for it on Saturday night. "

"Will..." I hate how my voice sounds, half whining, half pleading.

"Give me your address. I'm sending a car. You've got twenty minutes to pack what you need to be comfortable."

"You're very bossy, Mr. Power." And I like it.

"Well, I am your boss, and it pains me that you've not been fulfilling the duties outlined in your contract, so I'm changing your job duties. Address."

I tell him. "But I need thirty minutes."

"I'll be asleep by then," he jokes. "All you need to do is toss your toothbrush and a pair of clean underwear in your purse … how long will that take?"

"I'd like to shower—"

"Use mine." It's a command, not an offer. He stands from his bed and walks toward the camera. It's set with a decent zoom, so the whole top of his bed fills the frame, which I guess he doesn't realize.

"Will, you have to zoom out. All I can see is out-of-focus forehead wrinkles."

"Give me a second." The camera jerks left and then right and then goes black for a few seconds.

"What are you doing? Why are you breaking your camera?"

"Not breaking it."

It comes back to life, and I'm looking into a bathroom ten times nicer than any spa I've ever been to. The shower looks like it could comfortably fit five.

"Wow."

"Shower here." Will slowly moves the camera around the room and then holds it arm's length from his body so his face fills the screen. "Please?"

"I don't know. Rumor has it you have hidden cameras in all the rooms."

"The driver will text you when he arrives. See you soon."

And with that, Will covers the camera with his hand. I

can still see his bed from the remaining one on the wall, and I can still hear him, which means he can still hear me.

"Virginia Beach, I do not hear any rustling. Why are you not jumping out of bed?"

"You're impossible!" I ruffle my duvet so it makes extra sound, stomp the five steps from my bed to my door and open it. It squeaks. "Happy now?"

"Beyond words."

The camera feed dies, and I'm left alone with three thousand newly hatched butterflies flitting about in my belly.

I am not known for my patience. Not that I'm known for being *impatient*, but since I always get *what* I want, *when* I want it, patience is not a skill I've had to develop.

Until Virginia Beach breezed into my life.

I've been practicing Buddhist-worthy self-restraint in every interaction with her since the first day she swayed her hips for the hydrangea and whispered sweet nothings to the sweet peas in my office. And I'm done playing second fiddle to a fucking fiddle-leaf fig tree. I want those lips blowing *my* ficus. I want her to teach me how to test the moisture of her flora.

Jesus. I might not be a plant whisperer, but even I can tell that the plants in my office and apartment aren't just healthy and happy. They're fucking horny as hell. They've been getting all the action from Virginia "Blowing Every-thing But Me" Beach. Now it's my turn.

I hope.

My phone pings, letting me know my driver has Virginia and that she'll be here in fifteen minutes. I call down to the security desk and ask the on-duty guard to escort her up when she arrives. My plan is to be waiting exactly where she left me—standing in my bathroom but with the addition of steam. What she called a shower is also a steam sauna when the door is closed.

Saunas are relaxing, so I decide to take one and invite her to join me before she has her shower. I put the odds of her saying no at less than five percent since she told me she's dreamed of one day having a home with a cedar sauna. Mine is marble, but with your eyes closed, you'd never know the difference since it's equipped with a nebulizer, already primed with cedar essential oils.

I pull paper from my printer and a black marker from my desk to draw arrow signs that will direct Virginia to my en suite. I drop the first sign on the floor at the elevator. On the last one, outside the bathroom door, I write, JOIN ME, and place it on top of a plush towel I estimate is only just large enough to cover her breasts and ass. I sit with the same size towel draped over my otherwise naked lap.

I realize Virginia was right—no sleep will be happening tonight. At least, not if I get my way.

After what feels like an hour, I grow concerned that something has happened. She should be here by now, glistening skin taunting me.

I turn off the steam and am surprised to find the towel I left for her is gone. The arrow sign that had been pointing to my bathroom is now facing the opposite direction, out of my bedroom. I follow the reversed arrows straight to my guest bedroom, where the JOIN ME sign is now placed outside the closed bathroom door. But she's added, *"If you sing along with me."*

I sit my damp, towel-covered ass on the bed and listen to her sing the chorus from a Mazzy Star song she loves to hum. "Faaaaade into you," she belts out as though she doesn't care if anyone hears her. I only know the chorus. She sings a verse and I wonder how long she's been standing in my shower. And what other songs she'll sing. I decide to find out, so I toss the towel in the hamper, pull the blankets over me, and lie down to listen.

She sings the whole song two more times before a warm body presses against my side. Virginia's voice is quieter but clearer. Her breath warms my ear. It's the first good dream I've had in years, and I'm not going to ruin it by opening my eyes.

A hand lightly touches my chest, over my heart.

"Tonight you are not the boss," dream Virginia whispers. "Tonight you listen. OK?"

"Hmm," I moan, afraid to speak.

"Roll to your side, away from my voice." Her hand slides from my heart, over my ribs to my back, and gently nudges me to twist. "Can you feel my fingers on your back drawing the infinity symbol?"

Yes, I can feel her touch. I can see her touch in the darkness behind my eyelids, following as she swirls from my rhomboid up to my trapezius down and across my spine to my erector spinae, then lower to my obliques ... *fuuuck*. I can't help it. The energy passes from my back to my front ... and I grab for my growing erection.

Virginia's fingers stop moving for a second. I debate apologizing. But fuck it. I am not going to apologize for feeling good. Her hand flattens against my back and rubs in broad circles. I have a flashback to being small, lying in a single bed and having my back rubbed by ... I can't remember. Was it Dad or Mom? It's been over four decades. Did they rub Horse's back to help him fall asleep too?

I tense the muscles across my whole upper body and then release. This is relaxation on a whole new level.

"Is this OK?" Virginia whispers.

I still don't dare open my eyes. "Perfect."

"Did you know that humans, in fact, most mammals, will wither and die if they don't have touch when they're infants? Skin-to-skin contact is critical for our survival. And we still need it as adults, but most of us don't get the right kind of touch." She's drawing the infinity symbol again. "Or enough of it."

Virginia continues talking in her quiet, comforting manner. I'm not sure what she's saying when I fall asleep, but when I wake, my heart isn't pounding. No images of imminent death play in my mind's eye. Just an awareness that my body is wrapped around another and something is tickling my face.

A chaos of copper curls fills my vision when I blink open my eyes. I don't dare move; I don't want to wake her. Virginia's back is pressed tight against my chest. My arm hangs over her ribs and my hand holds her shoulder. I move my fingers lightly to see if I can feel straps. I do not. I am immediately aware that my cock is paying attention to my hands. Even if Virginia doesn't register the movements on her shoulder, there's no way she'll sleep through the sudden eruption of a tree branch pressing into her tailbone.

Her buttocks flex and she twists. Not, it appears, away from me, but to force more contact.

I moan and drop my hand to her breast, which is, as I'd imagined, naked. My fingertips brush her nipple and it responds, sending a jolt of energy to my growing hardness.

"Feels nice." She yawns. "You fell asleep. What time is it?"

"Hey, Alexa, what time is it?" I ask.

"It's six-fifty-three a.m."

"Wow," Virginia and I say together.

"Did you just sleep seven hours, Will Power?"

"I think I might have," I say and start to roll away from her.

Virginia whimpers. "Don't go."

"I'm not going far. I just need to stretch my arm. Permission to explore?"

Virginia answers with a sleepy sigh that carries a "yes" within. But it's the way she rolls, first away and then over so her breasts face me, and the way her thighs lay open in invitation, gives me an answer I consider consent.

Her skin is smooth and soft under my fingers, which I drag down her right side, over her hips, and along the outside of her leg to her knee. I cross to her other knee and run my hand up her left side until I reach her breast. I pause and ponder my next move.

Virginia had kept her touch Disney-rated. I don't want to assume the subconscious cue of her slightly parted legs is in synch with her conscious desires, so I ask, "May I touch you?"

She answers by taking my hand in hers, placing my fingertips over her nipple, and squeezing.

"Kiss me?" She asks.

I start by sucking her nipple into my mouth and tease it with my tongue. She responds with a moan, then places her palm on the back of my head to guide my face up to hers.

Her mouth is slightly open and her jaw is relaxed. She still looks half asleep, but when our lips touch, it's clear that Virginia Beach is awake and eager. I inhale the scent of her warm skin and press my mouth firmly against hers while I hold her chin.

She copies my movements, taking my face in her hands,

opening her lips when I relax my jaw, moving her tongue right as mine touches her teeth on the left. She is both pliant and firm in her actions and reactions. She responds to me exactly as I've imagined she would.

We kiss and explore each other's upper bodies with our hands and mouths until the sun is bright enough to be seen through my room darkening drapes.

"Virginia—" I kiss her belly. "I'd like to—" I slide my fingers between her thighs and she presses her knees open.

"Yes," she sighs.

20. *Virginia*

PININ' FOR THE FJORDS

"Will, should we maybe talk before ..."

He groans and leans away from me. "Do you need to talk? Because I definitely have nothing that needs to be said right now."

"It's just, we agreed we wouldn't have sex, so I thought maybe—"

"If you need something to think about, woman, think on this." Will takes my hand and guides it below his waist. He's semi-erect, so I wrap him in my palm.

"Oh, dear," I say, trying to sound disappointed.

"What?" Will sounds panicked.

"Look." I pull back the duvet so we can see what I'm holding. "I must have some Miracle-Gro residue on my hand."

Will growls and the sound vibrates right to my core.

"Condoms. At the other end of the suite. Wait here? Or come with me?"

"I am not letting go of this," I say with a squeeze.

"You don't know how happy that makes me."

Will and I stand, and after two clumsy steps with me

trying to hang on to his elephant creeper vine, he scoops me into his arms and carries me down the hall to his bedroom.

"You have to let go now," he says before leaning forward to place me on the bed. "Just repeat a couple of Will Power motivational quotes, and I'll be back before you even notice I'm gone."

As Will's naked butt disappears into his bathroom, I call out, "Consistent growth requires consistent activity. Get to business!"

"Good one." His muffled reply is followed by a distinct, "Cock-blocking motherfucker!"

Will comes out of the bathroom with an obviously deflating semi, a condom box, and a piece of paper. He hands me the note.

"These expired two months ago. I'll take my chances. You're welcome. A."

"A?"

"Aiden," he mumbles. Then he yells, "Fu-uck!"

The unflappable Will Power is visibly perturbed, standing naked in the middle of his room with an impressive but deflating dick.

"Is it broken?" I point and bite my lower lip to keep from giggling.

"No, it is not broken." Will scowls.

I chuckle.

He shakes his head, then smirks. "It's just restin'. Pinin' for the fjords," he says with a decent British accent.

"Fjords are wet, aren't they?" I lick my lips.

"Where are you going with this?" He steps toward me, his arousal returning.

"I don't know. Just wondering if my mouth might be moist enough to help with the homesickness for those fjords ... oh my, you weren't kidding. That was a quick rest."

I reach forward and pull Will toward me by his thigh. He steps as close to the bed frame as he can and I scoot down the mattress to position my mouth to take him in. I start by kissing his lower abdomen while my hand grips his now fully erect cock. He's breathing deeply and slowly, like he's trying not to have a panic attack. I look up to see his eyes are closed, but his mouth is open.

I slide my hand down his cock, grip the base and cup his balls. His hips tilt forward, and his soft head touches my cheek.

"Will. I haven't done this in ... a very long time. I'm not very good at it, so tell me—"

He reaches down, palms the back of my head and presses his cock into my mouth while I'm talking.

"You're perfect," he says.

And I guess I do okay since it seems like no time passes before Will grunts and pulls away, coming in his own hand. I'm both disappointed and relieved that he didn't thrust down my throat when he came.

"What a gentleman."

"You better not be calling me that after my mouth does what I have been dreaming of doing to you since the day you came up on stage."

"Tell me," I exhale, feeling the throb of longing.

Will shakes his head and moves to the end of the bed. "Power mantra forty-three." He pauses and looks at me with a delicious challenge in his eyes.

"Words are wind—"

He pulls my ankles and I drag forward until my bum is at the edge of the mattress. Before I can finish the quote,

Will has pushed my knees apart and is blowing warm breath between my legs.

"Finish," he says, giving me a long, soft lick.

"Your actions define you," I press against his mouth and he moans a sound that acknowledges I'm right. And then he rewards me with actions that clearly define Will Power as the most generous man to ever pleasure me.

He looks up, and though I can't see his mouth, the crinkle at the side of his eyes tells me he's smiling. He speaks so close to my sensitive skin that each word is a warm wind against me. "Focused." He swirls his tongue against my clit. "Hungry." He presses my lips open and presses his whole mouth over me. "Generous." His tongue and lips move in a rhythm and pattern that makes me dizzy.

Will pauses and says, "Insatia—"

"Shut up!" I cry.

Is it selfish to lie like a quivering lump while Will liquefies my body? I should be doing something other than moaning and thrusting my hips into his face. But my hands can't reach farther than the top of his head, and my spine has dissolved into the mattress.

Will uses his lips and tongue to bring me to the edge of ecstasy, then holds me there, my tiny muscles vibrating so fast and for so long, the euphoric pleasure becomes pain.

"Will," I beg.

He looks up from between my thighs and uncouples his lips from mine. The pain intensifies, and I buck my hips to force his mouth back to my skin. Will growls and finishes me with three long, slow, broad licks.

I come hard and loud and unapologetically animalistic.

Will climbs into bed and wraps himself around me. His heart is beating as fast and hard as mine.

"Was that okay?" He bites my shoulder and I shiver.

"It was fine," I deadpan. "I mean, if I was leaving a review of this experience on Yelp, I'd give you a solid four stars."

Will rolls away then coaxes me down so I'm on my back. He straddles me, holds my shoulders, and levels me with a serious glare.

"Four stars is unacceptable. This establishment has an iron clad satisfaction guaranteed promise. What can I do to earn that last star?"

My insides are still contracting and they need something to squeeze. "Get a condom."

Will jumps off the bed and is holding his phone with superhero speed. He clicks it on, then presses it to his ear. His jaw is tense and the crease between his eyes is as deep as I've ever seen it. When he speaks, there is no play in his tone.

"I don't care what time it is. If you don't have a condom—no, a box of condoms at my door within three minutes, you won't be able to use one for at least a month."

He drops his phone and his tough big brother attitude on the bedside table because when he looks at me, all I see is a man who would do anything to make me happy.

"Water? You're going to need it because my Power play is going to leave you panting."

We play. We make love. We fuck.

Will touches me in places I didn't know I had. After two hours, Will Power has created me, broken me apart, put me back together, and then shattered me. My body is full and empty. My mind is elated and wretched. My heart overflows with infinite joy and immeasurable misery.

So what do I do? I burst into tears. I sob, inconsolable and irrational.

Neither of us speaks. Will holds me while I shake and release every emotion known to humankind. Once I catch my breath, I start to laugh, just as uncontrollably. I laugh until I can't breathe, and then? I cry again.

Goddess bless the man, Will doesn't say a word through any of it. He cradles me through each humiliating sob and snort, handing me tissues now and then so I can wipe away the snot and tears.

When I am finally able to think and move, horrified about how red and swollen my eyes must look, I roll to face Will, only to find his cheeks wet and his eyes red.

He smiles. "Hell of a crymax."

"Sorry," I mouth, not confident that my voice will work beyond exhausted bawling noises.

"Sorry? For what?" He wipes a tear from my cheek. "I needed that apparently as much as you did."

"You needed someone to have an emotional meltdown in your arms?" My throat constricts.

"I guess so."

I try to process what has happened in the last twelve hours and how I've allowed myself to be so vulnerable with a man who is a billion times more everything than anyone I could ever hope for a future with. And yet ... it feels right. It works. We work.

Will and I lie wrapped together for several minutes until our breathing synchronizes into a rhythm adjacent to normal.

"Did you have a nightmare last night?" I ask.

"I dreamed. I remember ..." Will looks past me, squinting. "Something with a car going up a really steep hill that made me uncomfortable, anxious. But then"—he turns to me—"I looked beside me in the car, and you were there. Not you, exactly. Nobody in my dreams has a face. But it was your energy. It was one hundred percent you. And you, your energy—I sound like a flake—you smiled and laughed and next thing I was ..." Will looks into the distance again. "I don't remember, but it was nice wherever it was. Because you were still with me."

I sniffle. "How can my tear ducts store so much water?" I choke.

Will grimaces and tilts his head. "It's sucking the moisture from your face. I hate to be the one to tell you, but ... you're looking kind of like a dried-up, apple-face doll." He rubs my cheek. "Yup. Definitely from your face." He smiles.

I reach up to mask myself, but Will grabs my hands and holds them between us. Then he leans forward and kisses my cheek.

"I love dried apples," he says before planting his mouth against mine.

We kiss until I'm breathless again.

21. Will

A PRINCESS PLUNDERED

I cannot remember the last morning I stayed in bed past ten. And I'm certain I've never done so with company. I leave Virginia sprawled and satisfied and head to my kitchen to make us coffee. A platter of energy-boosting, Power power-balls sit on the table at my elevator door. A note lies on the tray. "My balls taste better than yours. ~A."

I'm not one for morning-after pillow talk and laying in bed with Virginia makes it clear that my issue isn't with pillow talk. It's that I've never woken up beside the right woman.

And at 11:12 a.m., when Mom calls to ask why I'm late for our monthly Saturday brunch, my overworked muscles are ready for real food.

"Mind if I bring a friend?" I ask.

Virginia's eyes widen and she shakes her head.

"Yes, a very nice woman named Virginia. You'll like her. She's the one taking care of all the plants in the building."

Virginia scowls.

"No, Mother, she isn't working today. She is my friend,

and we've been"—I mouth *'Fucking all morning'*—"hanging out."

Virginia looks as if she's going to burst an aneurysm.

"We'll be there in ten."

"Will, what if I had plans this afternoon?" Virginia says through clenched teeth.

"You do have plans ... to spend the day naked with me. I just forgot today was family brunch."

"Yeah, emphasis on *family*?"

I laugh and pull her into a bear hug. "My mother will be delighted to meet you. And it's not an inconvenience for her. Kitchen staff are paid to adapt."

"You're very bossy, you know that?"

"An hour ago, you were praising me for how I take control." I slap her ass, which, I've learned, is a serious turn-on for Virginia "Full of Surprises" Beach.

"I can't go dressed in—"

"Breathe. You wore clothes over last night. They're fine. You're perfect. And nobody is going to be looking at what you're wearing."

"Fine." She exhales and drops her feet to the floor.

"You want to know why they won't notice?" I slap her ass again.

"Will! Because ... they're men?"

"No, because everyone will be staring at your face. A face that screams you've just spent the last four hours being deliriously despoiled."

"I am definitely not going!"

I take her hand and pull her into my shower. "Come on. I have special soap to rinse away the look of euphoria. It's what I wash with every morning to give me my trade-mark scowl."

What I plan will be a quick rinse turns into shower sex. On the upside, Virginia agrees to eat with my family.

The downside?

"William Wallace Power," Mother barks as we step off the elevator. "I called you over thirty minutes ago. What the hell have you been—"

Virginia pokes her head out from behind me and waves to my mother.

"It's my fault, Mrs. Power." Virginia steps toward Mom with an arm outstretched. "I'm Virginia."

Mom looks confused for a few seconds, and then the penny drops. Her face lights up and she grabs Virginia's hand. She doesn't shake it, as I'm sure Virginia expected. No, she pulls her into a hard hug.

"Wonderful. Oh, this is wonderful. Let me look at you." Mom holds Virginia at arm's length. "Beautiful. Look at your eyes. She's lovely, isn't she, Will? Look at all that gorgeous red hair. I've always loved red hair. Haven't I, Will?"

"You sure have, Mom." I turn to Virginia. "Have you met all of my brothers yet?"

"No. And I can't wait to meet Aiden." She hangs her head.

Aiden is the last one I want Virginia to meet. Having him deliver condoms was, in fact, a blessing, since there's no way he can argue that he didn't know she's taken. He's an unapologetic playboy, and according to the gossip rags, the best-looking of the four of us.

Although Mom does not approve of his lifestyle, we all know she tolerates it since she secretly hopes he'll accidentally impregnate one of his conquests. With a son, of course.

Mom's place is technically twice the size of mine. But

her living space wraps around three sides of the building since 1,500 square feet are dedicated to live-in staff use.

We walk through the living room and down another hallway to the day dining room, the one that overlooks the harbor and mountains. Her evening dining room doesn't have a view—anymore. A newer building blocks it.

Our monthly, family dinner was changed to a monthly, family brunch, for that reason: All four of us agreed that we'd jump from the roof if we had to hear her say, "If your father was still alive, this never would have happened," one more time.

Yes, Mom is disappointed in us for pretty much every-thing—except the value of the business, which we've doubled in the last decade. Not that it makes one iota of difference since one-tenth of $30 billion divided by five is still ten times more than any of us need to continue to live like princes. And a queen.

"Does your mother live here alone?"

"Sort of. But she has staff who share space out the elevator door on the other side. And who magically appear when she snaps her fingers."

"Really?"

I chuckle. "No. That would be rude, even for Mom. She rings a bell."

We reach the day dining room and Virginia does nothing to disguise her reaction as she takes it all in.

Her free hand jumps to her heart and she gasps. "Wow! I've never seen anything so stunning ... like in a magazine ... incredible ..."

Aiden gets up in her face, smiling like a goddamned toothpaste actor. "Most handsome. Least photogenic of the Power brothers. Lovely to meet you." He extends his hand, but Virginia ignores it and looks past him.

"Mrs. Power, your plants. Is that ..." She drops my hand and beelines to the side of the room that blocks the outdoor view with inside greenery. "It is! I've never seen a desert rose in real life. It's even more beautiful than I imagined."

Virginia stands on her toes to see god knows what and says words that make no sense to me.

"Albuca frizzle sizzle? Tweedle dee begonia? Oh my gosh, and a polka dot begonia? Black bat flower! I can't believe your family. It's remarkable, Mrs. Power."

Aiden pats my back. "Good luck with that!"

Mom joins Virginia at the plants. "I am impressed."

"Holy shit!" all four of us blurt.

"Have you heard of the Shenzhen Nongke orchid?" Mom asks.

"Of course! I mean, yes, yes, I have, Mrs. Power."

"Would you like to see it?"

"No way. No! Way! *You're* the anonymous buyer? Oh my gosh." She turns to me and glares, as if I've been keeping some state secret from her. "Will, did you know your mom had the Shenzhen Nongke orchid?"

I can't decipher if Virginia is angry that I didn't tell her (even though I have no clue what she's saying) or if she's ready to jump my boner. What's clear is she thinks this is pretty fucking amazing.

Mom waves toward my brothers and me as if we're staff being dismissed, then takes Virginia's hand and drags her in the direction of her private hallway. "Will doesn't know a nun's hood from a dancing lady."

All I hear is shared laughter before they disappear.

"What the actual fuck just happened?" Horse asks.

"When was the last time you saw Mom laugh? If you don't marry her, I will," Brian says.

Aiden repeats, "Good luck with that."

"So that's the woman you delivered a box of condoms for?" Brian asks.

"Aiden. Jesus. You told them?"

My three pain-in-the-ass brothers laugh as if I've just delivered the funniest damn joke in the world.

"I've seen her before," Horse says. "She works for us, doesn't she? That will not play well with HR or Legal, Will."

"Fuck HR and Legal. I don't care. I'm going to find Virginia. Make sure Mom hasn't thrown her off the balcony."

This is not how I expected brunch to go. And I still haven't eaten. I'm hungry, and now I'm irritated. Not a good combination.

I stop outside Mom's bedroom. The door is open, and the two women have their backs to me. Virginia is holding the whatever whatever orchid.

"Gorgeous, why have you stopped blooming, hmm? What's wrong, baby?"

"Is this the infamous—"

"Shh!" Both of them turn to shut me up.

We stand in almost silence for at least two minutes while Virginia strokes the plant, pokes the soil, and hums now and then.

"Mrs. Power, when was the last time she was repotted?"

"I honestly don't know. I have people who do that. I'm sure I can find out for you."

"And the last time you remember she flowered?"

"Well, at least a year ago. Possibly two? She used to flower twice a year, so she's missed at least two flowerings."

She? Since when do plants have genders? I exhale, apparently too loudly, since I draw the stares of the two most intimidating women I've ever met. I did not realize how terrifying Virginia could be until she joined forces with Mother.

"If you let Will know when she was last repotted, I'll do a little digging, too, and then we can work to get her back in form for you. I would love to see her bloom. The pictures I've seen—stunning. Unique."

Virginia returns the underwhelming stalks of green to the table.

"Ready for brunch? I'm starving," I say.

I let Mom leave ahead of us and take Virginia's hand. Mom's private hallway is lined with family photos. Each Power man has his own section, starting with my great-grandfather and grandfather on one side of the hall, closest to the bedroom. Dad's gallery faces them.

We have only a handful of pictures of my grandfathers, plus their framed birth certificates. Dad's life in photos balances the OG Powers.

Virginia stops when we reach the colorful columns—pictures of my generation. They're all professional portraits from our birthdays and designated special occasions, high school and university graduations, that sort of thing.

Like the Power men before us, each of our sections has our birth certificate at the top of the column. To mess with Mom and Dad, we used to move around photos pretty regularly. At one point, when we were teens, they were such a mess that Mom had to contact the studio and have them compare all our baby pictures to negatives since even she couldn't tell Horse and me apart before we were six, and we all looked indistinguishable for our newborn and first-birthday photos. Dressing us identically was, in hindsight, a foolish idea.

"Oh my gosh, look at how cute you were. Oh my

goddess..." Virginia is focused exclusively on my two columns of portraits.

I take unusual pleasure in how she fawns over versions of me that are over twenty years old.

"Wait! That's Colt." She points to a picture of me, or maybe Colt, at thirteen.

I look, and she's right. Did one of the guys do this, or is the staff messing with Mom? The thought makes me laugh.

"How can you tell?" I ask.

She points to Colt's forehead. "There's no worry line here. You have a crease between your eyes. See?" She points to the thirteen-year-old in the portrait in Colt's area.

"Amazing."

"I am," she agrees. "Should we swap them back to their right places?"

"Nah. We should do this instead." I reach way above her head and pull the two birth certificates from the wall.

"Let me see." She reaches for a frame and reads: "William Wallace Power. Born on October 26, 1980, at 1:31 a.m. at Women and Children's Hospital. William Wallace, eh? They didn't have high expectations of their firstborn, did they?"

"Not so high."

"Let me see Colt's." She hands me my birth certificate, which I hang above Colt's pictures. "Colton Carter Power. Born on October 26, 1980, at 1:52 a.m. PST ... so you beat him to the punch by twenty-one minutes."

"The stupidest race I ever won," I say, reaching for my brother's frame and hanging it above my photos.

"Why'd you swap them?"

"Small pleasures. Not many ways to mess with Mom."

"She seems lovely."

"You certainly manage to bring out her good side.

That's no minor feat." I take her hand. "Can we please eat now? I am wavering between dying of starvation and dying to get you back to my suite so I can pick up where we left off. Which I think was right here." I bite her neck and deliver a hungry kiss.

"Should I sublet your bedroom? It's too quiet without you." Georgia stands in my door and watches me pack another bag to take to Will's. Over the last two months, I've virtually emptied my closet, one dress at a time.

"I'm sorry. He'll be going on the road in three weeks and then gone for nine. That's loads of time for you to get sick of me again."

My protective older sister purses her lips, scowls, and sighs. Loudly.

"I will never get sick of you. You're family. I love you. But I worry that this guy ... a man who publicly humiliated you and basically said you'd never amount to anything? Who called you a clown? I worry that ..." Georgia stops talking and lets me fill in the blanks.

"Will is nothing like Dad. And I'm not in some messed-up 'make daddy love me' relationship. I promise. Will is a complicated man. The way we first met was an unfortunate snapshot of a bad day. That's not him at all. He truly isn't concerned with what people think about how I dress or my crazy hair or—"

"Yeah, well, when was the last time you were out in public with him? Why is he keeping you hidden away if he's not embarrassed to be seen with you?"

I press my fingertips to my temples to soften the spikes embedding in my forehead.

"Georgia, he's hiding himself, not me. He hates being in the spotlight—"

My sister scoffs. "Funny way to show it, you know, being the most famous public speaker in the English-speaking world."

My headache intensifies. "Please don't worry about me. He's a great guy. And half of the reason I'm there every night is that he still has nightmares if I'm not with him when he hits REM sleep."

"An attractive trait," she mumbles.

"I need to go. I'll be back soon-ish."

"Which will be?"

"Soon-ish," I repeat.

I leave my tiny apartment, which in the last weeks, I've started to think of as "Georgia's place" since I'm feeling more and more at home at Will's. It took several days for me to relax and get comfortable using spaces it's clear he never has—like his kitchen—but once he gave me free rein (and a bottomless budget) to add cozy touches to his black, white, gray, and polished chrome decorating, his condo has become more welcoming. In addition to the dozens of plants that are now bringing life to every corner of every room, I've added a few wood tables, some nature-inspired art pieces, and loads of colorful cushions and accent rugs.

My dresses hang in the master closet and look perfectly at home with Will's custom-tailored suits. Well, in the quality department, at least. From a color point of view, my side looks like an explosion of a million flowers while his side looks like deep space.

Even though it feels needlessly decadent, Will insists I use a company car, with driver, when I want to run errands or when I care for Mr. Bernard's greenhouse in the British Properties. Will says that since he has a vehicle and man on twenty-four-seven standby who is paid whether he drives or twiddles his thumbs, I provide the guy a reason to get dressed in the morning.

"Sorry. That took a little longer than expected. My sister needed to vent," I say to Dawes, sliding into the back seat of the black Bentley. I schedule my rare appointments and errands around Dawes's. He's been working for Will Power & Bros. since it belonged to the previous William, and he loves telling stories about the old days.

"Will's birthday is coming up in just over a month. I have no idea what to get him. Do you remember what some of his favorite gifts were when he was younger? I'm thinking of something with a nostalgic theme."

Dawes hems and haws and taps his steering wheel as we drive toward the British Properties. "I can't say I can help. His father loved a good bottle of Cognac. He'd drink every time he was in my car. He joked that he had to be drunk to relax with my driving."

"Will doesn't drink, so that won't work."

"No. He is nothing like his father. Now, Mr. Aiden? That nut didn't fall far from the tree." Dawes chuckles.

"He is a bit of a nut, isn't he? But ..." I'm not sure how to ask what is now on my mind. "Was Will Senior um ... ahh ... did he have ... I mean, was he a ladies' man like Aiden is?"

Dawes laughs out loud and makes eye contact with me in his rearview mirror as he shakes his head. "No, no, no.

Not as far as I know, and I would know since I was with him whenever he left his apartment. He was a faithful husband. He and Mrs. Power enjoyed socializing. They were out three, sometimes four nights a week."

"It must've been quite a shock when he died. A big change for you."

"As a driver, it's not considered right to call an employer a friend, but Mr. Power and I were close. Closer than any other friend I had then or have had since. He confided in me like I was a priest—a priest who shared his love of fine Cognac when I was off duty."

"I'm so sorry."

"As for it being a shock? With his lifestyle, I can't say anyone should have been surprised. I suspect he would've been the most taken aback. He truly believed he could buy his health as long as he had the right doctors. His heart, apparently, disagreed. Shame it happened while he was away. Mrs. Power ... she's never been the same. And Mr. Will, still a boy, really ... being the one to find him. I believe he died a little that day, too. He adored his father. We all did."

Dawes and I sit in silence for several city blocks.

"Will worries that he's going to die within the next two years, like all the Will Powers before him. He thinks he's cursed by his name. What do you think?"

Dawes laughs again. "Have you ever listened to Mr. Will's podcast?"

"Every single episode."

"As have I. Did you know the quotes he loves to repeat were, for the most part, written by his *great*-grandfather?"

"No. I always assumed they were Will's."

"Well, some are, to be sure. But the one I'm thinking of is something Mr. Power told me he got from his father, who got it from his. 'Your task is to design your destiny, for destiny is not fate. Fate and failure are friendly bedfellows. But your destiny is your noble course.' Do you remember that one?"

"Honestly, just the first half."

"It's certainly not the place for an old man who's kept on salary for little reason other than loyalty to speak his opinion, but it's not often I'm asked for mine anymore, and since you asked about a curse on the name Will Power, I'll tell you what I think."

"Should I call Will so he can hear, too, or would you prefer to tell me privately?" I ask.

"This is no secret. I've already told Mr. Will my thoughts on the matter. Unsolicited." He laughs again. "Mr. Will has accepted fate as his destiny."

We stop at a red light and Dawes turns his body to face me. "The curse he carries is one of loyalty to a name, not the name itself. Both are things he could have changed. But he's had no reason to do so. Until ... maybe now?"

"I don't know. I hope so."

The drive to the British Properties is direct and so pretty. The fall colors bring me joy.

Mr. Bernard has been inviting Dawes in for coffee for the last three weeks while I work my magic with his wife's plants. The men are almost the same age and knew, or knew of, many of the same people from back in the day when these septuagenarians were young.

Since convincing Will to take a week and sneak off to a B and B in a little village in the mountains is proving a hard sell, I asked him to come by today to see the greenhouse so he'd have a better understanding of the power of immersing himself in living, breathing, relaxation-inducing nourishment.

After hand-shaking and other pleasantries, I set my plan in motion.

"Mr. Bernard, can we bring your front-hall chair into the greenhouse, please?"

Mr. Bernard had already agreed, and I've cleared a perfect spot in the corner farthest from the chatty older men since I don't want their reminiscing to distract Will, but I couldn't very well ask Mr. Bernard to have his afternoon coffee elsewhere.

"As long as that strapping young man carries it," he says. "Got his mother's good looks, didn't he?"

"And his father's pigheadedness," Dawes adds.

"I prefer perseverance," Will calls over his shoulder, heading into the house to get the chair. "And I do have the power to fire you, you know."

Dawes winks at me. "He has the power, but refuses to use it."

Will carries the chair into the greenhouse and stops by Mr. Bernard and Dawes. "I promise you're on my list. But HR will allow me only one dismissal per pay period. And there are bigger pains in my ass than you, dear Dawes. So I guess we're stuck with each other for a couple more years."

"As long as I can continue to drive this delightful young lady around, I'm happy to tolerate your obstinance, Mr. Will."

Will follows me to the back of the greenhouse. I point to where I'd like him to put it down.

"And I'm just supposed to sit here and ... what, exactly?"

"Meditate. Nap. Talk to me. Help me. I'll be right here repotting the plants on that table. Want to get your hands dirty?"

"Yes, but not the way you're thinking." Will bites his bottom lip.

My belly flips.

He presses his hand to his chest, then slowly runs it down his body toward his zipper, but just before he reaches his belt line, he shoots his arm out, grabs my hips, and pulls me against him.

His fingers tease the zipper on the back of my dress, down a bit, up a bit. Down a bit more, up a little less.

"Will ...," I warn.

"Virginia ...," he mimics my tone.

I try to wiggle free, but he holds me tighter. I can't say I don't like it, which makes it even worse.

"We can't ... can we?"

"There is a football field of forest between us and the two old men. Can you hear them talking? No. Can you see them? Again, no." He tugs my zipper, and I feel the cool air all the way to the top of my bum.

I look around to make sure we are, in fact, well hidden. There's little chance we'll be caught, but I can't make it easy for the man who always gets his way.

"All right ... you want to have sex in the wilderness? I'm game, but on one condition."

"I like your condition," he says, squeezing one of my butt cheeks.

"The condition is that before you go on tour, we go away for a few days, just the two of us."

"Dirty weekend away. I like it." He pulls my dress off my shoulders.

"Yes, but I want it dirty, not just at night, but during the day, too. Three dirty days where we spend time in actual nature and three steamy nights with you at a VRBO in Lily Valley. If you take me *there*, I'll let you take me *here*."

Will's hands release my dress. It floats to the ground with a gentle whoosh.

"Anywhere for and everywhere with you," he says before his lips crash into mine.

23. Will

LAST OF A LEGACY

I sit at my desk and hit "Send" on an email before putting the computer to sleep.

I love wrapping up my work day while Virginia whispers to the plants in my office. Before I met her, if someone had come in and stolen every single pot during the night, I wouldn't have even noticed they were gone. I might have wondered why there was more light coming through the window, but the greenery was nothing more or less than executive office staging.

As Virginia lifts a medium-size pot above her head—a *calathea roseo-picta*, which she's named Rosy—looking for signs of mites, I picture her holding a baby high in the air, cooing at the child the way she talks to her plant babies, as she calls them.

Virginia is the embodiment of life in all ways, shapes, and forms.

The way she nurtures it.

The way she celebrates it.

The way she saves it.

The way she's saved me.

I am a different man when I'm with Virginia. I feel like I don't have to be Will Power, I can just be a relatively normal guy who's allowed to goof around and make mistakes. To let my guard down around anyone other than my brothers? I've never experienced this before. It's disorienting, but not like a nightmare—more like racing a Maserati in the fog. Exhilarating, if not a touch terrifying.

My breath catches, and I become aware of an ache in my chest. I close my eyes and lean against my chair back, exhaling a long, slow breath.

When I open my eyes, Virginia stands inches from me, concern on her face.

"What are you stressing about? Anything I can help with?"

I pull her onto my lap and she pushes her arm between my back and the chair, rubbing small circles in the space between my shoulder blades. We've learned it's an effective way to relax me.

"I'm not stressed. I'm ... confused? No, it's more like bewildered or maybe befuddled."

She laughs. "The befuddled billionaire. That would be a fun name for a segment in your podcast."

"Hard to find high-net-worth guests willing to admit they ever experience uncertainty."

"You could lead by example."

"No. Only you ever see that side of me."

"Maybe more people should."

"Maybe. But it's not on brand."

Virginia pulls her hand from my back and cups her warm palm to my cheek before kissing me. And just like that, the anxiety that clenched my heart when I imagined this woman with a child—which most certainly could never be mine—evaporates.

She's never mentioned whether she wants children. It dawns on me that not knowing is a problem, since I am very clear about what I do and do not want.

Kids are unequivocally on my *do not want* list.

What concerns me is what is on my *want* list.

I want to spend the end of every workday with Virginia humming in my office.

I want to take the elevator with her to a condo she calls home.

I want to fall asleep and wake up with this woman until the day I die.

All my wants are selfish since she's thirty-eight and if she wants kids, every day and night she spends with me is time wasted not finding a suitable father.

"Anything special you craving for dinner?" I ask.

She grins. "Aside from an appetizer of Power balls?"

My groin responds accordingly.

"Anything the kitchen can make for us?" I clarify.

I want to have this conversation on a full stomach, before my dick gets a voice, since easy sleep has become somewhat of a Pavlovian response to evening sex.

"Something fast so we can get to the naked part before I'm too tired to appreciate it," she says.

A quick-to-prepare dinner of barbecued jumbo tiger prawns, saffron rice, and a gourmet salad are delivered within twenty minutes of making the call. I set the table while Virginia chats with some sickly succulents she's rescued from all corners of the building and brought into my suite to rehabilitate. She sounds upbeat and happy, as always. She insists that all life can read energy, so the energy she projects to unwell plants must be positive and hopeful.

At first, I thought she was crazy, but since I can feel her spark from across the room, I can't argue that she's wrong.

We eat without looking at our phones but without much talking either. When Virginia does anything, it's with her full focus, including eating.

"That was delicious," she says, holding her belly and leaning away from the table.

"Crash on the couch for after dinner tea?"

Sitting on top of the maple sideboard buffet, one of Virginia's additions to the living room, is a tray with two teacups with saucers, a matching sugar bowl, two teaspoons and a thermos that the kitchen staff deliver each night with fresh hot water when they drop off our dinner.

I'm distracted by my thoughts when I lift the tray and let it tilt too far to the left. One of the teacups slides off before I can catch it. It hits the polished concrete floor, shattering into a hundred pieces as the word "Shit!" escapes my lips.

Virginia yelps, startled.

"Don't move," she says, jumping up and running to the front door where she's left her shoes. She comes right back, hands me mine and takes the tray from me. "I don't feel like pulling porcelain from your toes tonight. I'll grab the broom."

Virginia disappears in the direction of the kitchen. I slide on my loafers and take this as a sign to not mention what's been on my mind.

But when she dances back, pretending the broom is a dance partner, I know I have to deal with this. Virginia deserves all the joy the world has to offer and if that means having kids, I need to break this off so she can find a man who'll give her that experience. I step out of the way and stand like a dolt while she hums and sweeps up my mess.

"We can share a cup tonight," she says after leaning the broom and dustpan against the wall.

I drop onto the couch and she stretches her legs out across my lap.

"Do you like kids?" I ask.

An easy opener. If she hates them, I'll be able to leave for my tour knowing she'll be waiting for me when I get back.

"I *love* them." She emphasizes the word *love* by tilting her face toward the ceiling, as if looking at heaven.

Shit. "Love them as much as you love, say, your plant babies?"

She doesn't answer right away. Instead, she leans forward and studies me, the same way I've seen her lean toward the TV when she's trying to decipher whether a person is guilty of a crime based on their body language.

"Will, you're acting weird. If I didn't know better, I'd think you were pregnant and afraid to tell me."

Why is this so damn hard? I can talk off the cuff in front of a thousand people, but for this conversation, my brain and mouth are smoking pot offstage.

"Virginia ... I'm trying to have a serious talk here."

"No shit, Sherlock. Have you forgotten I'm an astute observer of human behavior?" she says with a smile. "What are you really asking me?"

"Do you want to have kids?" I blurt.

Her eyes open wider than I've ever seen them.

"Um ... uh," she stutters. "Are you asking if I want to have your kids? Kids with *you*?"

"No. No, I mean, in general. Is your ..." I place my hand on my stomach. "Is your baby clock ticking or whatever?"

"My baby clock?" She jumps to her feet and spins, looking around the room. "Shit! I have a baby clock? Does it need to be wound? Oh God, have I left my baby clock unwound?"

"For fuck's sake, Virginia, don't make fun." I'm losing it, and she's acting like this is a big joke.

She stifles a small laugh. "You're very cute when you're nervous, you know. I've never seen this look on you. I kind of like it."

I grunt. I don't like it at all.

"Will, sweetie, baby, honey, I do not want kids. I never have." She grabs my hand and pulls me to stand in front of her. I don't know what she reads on my face, but her tone adjusts. "I thought you didn't want kids. Have you changed your mind? Is that what you're trying to say?"

I pull her close. "No, I still don't want kids, just clarity about what you want in your future."

"What I want?" Virginia tilts her head so I can see her face. "What I want is all the fun without the 'oops.'"

"I have good news for you, then. If you're naked with me, there'll never be an 'oops.' I had a vasectomy when I was twenty-five."

Virginia pulls out of our embrace and takes three steps away from me.

"Why are you scowling?" This conversation could not be more confusing.

"Are you telling me that for the last nine weeks, we could've been having sex *without* condoms?"

"You said no to sex without one."

"Yeah, before we knew each other's history. When I assumed this was going to be a short-term thing for you. Why didn't you tell me after we got tested?" She shakes her head. "You know, the nightmares you don't have anymore?"

I swallow, concerned by her tone.

"My equivalent is an accidental pregnancy. And an IUD, even though good, is not one hundred percent. So ..." She stares at me, unreadable.

"So ...," I repeat, not sure if she's upset or pleased.

Her furrowed eyebrows relax and she grins. "So, Mr. Power, I would not have believed it was possible, but you, sir, just got one billion times sexier."

I exhale and rub at my jaw to relax the tight muscles. "Is that so? What can I do to make it one billion and one?"

Virginia bites the side of her finger while she looks me up and down, clearly objectifying me. And I love it.

I mimic her stance but flex my bicep three times.

She drops her hand and bites her lower lip.

I drop my arm and drag my tongue over my top lip.

Her eyes travel from my mouth to my fly.

"Should I take these off?" My zipper is already coming down as I ask.

Virginia closes her eyes and inhales a full breath. She moans when she exhales.

"Open your eyes. I want you to see what you do to me." My pants are open, hanging on my hips, and my cock is fully engorged, pressing against my boxer briefs. Virginia's mouth is slightly open and she's taking quick, shallow breaths. "Do you want to feel me inside you, because if I have to wait more than thirty seconds to be skin on skin with you I'm going to pass out."

Virginia reaches under her dress and drops her panties to the floor. My slacks and underwear are right behind. She pushes me back on the couch and straddles me. I slide inside her in one easy thrust.

"Fuck me," I moan and close my eyes.

"Look at me," she breathes. "I want to see what I do to you. I want you to see what you do to me."

Virginia is in full control. She presses her body back, places her hands on my chest and grinds her ass in slow circles with me deep inside her.

"Sweet mother earth goddess," she whispers. "I love how you feel."

She tilts her ass up and away. Only the tip of my head remains inside her. She squeezes and releases then reaches behind her and takes my balls in her hand.

"Fuuuuck." It's been less than a minute and I'm seconds from coming. This won't do.

I push my hands up under her dress, grab her hips, and pull her down on my cock.

She squeaks. Her eyes open wide.

"Sorry," I say, worried I've hurt her.

Virginia smiles and shakes her head. "Fuck me hard, Will."

And without a thought, I press my elbows into the couch and push up fast and hard, still holding Virginia's hips. In one smooth move, I flip us around so I'm on top and in control. I am an animal with one sole purpose.

Virginia's eyes and mouth are open. She stays right with me in this moment.

"Let's see what you've come up with," Mr. Liu asks before I even sit down.

"I'm not sure this is what you're looking for." I push a stack of papers across the desk to him.

It's my twelfth week in the Power Broker Program, and according to my coach's analysis, I'm significantly behind where he expected I would and *should* be by this stage, the end of Q1 with him.

The problem is that his vision of my business and my vision of my business are quite different. Mr. Liu's definition of growth includes spreadsheets and ever-increasing dollars connected to a reduction in the time it takes me to earn that money. I see growth using different numbers—basically, how many green things I get to interact with in a week or month.

Following Mr. Liu's plan for The Other Side of the Fence, by the end of Q4, caring for plants will be a hobby for me. I'll instead be dirtying my hands with the management of contract staff who will be the ones actually whispering to the wisteria—and the ferns and the azaleas and,

and, and ... Thinking about that kind of corporate growth makes me sad and anxious.

"Virginia." He pushes my feeble marketing plan across the desk, *tsk-tsking* like a disappointed parent handing back a subpar report card. "You can do better."

I inhale a confidence-boosting breath, nod, and say, "You're right. I could do this differently. But the business plan we developed? It's not sitting well."

"A personnel issue? Do you need more tips on how to manage a contractor?" he asks.

"No. She's working out just fine. She's good. Clients like her. It's just that the next stage you've designed—"

"*We've* designed," he interrupts.

"Yes—we've come up with—has me training two more people to take on my contract in this building."

"You're having trouble finding the right people? We can use a few hours of HR time—"

"No. That's not it, Mr. Liu. I don't want to stop doing this contract. I don't want to give it to other people."

He looks confused. "But you're not giving it up. You're improving efficiencies. Your company will still be earning fifty percent of the contract. And that will free your time to go out and land even more lucrative contracts. Another building like this one, and you'll have your same income for just a couple hours' work a week, instead of thirty plus."

Mr. Liu and I have had this same conversation every time I've seen him in the last month, and I'm frustrated that he's not hearing me. I steel myself to say what I know I should've said much sooner.

"Mr. Liu, I am so grateful for all you've done to help me see the potential in The Other Side of the Fence. I never would've envisioned the kind of success you've helped me understand is possible."

"You had some significant upper-limit barrier beliefs when we first met," he says.

"Yeah, I guess."

"It's normal for you to backslide on believing you can be as successful as my financial projections indicate—"

"I'm not backsliding. I'm trying to say that I don't want that kind of success."

Mr. Liu smiles. It's the biggest smile I've seen from him. "Classic stage two." He chuckles. "You don't want that success because, at some level, you still don't believe you deserve it."

I want to pull out my own fingernails, which, I notice, have dirt under them, as per normal.

"Mr. Liu, it may be true that I'm in stage two of whatever process I'm going through. But please look, see, and believe that these hands"—I hold them up with dirty nails facing him—"are happiest when they're in dirt. *I* am happiest when my fingernails look like this. I don't need to be a millionaire to be happy. What I need is to be doing the work I love."

He's not smiling now. He's scowling at his own hand while tapping his knuckles on his aqua-colored, tempered glass desktop. He sighs.

"Virginia, Virginia, Virginia ..."

I wait. Watch his posture change from relaxed to rigid. I can tell before he speaks again that I'm not going to like what he says.

. . .

Will finds me in the sauna, which is where I've been for the last ninety minutes since leaving the twenty-sixth floor for what is likely the last time. Well, aside from visiting the offices that have plants, which do not include Mr. Liu's.

I should've known this would end badly when he refused to accept my thank-you gift of a fern and again when he declined having anything alive in his space, even if it was owned by Will Power & Bros.

"I missed you this afternoon. Seems wrong to end my day without my plants being whispered to," Will says, sidling up beside me and dropping the towel wrapped around his hips.

"Yup," I agree.

I spent the whole afternoon trying to figure out how to tell Will that I'm no longer in his executive coaching program. That, according to Mr. Liu, I hold the illustrious honor of being just the third person to be terminated. And the only Gold Ticket winner to toss away my free ride to success. Yay, me.

I've been wondering how much Will will care and if he's aware of the small-print details in the contract I signed when I joined. I didn't offer details when I texted that I wasn't feeling well and would see him back here after work.

He'd asked if I needed anything sent up.

A time machine, I thought. But I said I was fine, just out of sorts, and that once I saw him I'd feel better.

But I don't feel better. I feel much, much worse after considering all the different ways this conversation could go. Five out of ten results include Will looking at me with disappointment, three have him reacting with anger, one has him pitying me and my upper-limit problem. In only a single scenario does he pull me into his arms and tell me he doesn't care about contracts or his program's reputation or how he went out on a limb for me and let Mr. Liu and the rest of the team believe I was meant to be a success.

And in that one happy-ending scenario, Will is drunk.

"So ... Dawes tells me your father was a Cognac man. Do you have any interest in, you know, maybe sharing a drink—or twelve—with me tonight?"

Will grips my knee and guides me to face him. "What's wrong?"

"Tear the Band-Aid off, right?"

"Easier that way," he agrees.

"Let's see. To start, I'm sorry that all the planning and prep your staff has done with me to be a guest on your podcast will have been for nothing."

"What are you—"

"Will, let me finish ... it's a big Band-Aid." I try to smile. I suspect even through the steam, Will can see it's more of a serial killer's grimace. "I'm not in the Power Broker Program anymore."

"What?" Will stands, his anger palpable. "If it's not working out with Liu, I'll have another coach assigned."

I shake my head. "It's not Liu. Well, not really. It's me. I don't want what we've been working toward. I don't want what I agreed to. I don't want success. At least, not the way the program defines it. I am so sorry I let you down. I am so sorry that I'm a big, black stain on the Will Power brand. I'm sorry I let myself get caught up in believing I wanted ... Power Broker–level success."

There. I said it.

Will is still standing buck naked in the steam. He'd turned his back to me while I was talking, so I can only read his body language ... and even then, all I really see is the way he's breathing. Deep and slow.

He's trying to control his anger.

I mimic his breath to control my fear.

I stand, wrap my towel around my chest, and try to sneak by him. I want to leave him to process without me in his space.

I make it to the door, but the *swish* created by the change in pressure in the sauna pulls his attention to me.

"Stop," he commands.

I halt and let the door close again, but don't turn around.

"You're mad," I say.

His hand lands on my shoulder and he twists me to face him. "I'm fucking furious."

25. Will

It's been a week since Virginia dropped out of the coaching program. And in the last seven days, she's been visibly more relaxed. We spent hours talking about her experience. She had nothing negative to say about Liu, but that hasn't reduced my ire about the situation.

I check my watch. Time to go shake shit up at the executive level. Emergency board meeting with all the major shareholders, which includes my mother, my brothers, four non-family investors, and myself.

I'm going into this meeting knowing I have support from Horse, Brian, and Aiden—four votes of nine. I need Mother, or one of the OG members, to have these changes passed.

As the president and CEO, Horse is in the direct line of fire and the one to lead the meeting. But I'll be at his side, ready to dive in to take the bullets. Aside from Mom, the room will be all suits. I suffer no delusion that this will be an easy conversation, but it's been simmering for years. Horse and I have been discussing and planning to share a new plan for a while, just not this soon.

I stand at Savi's desk. "Do I look like a man ready to be eviscerated?"

She nods, then shudders. "I'm picturing your testicles hanging from a clothesline."

"Great pep talk. Jesus, if I ever suggest a new role for you, remind me of this conversation."

She laughs. "I've never been prouder to call myself your right arm. Go get 'em, Power."

As I wait for the elevator, she chants, "I am a winner. I am making shit happen. Nothing will stop me from success. I am a winner. I am making shit happen. Nothing will stop me from succ—" The elevator doors cut her off, and I'm on my way down.

I enter the boardroom twenty minutes early. Horse, Brian, and Aiden are already here, though I do a double take to make sure Aiden really is my youngest brother.

"You clean up well," I say, grabbing his freshly shaved chin between my fingers.

"This tie is choking me." His tongue drops over his bottom lip, and he coughs dramatically.

I pull my drama-queen brother into a one-armed hug. "I love you, bro. Way to step up. I have all the faith in you."

He shoves me away with a grumbled "fuck off" and loosens his tie.

Based on the energy in the room, you'd never guess we were about to stage a corporate coup. There are no nerves. It's more a sense of excitement I haven't experienced since we were all under ten, still naïve about what it means to be a Power. All the strings, the expectations, the limits.

If we succeed and get the fifth vote, we'll celebrate. If we fail, we've all decided we'll walk and let the remaining board members find new leadership. Sure, we'll lose some nice perks and several hundred million dollars each. We're not sure if Mother will allow us to keep our condos in the building, and frankly, none of us care enough to add that to the negotiations.

With five minutes until go time, Horse calls us into a huddle, just like when we were preteens, acting out our Power versions of the *Teenage Mutant Ninja Turtles*.

Horse throws his fist into the middle of our group. "Horse Power!" he barks.

"Will Power!" I say, bashing my fist into his.

"Brain Power!" Brian adds, while the rest of us mutter, "Try hard." He growls back, "Fuck you," punching my fist, then Horse's.

"Fire Power!" Aiden's fist collides with each of ours in turn.

"Go Team Power," we chant in unison.

Nothing makes me happier than having these guys as brothers, knowing they will always have my back and I will always have theirs.

The boardroom door opens. Top of the hour. Horse's executive assistant, Reshma, ushers Mother in first, followed by the suits who always enter in the same order—the man with the highest net worth at that moment in the lead, the rest following—and then Reshma takes her seat at the table as the official minute-taker.

Each spot is set with a glass of water, a binder, and a pen, as well as coffee cups and a carafe, and cream and sugar within reaching distance for every member in attendance.

There are no pleasantries, just head nodding and greetings of "good afternoon."

These men are not family to us. They were to Dad, who handpicked each member of his board. And Mom still feels some sense of devotion to them since they steered the Power ship until we were old enough and had the degrees—or in my case, the stage experience—to assume official roles at the table.

Mom is the wild card. And today will tell us where her deepest loyalties lie—to her flesh and blood or to the hired guns.

Once everyone is seated, Horse stands.

"I appreciate you all coming today and booking two hours out of what I am certain are busy schedules."

Lots of grunting and indecipherable under-breath comments.

"As you may or may not be aware," Horse continues, "Will and I will be celebrating our forty-second birthdays in just over four weeks, on October 26, if anyone cares to send a card ... or a car." He laughs in an otherwise silent room.

"Will has officially entered what we brothers like to refer to as 'the Calendar of Catastrophe,' that window of time when, if he follows in true Will Power footsteps, he'll unexpectedly and inconveniently stop delivering the Come Into Power seminars so he can deliver nutrients to the next generation of daisies."

Mom gasps. It was important to me that Virginia's influence be acknowledged, even if nobody other than Mother would recognize it.

As expected, Mom interrupts. "We are not having this conversation, Colt." She turns to face me. "Will—"

Horse knocks on the table twice, quieting Mom.

"You're right, we're not having a conversation about this. What we're having is a vote. You all have a package in front of you that outlines the proposal that Will, Brian, Aiden, and I have developed to change a few things in the programs Will Power & Bros. runs, starting with the Come Into Power seminars, touching the Power Broker coaching program, the Will Power Hour podcast, and even—you're going to love this," Horse says, exaggerating the word *love*—"changing the name of the corporation. Again," Colt adds for dramatic emphasis.

Nobody touches their binders.

One suit reaches for the coffee carafe. Another leans against his upholstered chair, arms crossed in front of his chest, as if bored.

After a minute of posturing, the head suit opens his binder and flips through the pages without reading more than a sentence on any document. The others mimic. He's the first to speak.

"Cut to the chase, Colt. What new name are you proposing?"

"Power Brother Industries."

He lifts a shoulder and says, "Meh. I don't have a problem with that. Anyone else?"

Heads shake. All except Mom's.

"Motion to change the name of Will Power & Bros. to Power Brother Industries. All in favor, raise your hand and say, 'Aye'," Horse instructs. A chorus of ayes fill the room. Mom's hand is not in the air, so he says, "All opposed?"

Mom nods. Reshma says, "Mrs. Power is opposed. All other votes in favor. Motion to change the corporate name to Power Brother Industries passes."

"I am not pleased," Mother says in her Mom voice. "Nor will I sign off on this name change. Colt, I'm disappointed and hurt that you blindsided me with this."

"It's just a name, Mother," I say.

"No, Will. If it was just a name, you'd leave it as it is. Names have power, they carry meaning. And that name isn't right for the future of this company."

I drop my head into hands and sigh. This was supposed

to be the easy win. The win to set the tone of the meeting to achieve more yes votes.

"Well, having my name as the company name isn't right for the future of anything or anyone," I say with a bit more frustration than I should.

"I agree. But with all the work you've all been doing to bring more women into the programs, and into senior positions in the company, I don't think the focus on the Brothers is the right way to move forward. I'm actually quite pleased to change the name, but I'd like to put forth an alternative." Mother stops talking and waits.

Old Guy Number One speaks, "Which is, Maureen?

"Power *Family* Industries."

My brothers and I have a silent confab and agree with the name. Horse says, "That works for us."

The other suits shrug and say they're fine with it. The name is put to a vote and is unanimously passed.

"Colt," the head suit says, "explain the plan for the seminars."

Damn it. We wanted to end with the seminars. I look at Horse. He nods and mouths, *We got this.*

"In short, Aiden will become the new face of—"

"No! Absolutely not," Mother says, getting to her feet.

"Love the vote of confidence, Mom." Aiden gives her a thumbs-up.

After a forty-five minute debate about this transfer of stardom, we vote. The four of us are in favor. Three of the suits, plus Mother, are opposed. And one suit abstains.

"Motion to replace Will with Aiden for the upcoming delivery of the Come Into Power seminars does not pass," Reshma says.

I'm pissed. "You realize that every other time the role has changed hands, it's been to a green presenter, right?

And if I keep doing this, you're guaranteeing the same outcome."

"William Wallace Power," Mother says. "I am so tired of your fatalist attitude."

"And Mom, I am so tired of your delusion that I can keep doing this." My tone has no anger, just fatigue.

The man who abstained interrupts what might have degraded into a very personal discussion. "I will gladly vote in favor—once Aiden proves himself."

"And to be clear, what will you consider proof?" Aiden asks.

He tents his fingers and squints at me, then smiles at Aiden. "If you can deliver a full run of seminars without anyone asking for their money back, I'll change my vote the next time this comes up."

"Sorry, and how am I supposed to achieve this perfect tour if I'm not delivering the seminars?" Aiden asks.

I'm wondering the same thing.

"You can't, obviously. Deliver them with your brother. Get the training you need, make it flawless, and I'll vote aye."

Horse, being the brilliant facilitator he is, jumps in while the energy is positive. "And that is a perfect segue to the next item we need to vote on: a total makeover of the Power Broker coaching program, which Will and I will oversee together."

A different suit chimes in. "That program generates a significant percentage of the company's income. It's working. I am absolutely not in favor of any changes."

"But it's not working as well as it could be," Brian says.

"The financials suggest otherwise."

"Sure, if you're thinking with your dicks," Brian argues.

"Bri-an!" Mother scolds.

"Mo-ther!" We brothers respond as one, just as we have for over thirty years. We are a Borg—pick on one, answer to four.

"You're going to love this, Mom. We have a plan that we believe could double the income of the coaching program in the next ten years."

"Impossible. We've saturated the market," says a third suit.

"Like I said, if you're thinking with your dick, that's true. But a simple review of the businesses, the *individuals*," he emphasizes, "who engage in the program make it clear that there is a massive, underserved market who does not approach business with dicks swinging."

"Bri—" Mother only says half his name. Her eyes dart to each of us.

"Mo—" Despite the pause, our hive mind allows us to answer in perfect time and tone.

Brian doesn't miss a beat, continuing as if nothing happened. "Female entrepreneurs. They are woefully underrepresented in our seminars and in the coaching program. That is money on the table. Data can be found on page twenty-five."

The suits and Mom flip to the page that delivers the stats and outlines the rationale.

This prompts the most controversial and challenging arguments—discussions—of the meeting. The old guard doesn't believe successful women approach business any differently from successful men. They come from the same school of thought that all our coaches have been trained in —that being the biggest (dick) and pushing the hardest (like a good dick does) is the only way to succeed.

I'm certain that we'll have Mother onside for this vote since she's the one who hired that artist, Catherine Clay, to build her nest in our lobby as a way to remind us that female entrepreneurs juggle more home life responsibilities than most men do. We all get that.

But until Virginia explained her perspective using a lot of flowery, earthy language, it had never occurred to me or Horse or even Brian that there might be a more holistic way to look at business development. That relationships, not transactions, can be the bellwether of success. That looking to nature's rhythms of growth and restoration can be applied to businesses to make them more sustainable and reduce founder burnout, which is a huge issue in successful enterprises.

Hell, I'm a walking, talking, time bomb example.

We brothers vote in favor of a virtual dismantlement and rethinking of the coaching program. The dicks vote as expected, all against the known quantity that has kept them all very wealthy. And Mother, goddamn it, joins them.

And it's not enough that she votes against her family, but she explains her rationale. "I don't disagree with you. I think it's an excellent idea that, as you know, I've invested my own money in trying to make happen. My issue is that you men are not the right people to lead that change."

"And again with the staggering support from Mother Dearest," Aiden grumbles. "Who, pray tell, would *you* have lead it?"

"A woman, son, dearest," she replies, confirming that our private joke is still safe from her ire.

As for the changes to the podcast, since neither Mom nor the old guys have ever fully understood the value, they all agree to our proposal to change the name and the format.

The room empties at the top of the second hour,

leaving my brothers and me to review what we won and lost.

"I'm relatively pleased," says Brian.

"I'm *relatively* insulted," says Aiden. "What the fuck, Mom?"

"I'm relatively surprised," Horse adds, "that we achieved as much buy-in as we did."

They all look at me since I've been the driving force behind the proposal we've been working on for almost two years. Not with the coaching program—that's new. But with the other three items on the agenda.

"Will?" Horse shoulders me.

"I am relatively *disgusted*."

"By?" Brian asks, looking confused.

"By the fact that every decision they made was based on the bottom line and their profit potential. Not one of them, not even Mom, considered the people who consume our programs."

"Sure they did," Brian says. "They talked a lot about the market." He looks at me like I might have stroked out for huge parts of the conversation.

"Spoken like a true bean counter." I shake my head and stand. "I'm hangry. Dinner at my place in an hour?"

"I'll bring the whisky," says Aiden.

"Bring the good stuff for a change. I think I might just partake tonight."

Virginia is spending the night at her place with her sister since tomorrow we're heading to Lily Valley so I can fulfill my promise to get away from the city and breathe forest air for seventy-two hours before I get on a plane and spend the next nine weeks breathing airplane and hotel air.

26. Virginia

A WILTING WISTERIA

"Oh, come on!" Will hits the steering wheel with his fist and knocks his head twice against the window of his Lincoln Aviator.

I stifle a laugh, even though his fit about being stuck in traffic while sitting in seats more comfortable than any chair I've ever owned and listening to music on a sound system that costs more than I earn in a year makes me think of a bratty toddler who's overtired but doesn't want to go to bed. It's not a sexy look on a grown man, but it is amusing.

"People posting in the Sea to Sky Traffic Facebook group say the accident's been cleared. We should be rolling again in ten minutes or less." I put my hand on his thigh and squeeze. "The scenery is pretty, isn't it?"

"It would be nicer from a helicopter," he grumbles. "Next time we go away for a weekend, we do it my way."

"I know. And I appreciate you slumming it—"

"Virginia," he threatens with a glare.

"Sorry. I really do appreciate that you're stepping out of your comfort zone to spend three days where I'm happiest.

Truly." I undo my seat belt and lean across the foot-wide console armrest that separates us to plant a kiss on his cheek.

He grunts and tilts his head to look in the rearview. I glance at my side mirror and see that our security detail is still standing in the rain outside their vehicle a few cars back, appearing as intimidating as I suspect they would be if anyone approached our car.

I booked the largest house available for rent in Lily Valley, so we'd have enough bedrooms for the entourage of six guards that Will insisted we bring with us. Lately, he's been even more concerned about being seen than normal. And it's started to leak into how much control he's taking over my comings and goings. He won't even let me leave the Power building without one of his guys within arm's reach.

Over the last almost three months that I've been basically living in Will's penthouse and working in his building, I've gotten a taste of all the things billionaires can't do due to their wealth. There are so many restrictions that never would've occurred to me. Will can't have a food craving and decide to order takeout from any restaurant that hasn't been vetted by his security staff. Not that he ever needs takeout, but when a girl wants her comfort food from the greasy spoon that basically fed her as a teen, a high-end, on-call chef just doesn't fill that need.

Will can't go to a general admission movie, ever. Not that he really cares. But, when a new Ryan Reynolds film drops, yeah, I want to be first in line to see it so I can gush on fan sites.

And I know from day one that he can't even go outside for a walk unless he's accompanied by at least one sharpshooter. In the last couple of weeks, he won't leave at all.

It's a life so far removed from my own that there are days I wonder if I'll be able to adjust, assuming Will and I stay together long enough to make that a question. I mean, he and I are great. But I'm not great at living in a greenhouse.

"Hey, look. Taillights. We're about to roll. Hooray!"

"Hooray," Will says with no enthusiasm.

"I'm sorry this is stressing you out."

"It's not your fault. And I'm sorry I'm so cranky. Having those guys"—he bumps his head against his headrest—"on high alert puts me on high alert, and it's uncomfortable as hell. Not that I expect anything will happen, it's just ..." He doesn't finish his sentence.

"Statistically, that's exactly when something bad happens. I get it. But we'll be at the house soon. And then I promise, you'll not feel anything except relaxed. It's so beautiful there. Peaceful. Full of life, but hardly any people."

"It sounds like heaven," Will says, leaning across the giant armrest to kiss me.

A polite double honk tells us our kiss has lasted a little too long.

Will puts the car in gear and rolls a few feet forward while the vehicles immediately ahead of us start moving. Within thirty seconds we're at highway speed again. Fifteen minutes later, two security men are checking the property around the house I rented, two are inside making sure it's empty, and the last two are hauling in our luggage and boxes of food.

It all seems like overkill to me since I'm not publicly connected to either Will or his company, and anyone in Lily Valley who knows me—which is a fair few of the two hundred residents—knows that I normally trade gardening services for free B&B weekends in the low season. In other words, the odds of me showing up with a man who earns enough to take me away for a staycation weekend, let alone the richest man in the country, are one in a billion.

"Pretty nice view, isn't it?" I ask. Will and I stand in a living room with a three-story ceiling and wall of glass overlooking the inlet with mountains across the water. "The sunset will blow you away."

Will grabs my hips and pulls me backward into him. "What blows me away is seeing how happy you are here."

"This is nothing!" I face the man who makes me happier than getting a one-of-a-kind orchid to bloom again after being dormant for two years. "There's a bluff in the forest that overlooks Howe Sound without any obstructions. It's like standing on top of the world. We can have a picnic there this afternoon."

"Kind of chilly for a picnic, isn't it?"

"You won't be cold. It's a proper hike. You'll be glad for the rest. At least, I will. You'll probably just be happy for the food."

Since Will is leaving to deliver the European dates of his seminar tour in under a week, he's warned me he'll have to work a little this weekend, mostly responding to questions from his travel team.

"Now's when you can take thirty minutes to work and I won't even notice," I say. "I'll prep some snacks for the picnic, then we can get dressed in hiking clothes, and I'll show you my favorite place on the planet."

"Let security know, OK? We'll need two guys with us."

Now I'm the three-year-old, wanting to bang my head on the wall to protest this unfair treatment.

"We'll be alone. I've never seen anybody else where I'm

taking you." I stand on my toes to look right into his eyes. "Can't we do this *one thing* without chaperones?"

"I wish." He tilts my chin up and kisses my lips.

"I'd planned a surprise," I whine. "A *naked* surprise."

He smirks. "That's not happening. And not only because we'll have two guys within earshot, but because there is no way in hell I'm exposing any part of my body to be attacked by nature again. As much as I love your ass, I am not sucking thorns from it."

"No roses where we're going ... though ... there are blackberry vines. Those can tear your arm off if you move through them too quickly."

"You really need to work on your pitch."

A few hours later, Will, Liam, Jake, and I are standing shoulder to shoulder on a rocky outcrop, a mile above sea level overlooking forest, ocean, and mountains in the distance. The air is crisp and smells of dirt and cedar trees.

I pull off my backpack and place it on the picnic table that, the story goes, was carried here a decade ago in pieces by a besotted young man. His lover told him she wanted to have a picnic at the top of the world, so he granted her that wish.

"Do you love it? Don't you feel relaxed here?" I ask Will.

He leans down and whispers in my ear. "I'd feel a lot more relaxed if you hadn't planted the idea of making love to you here."

I mouth, "Make. Them. Leave."

Will inhales a couple of deep breaths as he stares out

into the gorgeous vista. Then he turns, wearing his man-in-charge expression.

"Jake, Liam, I don't see any imminent threat here. Do you see anything different?"

"No, sir," they say in unison.

"Good. I'd like one of you to leave me a radio and then for both of you to head back to the main trail, where we turned to come up here. Protect me from that distance, please. Ms. Beach and I would like to have our picnic without your fine company."

An anthill forms in my belly. An anthill filled with hundreds of very happy little legs, dancing at the thought of the feast that is about to be spread before them. The feast of the world's most beautiful man.

Will stands by my side until I can't hear Liam or Jake on the trail anymore. He steps in front of me, unzips my jacket, pushes his hands under my shirt, and grips my waist.

The warmth of his palms melts me.

Will's lips graze the shell of my ear, sending shivers down my spine and a deep pulse of energy into my core.

Nature meet nurture.

"How did you envision this fantasy unfolding?" Will hums in my ear. "Actually, don't tell me. Show me."

"Really?" I stare at him, worried that he might judge me for being too woo-woo or worse, too kinky. I inhale courage and one of his mantras pops into my head, so I say it. "If what you're doing makes people uncomfortable, keep doing it."

Will tilts his head, eyes questioning.

I inhale courage. "I want us to connect with nature ..." I pause, since I can imagine what I want but can't find the words to describe it.

Will waits several seconds then asks, "Should I take off my boots?"

The ants in my belly, which had stopped dancing and were waiting on all their tippy toes while I formed my thoughts, faint. His question makes me feel relief and joy and so much love because I know that even though my fantasy is so far out of his comfort zone that I can at least tell him. And even if he isn't game for everything, I know he's started to understand and accept all of who I am and what's important to me.

I blink away the happiness that's welled up from my chest and into my eye sockets.

"Yes, I would love for you to take off your boots, but first I want to gather some soft pine and cedar branches and some moss."

"Are we building a fire?"

We are, I think, but not the way you mean it.

I shake my head no. "We're making a bed. A bed that's filled with plant energy and life and—"

"And bugs and spiders and sticky sap," Will interrupts.

"Probably."

"Sexy," he says.

"I think it is."

Will shakes his head but he's not hiding a small smile. "I imagine you have a knife in that bag."

I nod.

"Then let's make a bed fit for Virginia 'Full of Surprises' Beach," he says.

"Good surprises?"

"The best."

Will and I walk several yards into the forest and set to work. He cuts young branches from the yellow Cyprus and lodgepole pines that stand tall. I fill a body-sized, hemp pillowcase with moss and fallen pine needles. Because nature makes me so happy, I'm humming "Walking on Sunshine" and dancing—just a little, because who can not move their body when there's music, even if it's only in your head?

I register a change in the sounds around me and look over my shoulder to see that Will has stopped snipping branches and is laying on top of the pile he's gathered. And all he's wearing is a look of invitation.

"Is this the way you see your fantasy unfolding?" he asks.

"Is it yours?"

"My fantasy is to make you so incredibly happy that you forget what an asshole I was on the drive up."

"Then ... we have to carry this all back to the picnic table. I want to make love in the sun with an unobstructed view of forever."

Will's smile is replaced by a look of relief and he jumps up and pulls his hiking pants back on. "Thank Christ, because honestly, I'm kind of freaked out that a giant ass black widow or worse, one of those hobo spiders could decide to make this a threesome."

"I've actually walked face first into a web with an orb spider in it on one of my hikes." I wrinkle my nose since, as much as I love nature, I could do without having that experience again.

"Don't tell Horse if you ever want him to hike with you," he says, tucking his boot laces behind the tongues.

"Arachnophobe?"

"Top point-one percent."

Will finishes haphazardly pulling on his T-shirt and jacket and we haul the load back to the rock outcropping.

Once we have branches arranged on top of the picnic table, I lay an old Hudson's Bay wool blanket over it all.

"To keep the creepy crawlies out of my hair," I laugh, only half joking.

"You really know how to set a mood, Beach. Can I get naked again?"

"Actually ..."

"Oh, for the love of—"

"Relax!" I coo. "Take a deep breath." I lift my chin skyward, inhale, and raise my arms to demonstrate the expansion. "Doesn't the air smell good?"

Will copies me and wiggles his eyebrows. "Do that again."

"How about I do one better?" I slide my jacket off my shoulders and drop it on the picnic table's seat. "Help me with the rest?"

Will grabs the hem of my T-shirt and slides it over my head. He looks at my bra with questioning eyes. I nod.

My exposed nipples are quick to make their opinion of the cool October air known. Will cups my left breast with a warm palm then gently presses the pad of his thumb to my enthusiastic nip.

"Let me warm that up for you," he says before placing his mouth against my skin. I am in heaven. Or hovering just below it.

"There's an experiment I've been dying to try ever since I read about it, like five years ago," I say, stroking his head.

He lifts his face. "Tell me."

"I get naked—"

"Liking it so far—"

I step on the bench of the picnic table, then swing myself on top of the blanket and lay back on my elbows.

"Then I lie on the branches, the moss, the hemp, the wool. All natural, earthy things."

Will mumbles acknowledgement against my belly, which he's now kissing.

"And you stand on the rock with bare feet while we make love. I want you to be looking out at the ocean and sky and mountains across the sound. I want you to really connect with nature while you're really connecting with me."

Will pulls my boots off, undoes my pants and slides them, and my panties, down my legs. He resumes kissing my belly where the waist band had stopped him and moves his lips lower.

I arch toward him, then pull away.

"You need to take off your boots." My voice is little more than a hoarse whisper. "And your socks."

Will nods, almost imperceptibly. The lines in his forehead, between his eyebrows, deepen just enough to tell me he wants to argue but is stopping himself. He kicks his hikers toward the forest. Throws his socks behind him with a dramatic flourish. Points to the zipper on his pants with a question in his eyes.

I nod. "I promise this will be unforgettable."

Will takes his time, connecting earth energy with ours. Once he's inside me, I grab the picnic table, my nails digging into the wood as I ride the waves of pleasure. It's even more intense than I'd imagined it would be. But Will isn't appreciating the view—either of me writhing below him or the landscape spread out in front of him—his eyes are pressed tight and his mouth is open.

When Will comes, he makes a sound I've never heard before. It's raw and guttural and entirely unashamed. He's breathing hard when he opens his eyes, first looking at me then out at the expanse of nature. I stay quiet and just watch him settle. He doesn't move. Doesn't pull out, though that's happening on its own.

He speaks first. "B-plus."

I laugh. "How disappointing."

"Not at all. I messed up. Didn't follow your instructions. Let's eat and try for the A-plus experience in twenty minutes."

Oh my goddess, I love this man.

27. Will

SUSHI-TASTROPHE

I admit, for a man who's traveled to every major city in the US, Canada, and Europe, I may have led somewhat of a sheltered life. But when I agreed to spend three nights in a house without staff (aside from six pain-in-my-ass security guards) in a town so small it doesn't even have a place to get takeout, I had no idea what I was agreeing to.

Just weeks until my forty-second birthday and until yesterday I'd never had to concern myself with things like not having exactly the food I want to sate a craving, or sleeping in a bed with a dollar store mattress and sheets made of sandpaper, or running out of hot water while showering.

That said, until yesterday, I'd never experienced the astonishing pleasures of eating blackberries straight off the vine, naked sunbathing on a mountaintop, or carving my initials into a picnic table to memorialize the most intense sexual experience I've had in over twenty years of sexual experiences.

Virginia's world is one of extremes that annoy and delight me in equal measure.

"I want to take you to my favorite sushi restaurant tonight," she says after we step out of the tepid shower, post-hike number three.

"It's such a pain to go out. Let's order in," I suggest, wrapping a towel around my hips. My chest tightens at the secret I've been keeping from her for weeks—that during one of our "become one with the soil" park walks, someone took our photo and figured out who she is. And that they've made a threat—with the requisite request for money, of course—that's got my security team on edge. Which is why I'm on edge. I couldn't give a rat's ass about someone threatening to kidnap me. But threaten Virginia? I have to tell her this weekend but want to wait until the end so she can enjoy this time in her personal definition of the happiest place on earth.

"Come on!" She tugs at my towel. "Half the fun is being able to order one thing at a time. And I never know what I want until I walk in. Will it be grilled hamachi or tuna sashimi?" She smacks her lips and looks longingly into the air, oblivious to the towel I'm holding out for her.

"Then we'll order both. No, we'll order one of everything on the menu, eat what we want, and let the six hounds of hell finish the leftovers."

She accepts the towel and keeps her eyes focused on the part of her body she's drying while she talks. My attention follows hers.

"The fact that you call your security detail the hounds of hell suggests you feel like you're trapped in the underworld." Virginia looks up from her now-dry upper thigh. My interest has wandered a little higher.

"Ahem!" She clears her throat and I look up to her

smirk. "The other half of the fun is people watching and being in a different energy environment from what you have at home."

"It's such a hassle," I complain, following her into the bedroom.

Virginia riffles through her suitcase, butt naked, while she continues to press the subject. "Why are we traveling with six assassins if not to have the freedom to enjoy some time out in the real world?"

She has a point. Three of them could've left if we were just planning to stay in this strange little village.

"Fine. We'll go out. Make a reservation for seven."

She shakes her head as she pulls on leggings. "The thing is, you can't reserve a table at this place. It's best to arrive early."

"What? Is it like a fast-food joint? I am not eating sushi from a chain restaurant."

Virginia levels a silent stare at me. I take a step back.

"Have you been hanging out with my mother? Is she training you in all the looks that disempower the Power men?"

"Not *all* of them." She winks and blows me a kiss. "And it is not a fast-food restaurant. It has the best sushi between downtown Vancouver and Whistler. They just choose to not book it up for months in advance ... so, no RSVP."

M y six security guys, dressed in matching outdoor gear versus the usual black suits, look farcical getting out of their identical BMW X5s. But Virginia insists they at least try to look like normal people out to eat. Everything about them, however —from their posture to their scowls—screams that these are men trained to be hyper-observant, no matter how many dirt stains they have on the hems of their hiking pants.

Of course, there's a line to get a table. Virginia goes in and requests two tables for two and a table for four—in that order and all within view of each other so that I won't be left unprotected. Was it a hassle? Sure. But the thing that irritates me most is having to wait to sit. I wrack my brain for the last time I arrived *anywhere* and wasn't immediately taken to wherever the fuck I wanted to go.

As Virginia tries to chat with the stone faces that stand two in front, two behind, and one at each side of us, I bite my bottom lip to not voice the question running through my mind—

Do you know who I am?

This is, perhaps, the first time in my life when it would not be a benefit for anyone to acknowledge my privilege, my importance, my goddamn power.

And yet, here I stand, like a schmo, waiting to eat food that will probably not even be that good. As soon as the *Why?* pops into my incensed head, a laughing Virginia grabs my hand and kisses my knuckles.

"Thank you for coming. I've been craving their seafood salad for I can't even tell you how long. It's so good. You'll love it—maybe even more than you love me!"

That smile. She melts my cold, hard heart with her joyful energy. Virginia tilts her head up for a kiss. I don't kiss in public. I don't emote in public. I try not to do anything in public. But I can't say no to this woman.

I press my palm against her nape and tangle my fingers in her loose curls. The kiss is G-rated, but still ignites my blood.

Who am I? When I'm with Virginia "Free Spirit"

Beach, I am not the same man. My body sighs a quiet "thank you," but my brain screams "Danger!"

After forty minutes and a frustrating number of people who arrived after us have gone in, our entourage is invited to be seated. I give the hostess points for the table assignments. My back is against the wall, and four of my guards have a clear view of both the front door and the hall to the bathroom. I settle in and relax.

For about twelve seconds.

A small child screams. I look around to see what appears to be a five-year-old throwing a fit and the adults at his table totally ignoring him. I stare. The hellion continues to voice his displeasure at whatever the fuck a kid can be upset about with a plate full of food in front of him. His parents appear to be stone deaf.

"Seriously? Why is there a screaming child here?"

Virginia wrinkles her nose. "Family-friendly until nine o'clock."

"What's wrong with those parents? Are they not aware that their devil spawn is disrupting the entire restaurant?" I wave my hand to get the waitress's attention.

Virginia half stands to reach my arm and pulls it down.

"It's a thing in this town ... it's called permissive parenting. And the parents are referred to as jellyfish by, well, anyone who isn't into letting their kids run the show."

"You have got to be kidding me. I can't do this. First the wait just to have to listen to that? We're leaving." I push back my chair and nod at the security detail. They stand in unison, with military precision. But Virginia has crossed her arms and is shaking her head.

"Wow," she snarls, "I never would've guessed that your mother was a jellyfish too. Or wait—" She opens her eyes wide and points a taunting finger at me. "Was it your nanny who taught the great Will Power that he can get whatever he wants by throwing a fit?"

When my focus is no longer on Virginia, I realize the restaurant has gone silent. Correction, the brat has stopped bawling. But it's not quite silent. The whispers that carry my name from table to table sound like wind in a haunted forest.

One of my security detail leans close to me and says, "We have to go now. The space is no longer safe."

I can't argue that Virginia is wrong. I can't remember a time when I didn't get my way—aside from the whole "you are Will Power, therefore you are a motivational speaker" thing. I unclench my fists and breathe out, glad that I now have no choice but to leave.

"I'm sorry," I say, "we have to go. Everyone knows who I am."

Her eyes go glassy, but she squeezes them tight. When she opens them again, I see anger in her look. "Go. You got your way in the end. You always do, don't you? But I'm staying. I'm having dinner, and if you decide it's safe enough to stay at the rental, I'll see you back there. Otherwise ..." She trails off and looks away.

"Otherwise?" I repeat, wondering if she's going to make a threat about leaving me or if she'll interpret my absence as me leaving her. I don't like either option.

I crouch to her level. "Please come back to the house with me. We can order takeout and one team will bring it home with them. I can't leave you here."

She finally faces me, and her cheeks are wet. I wipe away a tear with the pad of my thumb.

"You're right." I swallow my pride. "I *am* being as much of a brat as the brat, just more mature in my delivery."

She coughs a laugh and mutters, "Quieter, maybe, but no more mature."

"Virginia, I don't want to fight. I'm sorry. I am. This is hard for me."

"Welcome to life as a mere mortal where we have to wait in line, and sometimes people make noise we don't like, and things don't always go our way."

"That's not what I mean—even though you're right about that, too. You know I don't go out. I find being in public ..." I pause, trying to find a word that doesn't make me sound as anxious and vulnerable as I feel. "I find it stressful. I'm on edge. And that doesn't excuse my reaction to a crying kid, but ... please understand?"

"Mr. Power." A hand touches my shoulder. "Sir, the cars are warmed up. We need to leave."

Virginia's face softens. "Well, having six hellhounds at our table with us doesn't evoke a spa-like relaxation for me either."

"Come with me?"

"I was really looking forward to the sashimi. And edamame. And gyoza. And a miso soup. And—"

"We'll get it all for takeout." I stand and make eye contact with our waitress. She comes over while Virginia is pulling on her jacket. "One of everything on the menu." I tilt my head toward my wolf in hiker's clothing. "This guy will pay."

"Yes, sir," he replies.

I stand tall as we leave, aware that everyone is looking at me. Outside, the partner of the security guy still in the restaurant nods me toward my car.

I stop. "What's the limit on your expense card?" I ask.

"Five thousand a day, sir."

"After I leave, talk to the manager. Pick up the tabs for everyone who had to experience that shit show."

"Yes, sir."

"Wait. Everyone except the table with the screaming brat. Those people need a lesson in appropriate behavior for a kid in a restaurant."

"Quite right, sir."

28. *Virginia*
THE POWER GOES OUT

Will is quiet for the first ten minutes of the drive back to Lily Valley. I'm quiet, too, processing what just happened. I can't decide if I'm more angry about his outburst or sad that Will has no idea how to function as a normal person outside of his ivory tower. One thing I have decided is that I'll forgive him once the food is delivered.

Thinking of the food, I realize how outrageous it is to have ordered one of everything. So much of that food will go to waste. I check the time. Just after seven ... the order will probably take forty minutes to prepare, another twenty to get to Lily Valley. Dinner at eight on a Saturday night isn't too crazy.

"Hey," I break the silence. "Want to play a round of pool? Or darts?"

"I didn't see a pool table in the house." He doesn't take his eyes off the road.

"There's one at the firehall. I know the chief. She's really cool. So is her husband. He's like you—well, not a bazillionaire, but he's from a moneyed family and has three brothers. I think you'd like them. We can have the sushi delivered there and let some of the volunteers eat so it doesn't go to waste. What do you think? Kind of nice to end on a better note than we're at right now?"

He grunts but doesn't answer.

More silence until Will taps his finger on his steering wheel. The computer screen on the dash changes.

"Call CSO," he says.

"Mr. Power?"

"Turn in at the firehall in Lily Valley. Tell the team at the restaurant to take the food there."

"Yes, sir."

"It's a good plan. I hope your friend the chief is home, or this will be the first tailgate party a Power has ever hosted."

"Thank you," I whisper and squeeze his thigh.

"Thank you." Will lifts my hand and kisses each of my knuckles.

The firehall is alive with party energy. Takeout containers cover the entire eighteen-foot-long table in the meeting room on the main floor. That's where most of the action and people are. We can hear them from the smaller room upstairs that's home to a big-screen television, a pool table, a couple of couches, and a kitchenette.

The TV/pool room has one way in—up an enclosed stairwell—so we only have one guard with us, which is good since that leaves space for ten firefighters to relax without being cramped.

Sophie, the chief and my friend, and her husband Nick are taking shifts between hanging out with us and being responsible parents, not leaving their sleeping toddler home alone.

It's Nick's turn to have fun, and he's cleaning up at the pool table. Turns out there's something the great Will Power can't do—and that's drop a ball in a pocket.

If anyone knows who Will is, they're hiding it with perfection. I told Sophie he just wanted a night where he could be like everyone else, and she let the men and women of the department know that's how they should treat him.

The guys are crude, the way guys can be when sticks are being swung and balls are the center of attention.

"I hope you're a better stick handler away from the felt, Power," Nick teases.

"Nick, cut my man some slack. Will hasn't had to handle his stick since I met him," I say.

All the guys groan in discomfort.

Lynn steps up to the table and drops a ball in a pocket. "Someone want to start the generator?" She pauses, looks around the room, then says, "Because it looks like the Power's going out tonight," Lynn bows to applause.

I clap along with everyone and notice that the security guy's scowl has relaxed and he's not above joining the mockery of his boss.

The huge screen is streaming *Backdraft*, a classic firefighter movie starring Kurt Russell and William Baldwin. It's obvious the whole crew has seen the film before since lines are yelled in time with the actors' deliveries, and each time a fire scenario gets something wrong, the room erupts in jeers and calls of "Drink, motherfucker!"

The happy, relaxed energy is contagious. The easy way these volunteers, who may not be friends outside the department, get along when they're here is why I love small towns and Lily Valley, in particular. In my perfect world, I'd have a small house and a big piece of land to garden here. With a greenhouse just like Mr. Bernard's.

A chorus of hoots and hollers erupts from the pool table. I look over to see Will bow and return his stick to the cue rack.

"Thank you, gentlemen and ladies, for not giving a rookie even one ounce of opportunity to look good in front of his girlfriend. You all suck." He's laughing. They're laughing. I'm laughing.

Will drops onto the couch beside me as a new team of four rack the balls.

"Having a good time?" I ask, knowing the answer by the deep smile on his face.

"The best." He pulls me tight against his body, and I snuggle into him.

"Can you see why I love it here?"

"It's like everyone in this town is a variation of you and your easygoing energy," he says.

"I think it's called authenticity."

He raises his brows, and I realize I might have just suggested he doesn't live with authenticity. "I'm sorry. I suspect it's a lot easier to be yourself when nobody's judging you."

"Or when they're judging you to be *the worst* pool player they've *ever* competed against—and they've played with drunken Santas and kids who need a stepladder to see over the table."

"Ouch." I chuckle.

"I like seeing you in this environment. It suits you," he says.

"It suits you better than chrome and concrete, too, you know."

"I wasn't referring to the physical environment. I meant these people."

"I know. Same. The people in your building are kind of chrome and concrete compared to the people here, don't you think?"

We both turn toward the guard, who at that moment is as perfect a statue as any punch line could ask for.

"You ready to head back to the house?"

"You ready to let me remind you that, without an audience, I'm pretty talented with a stick and balls?"

I groan. "Good thing you don't earn your living onstage … oh wait …"

Getting Will to agree to a digital sunset and to turn off his phone at nine p.m. once we started spending nights together required my best negotiation skills—and not a small number of sexual favors. Not that I don't fully enjoy the trade-off.

It's after midnight, and I am too tired for that part of our goodnight routine. But to escape the nightmare portion of Will's evening, I have to open my e-reader before I can close my eyes.

"What's your pleasure? Fiction or nonfiction tonight?" I roll on my side to face him. He's on his back with his hand behind his head, appearing to stare at the ceiling. He doesn't answer.

"Will?"

"Can we talk instead?" he asks, still looking up.

His tone—and that he seems to be intentionally not looking at me—turns the sushi in my belly into a spiky puffer fish.

"Words no woman ever wants to hear from a sexy, naked man in her bed."

He makes a weak effort at a smile.

"Roll on your side?" He twists his body and bumps his knees against my thigh to nudge me to curl in the other direction. Once I'm wrapped in his arms, his chest and stomach totally enveloping my back, we take three deep breaths together. We've got this evening relaxation thing nailed.

After what feels like too long, Will still hasn't spoken, so I break the silence.

"Fun night, eh?"

"Mm."

"No?" I ask, confused by his noncommittal sound.

"Yeah. It was fun. It was ... I've not felt that relaxed with a group of strangers ... well, ever."

Excellent! I knew he'd like Nick. Even though they're not quite the same species, they're both from the same family-money planet with all kinds of expectations on them.

"Nick's a good guy," I say, hoping to speed up this chat since I'm bone-tired and being wrapped in Will's arms is not helping me stay awake and focused.

More minutes pass, and when Will speaks, his voice startles me. I'd fallen asleep.

"Thanks for casting whatever magic spell you did to make everyone pretend like I wasn't me. It was nice to be treated like a regular asshole for a night. Like I was the same as these guys—and women."

"You kind of are." I yawn. "I mean, one bankruptcy and you would be."

First, he laughs. Then he sighs. "Bankruptcy actually makes the super rich even richer. It's a fucked-up system."

More silence.

"Will, I am so tired. What do you really want to talk about?"

"Us. What we think we're doing," he says.

I never expected to know what it might feel like to swallow the thousand thorns of a blackberry vine, but the sharp pain in my stomach suggests I now have a very good idea.

29. Will

LOCKED IN A TOWER

Virginia tries to twist out from under my arm, but I hold her down. I can't face her for this conversation.

This entire night has been a case study in why a long-term relationship with anyone who can't fully accept and embrace my lifestyle will never work.

Virginia will never be happy living the way I have for my adult life, locked in a climate-controlled tower except when I'm traveling and then locked in private jets and luxury hotels. She'd never be happy giving up the freedom she has to explore forest trails without an entourage or to literally stop and smell the flowers when she's out walking in a park.

And I would never ask her to give that up since she wouldn't be Virginia without dirt under her fingernails and twigs in that mess of red hair she prefers to leave wild.

I reach up and try to touch her head. But she shakes it and enunciates, "No. Will, let me go."

The irony of her statement is not lost on me; that is

precisely what I'm trying to find the words to do. I don't speak until she relaxes into my hug.

"There's a quote I never thought I'd say. But it's playing on repeat, so I guess—"

"Will." She twists again. "Pull off the fucking Band-Aid."

I've never heard her swear in anger.

"If you love someone, set them free," I say, cringing both at how lame that sounds and how apropos of the situation.

Her shoulder thrusts upward into my armpit and I recoil. She's free, feet hitting the floor with a thud.

Virginia stares down at me, hands on her hips.

"I'm not sure how to interpret this. You hold me in a bear trap and then say if you love someone, set them free. So, are you telling me in some fucked-up way that you don't love me? Is that what's happening here?"

I pull myself up, my back against the headboard, and turn on the reading light so I can see her better. An inferno blazes in her eyes.

"You know I love you. But this weekend, hanging out like a normal person ... this was a one-off thing. You know that, right? It's not my life. And as long as you're with me, it can't be yours, either."

I expect her to cry, to see tears. But fire and water don't mix, and the flames are winning. She stomps to the dresser and yanks out one of my T-shirts, pulls it over her head, then crosses her arms.

"Nope." That's all she says.

Is she agreeing with or challenging me? I can't tell from the single syllable. I know if I wait, she'll clarify.

Virginia walks back and forth a few times at the foot of

the bed, staring at the floor, shaking her head, muttering. She stops and points at me.

"I have just spent the last four months convincing you that your name did not come with a predetermined date on your death certificate. Do you have any idea how much fun that *wasn't*?"

"I—"

"That was a rhetorical question, Will. It was hell. Seeing you suffer was hell. And because it hurt me so much to see such a smart, kind, generous, funny man in so much pain, I did everything I could to help you. *Before* I fell in love with you."

She turns away, faces the wall.

"Virginia—"

She spins. "I'm not done. You knew my story. You knew the one thing—the *one thing*—that would hurt me most would be to be dropped because I'm not good enough for a man who has everything. You know that, Will. And I trusted that because I told you my biggest fear you would act with—I don't know, integrity? Or is it just plain old fucking human kindness?"

She stops and inhales a jagged breath. I hold mine.

"Well?" she asks.

"Um, sorry, so that wasn't a rhetorical question?"

"Fuck you, Will."

"Can I say something?"

She shakes her head, looking anywhere but at me. "Whatever. The great Will Power will do what he wants, anyway."

With that one sentence, I go from wanting to soothe Virginia to wanting to eviscerate her the way she's just shredded me.

"The great Will Power does whatever he wants," I echo.

"Do you seriously not see how this whole situation is precisely because the great Will Power," I say, dripping with sarcasm, "can't do *anything* he wants? When he wants? How he wants? Fuck, not even with who he wants?"

"Right. So we're back to me not being good enough."

"That is not what I said."

"The part where you don't get to do anything with who you want? Since this is all coming up after spending one day with me in my world, it kind of feels like you *do* mean me."

"No. Not even close." I can't believe how badly this is going. I didn't expect it to be easy, but this is not the direction I anticipated. "Please, sit." I pat the mattress.

"Thanks. I've been standing on my own my whole life. I'm fine."

"I meant the six hounds of hell shadowing our every move. I meant my job and all the people I work with, aside from my brothers. Men like Liu." I pause and wait for that to sink in. Virginia knows how angry I am at her former business coach, since she's the one who convinced me not to fire him.

She looks up from whatever interesting spot on the floor is holding her attention with a question in her eyes. She's softened—even someone who hasn't watched a thousand hours of true crime documentaries would see that.

"Virginia, I love you."

"Interesting way to express it," she mumbles.

"I love you, and I want nothing more than for you to be happy."

"I am happy. Why would you think I'm not happy?" Her tone bites, but it's not as vicious as the rabid cougar she embodied a few minutes ago.

"I know. This weekend showed me what you're like when you're truly being Virginia Beach without all the walls I usually see around you. This place, this town, these people—they make you happier than I've ever seen you. Even happier than being in that monster greenhouse."

The fire is out. Tears have pooled and overflow their banks.

"Please come back to bed? Please let me hold you. If not for you, for me. I need you. This is worse than my most distressing fucking nightmares."

She pulls off my T-shirt and drops it on the foot of the bed, crawls back under the duvet, and presses her back to my front. I hold her tight and feel her sob. She is breaking my fucking heart, but better now than in a year, after I've broken her spirit by keeping her locked in my fucking tower.

"Breathe," I say, taking a long, slow inhale myself. I wait until she sighs, her breathing back to normal, before I talk again.

"You know, my mother wasn't from money either. She met my dad when they were, like, fifteen or sixteen. She went to the local high school, was just a normal kid. Dad wasn't billionaire class back then, but the Power family was the wealthiest in the city. Mom's dad worked for the company. That's how they met."

"Like a 'take your kid to work' thing?"

I can hear the smile behind her question.

"No. Mom actually got an after-school job cleaning the bathrooms. It was an older building. She said it was the worst job ever. Can you picture *my* mother cleaning fifty toilets a night?"

"That is ... no, unimaginable."

"Yeah, well, the story goes that Dad was escaping from one of those bathroom windows that opened into an alley so the guards and doormen wouldn't see him."

"Your mom caught him?"

"She did more than catch him. She showed him all the places teens hung out—the places parents knew about *and* the ones they didn't. And ... the rest, as they say, is history."

Virginia rolls to face me. "I'm confused. You're saying you and I have a relationship that's the same as your mom and dad's, but that this will never work between us. Doesn't make sense. Why tell me that story?"

"It's not exactly the same. Dad wasn't free to roam around as much as he wanted, but he didn't have guards twenty-four seven. There weren't death threats against the family back then. It was a different time. And I'm telling you so that you believe, whatever this conversation is about, it has literally nothing to do with the amount of money you have, have had, or will have. Please, please, please believe that."

"But it has everything to do with how much you have." She shrugs.

"Yes."

"It's not fair."

"No, it's not. And you know what else isn't fair? How unhappy Mom is. After Dad died, she lost the joy of life. And I can't, I cannot, will not, do that to the woman I love. Put her through what Mom went through, losing the love of her life when she was only forty."

"Stop it. You're not going to die at forty-two."

"Maybe. Maybe not. That's beside the point. But if you had to give up this life, these friends, your freedom, you'd be dead in a year. Maybe not in-the-ground dead, but soul dead."

Virginia rests her head against my chest. I stroke her hair.

"I do love the dirt," she says. "Being in the ground dead

would be better than soul dead." She looks up with a sad smile.

"I'd certainly prefer it," I agree. "There's something else I have to tell you."

"Is it a good or bad something?"

"It's not good." A pain in my chest tells me how much of a lie that is. It's fucking awful, but I'm not going to let on how bad, hopefully ever.

"Will you be able to sleep if you wait to tell me tomorrow? I'm so tired. And right now, I know that whatever you say is going to sound ten times worse than it probably is." She presses her back closer to me. "I just want to be held right now and fall asleep in your arms. Can we do that?"

"Yeah," I whisper. "We can do that." I release the breath I didn't realize I was holding.

"And, can you, maybe, try to stay awake until I'm asleep and make sure my subconscious mind doesn't play dirty when I hit REM?"

I wrap my arm just a little tighter around her ribs. "Sleep knowing that I love you and that all I want in this whole fucking world is for you to be happy."

Virginia's chest heaves a few times before she relaxes and her breathing tells me she's asleep.

Fuck. Fuck. Fuck.

When I wake, it's still dark. I wiggle my shoulder and it's free to move. Will has rolled away. My mind kicks into gear and I replay our conversation from hours ago. I imagine what he's going to tell me next and where we can possibly go from here.

Georgia's cautions about men like Will reverberate in my brain like a brood of cicadas, a background cacophony that is impossible to ignore, drowning out my own thoughts.

I need to move, to make noise, to distract myself. I slowly roll from bed, dress in yesterday's clothes, and slide my feet across the floor toward the door so as not to press on a creaky floorboard. I need to ground before I try to figure out what to do. My plan is to go for a walk, get my heart rate up, and replace the noise in my brain with the thrum of my blood pumping.

I reach the living room and see a light on. Peeking around the corner, I spot one of the guards, the same guy who was with Will and me on our first walk in the park. I try to sneak by him, get my shoes and go outside. Despite using my stealthiest movements, the floor creaks right when I'm in view.

Bruce looks up from his phone.

"Ms. Beach, can I help you?"

He stands. My heart falls.

I point at the door and whisper, "Just going for a little walk."

He nods and grabs his jacket from the back of a chair as he passes.

"I'm fine," I say, holding up my hand. "I don't need company."

He smiles but says nothing as he continues toward me. Correction: toward his boots. He has them on and tied before I've finished doing mine up. I notice him texting.

"Please, I'd like to walk alone," I say, standing at the threshold.

"Unfortunately, I can't let you do that." He presses a hand on the door, opening it enough for him to get by me. Once outside, he holds his palm up in the stop position and looks from side to side, shining his phone's flashlight into the dark.

Ignoring his silent command, I push past him. "Bears and cougars are all tucked in bed. I'll be fine." Even though I'm not a runner, I start to jog away.

"Ms. Beach," he calls. In under ten steps, he's a wall blocking my path.

"Seriously?" I stare at him. He doesn't break eye contact. "Please get out of my way. Leave me alone."

"I can't do that."

"Yeah, you can. I've been going out at night by myself for a long time. I'll be fine. Go watch over the man who needs protection from life."

I move left to get around him. He blocks me. I take two steps backward and then bolt to the right. He blocks me. I cross my arms in front of my chest and push directly into him. That works. He steps out of my path. Then back into it.

"Come on!" I snarl, wanting to yell, but not wanting to wake anyone up.

"Ms. Beach—"

"Virginia. My name is Virginia. I'm not Ms. Beach."

"To me you are."

"To you I should be nothing." And just like that, Georgia's voice is in my head again. My resolve to get away from this man evaporates and exhaustion takes over. Physical, mental, emotional. I'm wiped out. Brain drained. And worst, soul sad.

What starts as a sigh ends as a sob.

"I just need to go for a walk," I whine. "Why won't you let me go for a walk?"

"I'm not stopping you from walking. I just need to accompany you."

"But I want to be alone."

"I understand. And I am sorry to ruin that for you. This is for your safety."

And then, in the dim light of a streetlamp, I read Bruce's expression. The penny drops. Will's reluctance to let me do anything on my own in the city, his irritated acceptance of this NHL-worthy lineup of body guards, and his edginess about being stopped in traffic on the highway in a place with no escape route all make sense.

"Has there been a threat against Will?"

He shakes his head. "I'm sorry. I'm not at liberty to talk about that."

"You're not at liberty to tell me why I have a six-foot-four, 250-pound walking wall of muscle shadowing me at one o'clock in the morning in the middle of nowhere?"

"Correct."

"So, who is 'at liberty,'" I ask with sarcasm, "to tell me?"

"Speak to Mr. Power."

I squeeze my eyes shut, inhale, and hold my breath so I don't scream.

I'm not ready to talk to Will. I need to think. But I can't think with Bruce the Moose tracking my every step. It's clear he's not going to leave me alone.

"Fine. You win. Tell me—did you get your own room?"

He nods.

"Then this is the compromise, since you won't let me have time on my own out here. I am going to take a bath in your en suite. I can't take one in mine because I'll wake Will. What time does your 'make sure nobody comes or goes' shift end?"

"Six," he says.

"I'll be done long before then."

We walk back to the front door in silence. Take off our boots in silence. Head to his room in silence.

"Wait here, please," he whispers. After a minute, maybe two, he ushers me in. His bed has been made, there are no clothes in sight, and the bathroom looks as if it's not been used.

"You didn't have to clean up," I say.

"The towel on the hook is fresh. Leave the bathroom door open when you're done, so I know you're not still here." He nods, then turns and leaves.

I start the water, undress, and kill the light. The bathroom is pitch dark—no window, no ambient light. I inch my way to the tub, step in, and crank the dial so it's delivering steaming hot water. I picture my skin turning bright red and feel the perspiration bead on my face as the tub fills. Using my foot, I turn off the tap lever and settle in.

My body relaxes and with it, my mind. I can finally think clearly, see my options, visualize the paths I can take from this crossroads.

In the way I replay the conversation with Will, he didn't break up with me. He strongly suggested I wouldn't be happy if I stayed with him. I choose to believe that he's giving me the choice to stay or leave since my happiness, not his, is what's in question.

Haven't I been happy?

I was happy hiking in the forest with him. Hanging out with my friends at the firehall. But that was holiday happiness. That could never be my every day life, not with us living and working in a big-city high-rise.

The number of times I've dreamed about being able to work from home, having a greenhouse where I'd spend my hours growing special plants and resurrecting sick ones for well-intentioned, albeit inept, clients—it's a dream I'd started to actually taste with Mrs. Bernard's flora. Aside from the end-of-day visits to Will's office to check on his plants, visiting Mr. Bernard has been the highlight of my workweeks.

A future locked in a high-rise, even a luxury high-rise with thousands of plants in hundreds of rooms on thirty-two floors, does not ignite joy in my heart. I imagine myself as a silent songbird in a gilded cage.

Maybe I could be happy if I were to spend my days outside in my dirt-on-the-ground world and my evenings in Will's chrome-and-concrete world.

I submerge my head under the water to block out the ambient noise of the sleeping house, so I can listen to my body as I consider that option.

I'd never sleep with the fresh air of an open window.

I'd never hear the pitter-patter of rain on the ground.

I'd never smell the petrichor rising from cool drops falling onto parched pavement.

I'd never sip my morning coffee while watching robins pull worms from grass or Steller's jays flit from tree to tree.

I'd never be able to pad out to a sunny wood deck in my bathrobe and sit with my face in the rising summer sun.

So many things I'd never be able to do again if I officially moved into the Power Industries private residences with Will.

As much as I love the man, the dread that fills my heart at all the things I'd have to give up weighs like a March snowfall, burying sweet, optimistic, early-spring crocuses.

I love those flowers. I relate to their enthusiasm about life, pushing up from the cold ground as soon as it's soft enough to break through. But I never want to experience the crushing disappointment of being smothered, left broken and bruised by whims of uncontrollable outside forces.

An image of the security team pops into my head. A life being guarded and on-guard would destroy me. How could *anyone* live like that?

My tears mix with the water that covers my cheeks as I realize that my father was half right—I am not the kind of person who can live in a wealthy man's world, but not, as he said, because I'm not worthy of wealth. It's because the things money buys don't make me as happy as down-to-earth, grounded experiences.

I pull myself up and wipe my eyes.

"Hi," a deep voice says from the dark.

31. *Will*

UNSOLVED CRIMES: OUTSTANDING

Virginia screeches, then sounds like she's drowning.

I throw the switch. Blinding bright light floods the bathroom, but I need to see to help her.

I reach under her armpits and pull her up into my arms to clap her back several times.

"Sorry, sorry, sorry," I whisper like a broken record.

Her coughing slows, and her breaths regulate.

"You scared the crap out of me. How long were you standing there?"

"Seconds. I debated turning on the light, but didn't want to startle you." I release her from my hug and lean her back from me so I can see her face. "You OK?"

"Just surprised me." Her lips curve enough to tell me she's not mad.

"I woke up. You were gone. I worried that ..." I stop myself.

Virginia kisses my cheek and pulls away. "Yeah, we need to talk about that." She points to the towel.

I wrap her in it, kiss her wet hair, gather her clothes off the floor, and follow her back to our bedroom.

I change into a dry T-shirt and boxers while she pulls on a version of the same. Once we're mostly covered, Virginia gets in bed, sitting up under the duvet, arms crossed, head tilted and eyes demanding answers.

I sit on the mattress edge so I can face her.

"Two, three weeks ago, the team received a credible threat from someone who knew that you are very important to me." I pause to let that sink in. And so I don't tell Virginia more than she needs or wants to know.

Her forehead wrinkles. I wait for the questions.

"Why didn't you tell me?"

"I didn't want you to worry."

She nods but still has her thinking face on.

"So, traveling with six security guys isn't normal for you?"

Not the question I was expecting. "No. Usually just one guy. And if I'm with Dawes or another driver, that's usually adequate. Even though they're not trained to protect me, the car is built to."

Virginia twists the edge of the duvet between her fingers, staring at it like she might squeeze out answers to her thoughts and questions.

"How often do you have threats like this? Do you get them when you're touring?"

She's not going to like this answer, but it's the truth. "I actually don't know. When I'm home, I reduce the risk—"

"By never going out," she interrupts.

"Yes. And when I'm away, the security team is always the same size. My protocol is always the same. So if there is a threat, I don't see or hear about it."

"I guess that makes sense. It would be hard to focus on

doing your job if you were always worried that someone in the crowd might be out to get you," she says. "What made this threat credible? What was the threat?"

I don't want to answer these questions. I take my time to consider how to tell her enough, but not too much.

"What made it credible was the level of detail the ... uh, the person had about our plans to get away for a weekend." That's all I want to say.

"What was the threat?"

"Virginia—"

"Will—"

"Your standard kidnap and ransom deal," I say, even though that's not the full story, or even the truth, since the details of the threat were a little more gruesome than that.

"Someone threatened to kidnap you? Seriously?"

I squeeze my eyes tight and wish to wake up in an alternate universe where I'm just a regular man and Virginia is exactly Virginia. There's no point lying; unless the kidnapper is caught before I leave on tour, I'll have to tell her, anyway, since she'll be living with a twenty-four-hour security detail.

"Not me. You."

Her first look is of surprise. And then she laughs. "As if! I mean, our new recliners are nice, but kidnap-worthy?"

I can't tell if this is a stress reaction, the way some people laugh when they're scared, or if she doesn't understand that she's a target because I would pay any amount of money to keep her safe. My answer comes soon enough, since her eyes pool and tears roll down her cheeks.

"I don't like this life, Will. I love you, but—" She chokes in a ragged breath.

I push into the bed beside her and wrap her in my arms.

"I can't live like this."

"I know," I manage to say past the painful lump in my throat. "I am so sorry I put you in danger. I was a fool. I knew better. I was being selfish."

I stroke and drop kisses on her tangle of wet hair, trying to imprint our connection into my very DNA since I know this will be one of the last times I'll be able to hold Virginia like this. When she tries to pull out of my hug, I squeeze tighter.

"I'm so tired. I just want to fall asleep in your arms," she whispers.

We strip out of our clothes, and I curl myself around her warmth. She falls asleep before I do.

When the sun starts to light the room, I'm not sure if I've slept at all. Virginia continues to dream, still pressed tight against me. In four days, I'm leaving for six weeks in Europe. I try to tell myself that I'll be too busy to miss her. And that once I've been away for that time, I'll be over my addiction to Virginia's voice when she whispers and sings to plants, her laugh at the most mundane things, her scent in my bed, the taste of her on my lips, the feel of her curves under my fingertips.

I tell myself it's for the best—if not for me, for her. I love her enough to set her free.

Though she won't be truly free until the fucker who made the threat is found, charged, and hopefully imprisoned for the rest of their lousy life. I'll never learn the identity of this person since I cannot trust myself not to take justice into my own hands. But the team will let me know when the threat has been neutralized. Until then, Virginia will have to live with the same level of protection I've endured my entire adult life. More, actually.

I pull her tighter against me. She's all but enveloped in

my hold. I guess I squeeze a touch too hard, since she squeaks, wiggles, and rolls to face me.

Her eyes blink open in the dim, early light. "Good morning." Her smile tells me she's not fully conscious yet because once she remembers last night, I can't imagine she'll be so happy to see me.

"Hi, beautiful," I reply, wishing I could capture the peace of this moment and stay here forever.

Awareness dawns on her face. Her eyebrows pinch together and her tension crushes my heart.

"Do you think for the next twenty-four hours, we can just pretend the hounds are more of your brothers and have a normal day?" she asks.

"I'd like that very much."

"Me too." Virginia kisses my neck, my chin, my lips. "You know what else I'd like very much?"

"I think I do."

I push myself away from Virginia's side and straddle her body, holding myself entirely above her so no parts of us touch. She sighs and closes her eyes. Her jaw relaxes and she yawns. She makes fists and then starfishes her fingers. Her shoulders fall closer to the mattress. Her hips rise just enough to touch me, then fall. I can't see her thighs, but I know she's relaxed her legs too.

She's ready.

I was born ready.

I lean forward and kiss her forehead. She opens her eyes, smiles at me, then closes them again so I can kiss each lid. Her temples, first the right, then the left. Her cheeks, right, then left. Her lips.

Normally, she lies still, but for the rise and fall of her breasts. This morning, though, she cups my face and holds our lips together. Her tongue probes, and I open them. She keeps her lips soft, her survey slow and deliberate. Her fingers massage my cheekbones and then slip to the corners of my mouth and gently push our lips apart.

"I love your face," she whispers. "I want to remember all the textures, the details, the softness of your lips and the coarseness of your weekend beard." The pads of her fingers and hands explore every inch of my face, my ears, my neck. Virginia closes her eyes again and a fat tear rolls from the corner of one. I kiss it away, then continue my own study.

I tease her nipples, tickling her ribs with my scruff. She squirms but in a slow, responsive way, her body and contented sighs communicating her delight. When my mouth tracks to just below her belly button, her hands tangle in my hair and direct my face lower. Her invitation is crystal clear, and my gentle exploration turns merciless.

I push her legs apart and nip at the top of her inner thigh. She exhales breathily, sending too much blood to my cock. I bite again, harder this time. Her hips push her apex against my cheek. Before I spread her lower lips to lick her into a frenzy of euphoria, I look up her body to see if she's watching.

Her eyes are closed tight, and her mouth is pinched in a grimace, like she's in pain. It's too soon for the pain of ecstasy just before she comes. She is in emotional pain.

My abdominal muscles contract so tightly, I feel like my spine might crack. I can't continue.

When I pull myself away, her eyes open. She gasps for air as if she's been holding her breath and releases a long, low moan filled with more grief than one body should be allowed to carry.

I did this to her. I led her to believe this could work, knowing from that first moment she stepped onto the stage —and all I could think about was touching her wild hair and taking off the dress that hummed with a life and joy that could never be mine—that this was the only way a relationship with me could end.

I hate myself. I leave her to recover on her own while I will myself to drown in the shower. When I finally step out, the bedroom is empty.

She's gone. And not just from the room. Bruce and his partner have taken her back to the city.

32. *Virginia*

COMPOSURE OR COMPOST

Convincing the security detail to drive me back to the city without Will's blessing required I unleash my inner brat. I stormed from the house with my backpack, walked to the highway, and thrust out my thumb. I've never hitchhiked and was secretly glad when the guy who followed me radioed his partner, Bruce, to bring the car down.

The highway doesn't have an exit or a turnaround for twenty miles—an exasperating thing when you're stuck behind an accident, but great when you need time to convince two guys to take you home, not back to the man who you can't be around right now.

"I'm sorry I woke you," I say to Bruce. "And thanks again for letting me use your tub last night."

He nods but doesn't reply.

"Ms. Beach, are you not aware—"

I cut him off. It's not like me to be so rude, but I'm done with all this cloak-and-dagger secrecy. "Listen, Paul Blart, my name is Virginia, and if you can't call me that, I will be deaf to your words. Number two, I am aware of the threat. At least, that there is one. And frankly, as I told Will, I can't do this anymore."

Bruce makes eye contact with me in the rearview mirror. He's smiling for the first time in my presence. "Virginia, this is Aziz. Don't think he was ever a mall cop, but—"

"Never," Aziz growls.

"But he's been with the Power family longer than I have."

"And we have to take you back to Mr. Power in Lily Valley," Aziz grumbles.

I am pretty certain there will be no winning an argument with Aziz unless Will is on my side. For the first time in my life, I wish I was in a car with a privacy window. I could text Will, but I need to hear his voice. He answers on the first ring.

"Virginia. Are you OK?" He sounds frantic.

"I'm sorry I left. I just couldn't ..."

"I know. I'm sorry too. But can we finish ..."

I let the silence hang between us, wondering if he wants to finish the action he was in the middle of or the conversation that was interrupted before he went down on me.

Finishing either would kill me right now.

Will inhales loudly and pushes out a long breath.

"How far are you?" he asks.

"About five minutes from the turnaround."

"OK." That's all he says.

Four minutes from the turnaround.

"Will?"

"Yes?"

"Can you tell Aziz that it's OK to take me home?" Despite the pep talk I've given myself, I still shudder out the last part of the sentence since I'm trying not to cry.

Three minutes.

"Will?"

"It's safer for you at the condo."

"I need to be home. I need to think. I can't do that if …
" The constriction in my throat stops the rest of my words.

Two minutes.

"Please, Will."

"Hand the phone to Aziz," he says.

I do as Will asks. Aziz says hello, followed by a series of
"yes, sir."

We drive past the turnaround point, and I release my
breath, feeling relief and grief in equal measure. Aziz hands
my phone to me.

"Thank you," I say. There's no reply. "Will?" Silence.
"Are you there?"

He's hung up.

I don't even try to hide my emotions. I allow myself to
cry. Bruce and Aziz speak quietly, maybe to drown me out.
The only acknowledgment I get is a hand reaching back
with a travel pack of tissues.

In the city, Bruce walks me to the door of our basement
suite.

"Can I come in? I need to update you on what's going
to happen now."

I'd texted Georgia to let her know I was on my way
home and that I'd need her to not ask any questions until I
had some time to process.

She's at the door when I open it.

"Sweetie, I am so, so sorry," she says, pulling me into
her arms. She notices Bruce and releases her grip, turning
off her mom voice. "Oh, I didn't realize we had company."

"Georgia, this is Bruce, one of Will's many bodyguards.
Bruce, my only sister, Georgia. Excuse me, I need to pee."

I leave the two standing at the open door. Since our apartment is so small, I overhear Bruce telling Georgia he needs to come in to explain some things. She asks if he'd like tea. He says no, but a minute later changes his mind.

I'm stalling, not eager to hear anything related to Will Power or the reason I'm a person of interest to bad guys and what that means for my freedom.

"You OK in there?" Georgia taps the bathroom door after a few minutes.

I come out. Shrug. Curl into my fancy chair.

The long and short of my situation is that I will have a shadowy man within spitting—or shooting—distance, twenty-four hours a day, until the threat has been neutralized. That's what Bruce tells us. And what that means in practical terms is that either he or Aziz will be in my business when I'm out and about. A third guard will take some overnight shifts parked outside our building.

And the best part? Our apartment is now bugged so that while the guys can't actually see me in my bed, they can hear what's happening in my home.

To her credit, Georgia is less annoyed than I am by the intrusion on our privacy. I excuse myself once we've been told what the rules are for me coming and going. Georgia and Bruce continue their conversation, which I don't hear from my position in my bed, head buried under pillows, as I will the last day to be a nightmare I wake from soon.

. . .

I spend the next two days in bed. Will and I have texted short, friendly messages a few times, but I don't have the stomach to see him. He's leaving in two days, and once he's gone, I'll have six weeks to do my job without the fear of bumping into him and disintegrating like fragile dandelion seeds.

Wednesday morning, Aziz meets me at my apartment door to drive me to work. I feel bad for Bruce, learning that he was the guard who had to sit in his car all night watching for body snatchers. One definite upside of Georgia's and my obsession with true crime shows is our naturally dark sense of humor. Aziz, however, does not see the humor in the jokes we've been making about how I could put my keen observation skills to a real test if I allowed myself to be kidnapped.

Aziz doesn't leave my side until I'm in an elevator and have promised I won't leave the building without him. As much as I dislike the idea of being taken away by bad guys, the dread I feel in this tower, where the nicest guy I can't be with lives, works, and breathes, is just as uncomfortable.

I go through the motions in all the offices, polite hellos to employees, lying that I'm doing well, and hoping my dear plants don't absorb my sadness. Otherwise, I'll be dealing with a thousand pots of compost in a week.

At about three thirty, the anxiety sets in. I have one floor left before I have to visit Will's office. Half of me hopes he's there; the other half prays he's not. When I step into the special elevator to the floor Will and his brothers' offices occupy, I can't make myself punch in the special code. The doors close, and I lean against the wall until I'm too tired to stand. I sit on the floor. It's ridiculous, I know, but I'm frozen with a decision that feels like it only has bad outcomes.

The elevator moves on its own, heading up. Decision made for me. I stand before the door opens. Colt is waiting.

"Come to my office." He touches my elbow and directs me down the hall.

I assume he knows everything since he and Will don't seem to have any secrets between them. Colt doesn't appear to be upset, but maybe he's waiting until we're alone to give me hell for ghosting his brother.

He motions for me to sit on the couch and finds his place beside me. He pours me a glass of my favorite juice without asking if I want any. Pours himself a shot of whisky.

"Cheers," he says, holding up his tumbler, waiting for me to lift mine.

We clink. He swigs. I sip.

"We're all worried about you."

I shrug. "No need. I'm taking this seriously."

"Virginia, you just spent twenty minutes sitting on the floor of an—"

I straighten. "Wait. How do you know how long ..." It dawns on me. "Cameras."

"Security called Will."

"And he called you, instead of ..." I can't seem to finish my sentences.

"He did. He's here—there." Colt points as if toward the other side of the building. "But he thought that if you weren't getting off, you were worried about seeing him. So, you get his better-looking brother instead." Colt looks apologetic.

I shrug. "You kind of are, since you don't have that scowl line Will has." I point to the spot between my eyebrows.

"Sometimes I wish I did. He's had a much harder life

than I have ... for, you know, a man who's had a ridiculously easy life in most ways."

I take a sip of the fresh-pressed mango juice and am
overcome by grief. Mango juice means breakfast with Will.
Or did. I put the glass down and bite my lip.

"You can cry in front of me. Will does all the time,"
Colt jokes.

"I've never seen him cry."

"Actually, neither have I. Will inherited more robot
genes than I did. Gets that from Mother's side of the
family."

I'm frustrated at Colt for trying to be funny. "Colt, you
don't need to babysit me. I'm fine. Really. I was just having
... a moment. I didn't think about the cameras. I'm sorry I
worried anyone."

"Virginia, he's miserable. Even though I haven't seen
actual tears, I know he's crying on the inside."

I flip from anguish to anger in a nanosecond.

"And that's supposed to be helpful, how exactly?" I
snap. "*You're* the people with all the power. Don't look at
me to fix this. I'm just the idiot who thought, for one hot
minute, that aspiring to have more than just a 'getting by'
life was something I was worthy of. Silly me." I only stop
ranting because I run out of air, and Colt uses the seconds
of silence I need to catch my breath to interrupt my tirade.

"Virginia, you're the one who ran, who left without
even a goodbye and then sat in that goddamn elevator as if
getting out on this floor was some kind of torture," Colt
matches my tone.

"Because seeing Will would be torture! And in case he
forgot to mention, he's the one who ended it, not me. He's
the one who said, 'If you love someone, set them free.'" I

stand and storm to the window. I'm filled with fury. I need to scream or punch or tear something to pieces.

Colt's hand touches my back. It's a soft touch. He doesn't rub, just lets it rest against my ribs. He's standing so close I can hear him breathing in a slow, calm rhythm.

"He said that?" Colt asks. "If you love someone, set them free?"

I answer with a nod.

I see his reflection in the window. Colt responds by crossing his arms in front of his chest, exhaling hard, and muttering one word: "Fuck."

33. Will

Two-and-a-half weeks into this tour, I'm only barely present and beyond grateful to have Aiden along, taking over on stage while he learns how to be the new Will Power ... or Fire Power, as he wants to brand this next generation of the Come Into Power seminars.

Works for me. Hell, he could call himself Fucking Power and I wouldn't argue, as long as I never had to do this again.

Aiden and I share suites in every hotel. His idea, and I'm not sure if it's because he doesn't want to be alone or doesn't want to leave me alone. I suspect he's worried since I've joined him in having an alcoholic beverage at the end of each day. Just one. Or two. Enough to take the edge off this feeling that I waited far too fucking long to take control of my life.

The upside, I've noticed, of having three or four drinks, is that if I dream, I'm not waking up with nightmares anymore. They say alcohol is a trigger for having bad dreams. They also say parasomnia has a genetic factor. So maybe, if you're genetically coded to have nightmares, alcohol does the opposite. Don't know and don't care. All I know is that none of it matters if it's too late to make things right with Virginia.

She's been replying to the two or three texts I send her each day, but she hasn't called me. My calls go to her voice-mail. I don't even know if she's listening to them.

I'm not upset with her. I understand self-preservation —in theory, at least.

Aiden joins me in the suite's living room. He's dressed in workout clothes and has a small duffel bag over his shoulder.

"Come with me. I've got the gym reserved for forty minutes. The entire team will be there."

"I'll pass."

"Not an option, Will. You're getting flabby. It's a lazy look on the family. Doesn't show much ... *will*power," he jokes.

"Fuck you." I'm in no mood to be the butt of the most overdone joke in the universe or to give a rat's ass about whether my appearance makes the all-powerful Power family look bad.

Aiden gets up in my face. "Hey, I'm the good guy in this scenario. You want to be pissy with someone, get your ass to the gym. There's a punching bag with Colt's face on it."

I laugh. "Fine." Aiden's right, of course. Sulking and being a slug are not good for me. The exertion of lifting weights and punching a bag—even without my twin's face —seems to reset my neurons from their "fuck the world" position to a slightly more optimistic "fuck you, world." A subtle change, sure, but I'm feeling a little more empowered and hopeful when I step from the shower.

Aiden and I go over our cheat sheets for tomorrow's seminar. For each of the six times we've shared the stage so far, Fire Power takes on a bit more of the script. He's a natural. It's obvious he loves the attention—in an alternate universe, he would've been groomed to be the ringmaster of our family circus.

And me? Who knows what I'd have become? After forty-two years with no choice, I can't even begin to imagine where my interests might lie—except for one thing. Well, one person: Virginia "Can't Get Her Off My Mind" Beach.

"So, are we done here?" Aiden asks.

I realize I've zoned out and have no idea whether we're done or not.

"Yeah. Whatever."

We deliver the Hamburg seminar over the next two days, and it goes well. I dial it back, and Aiden picks up my slack with his own style. The audience responds with enthusiasm, and so far, we've had no complaints or refund requests. That's all I care about—I don't want any reason that might persuade the board to vote against Aiden replacing me on stage.

Next up, my second-favorite European city—Copenhagen. In past years, I'd be enthusiastic about this stop. I always book an extra two days to visit a museum or an attraction, to eat out, to relax and recover at the halfway mark on the tour. This year, I regret being forced to stay away from home for these extra days.

I text Virginia to let her know I've landed safely at Kastrup International airport. It's after eleven p.m. in Vancouver, so I don't expect a reply and pocket my phone.

A car meets us on the tarmac to take me, Aiden, and two of our security detail to a line-free customs check-in.

The rest of the team has to go through the normal process.

As always, I've invited Savi to be a tourist with me. And for the first time, she declines.

"I'd rather risk being mocked for my abysmal Danish than spend an extra minute around your sad-sack energy," she says.

I tell her she's fired. She rolls her eyes and gives me the finger. Right to my face.

"Telling the truth is not a fireable offense, but flipping your boss the bird is. I read the employee contract before leaving," she says. "So, is my firing immediate or once we get home?"

"2050," I say.

"Do something that makes you smile this weekend, Will," she says. Then she waves and joins the rank and file customs line.

Aiden and I breeze through VIP customs and are escorted to a waiting car. The driver opens the door. One security guard gets in, then Aiden, then me, and then the final security guy.

I notice a second person in the front seat, right in front of me, and tilt my head toward my brother. "Who's that?"

"Oh yeah," he says, "Surprise!"

The hooded head turns to face me.

"Aiden says you've been impossible to be around. Thought it would be fun to come and poke the wasp's nest," Horse says.

He pulls down his hood, and I do a double take. He's had a haircut and shaved his beard.

"That is just too creepy," Aiden says.

"Seriously," I agree. "Turn around, bro. I can't look at you."

Horse drops the vanity mirror and makes faces at himself. "It is weird, isn't it? I had it done on the flight. I left Vancouver as myself and arrived in Denmark with a plan to assume another man's identity."

"Meaning?" I ask, but Aiden taps the driver on his shoulder, interrupting the chance for Horse to reply. "You have the itinerary for the day?"

"Yes, sir. Starting with a breakfast reservation for six at Lækker Mad."

"Helmets on, boys. Let's have some fun!" Aiden cheers. He slaps my leg. "We'll fill you in over breakfast."

The plan is as brilliant as it is crazy.

"That's a lot of details," I say, between bites of the most delicious Æggekage I've ever eaten. I'm not sure if the omelet is in fact the best bacon, cheese, and egg I've had or if it's the prospect of pulling off a twin swap with Horse that makes this such a good meal.

"Nobody knows about this other than us? Not even Brian?" I ask.

Both Horse and Aiden level a stare at me. "Mr. By the Book? Are you kidding?"

"Right. Brian would fold like a cheap card table if pressed." I agree. "I feel bad he's left out, though."

"We'll make it up to him once everyone is back in their rightful trousers." Aiden laughs.

"What about Virginia?" My abdomen tenses at the thought of having to lie to her, knowing I could never get away with it.

My brothers shake their heads.

Horse speaks first. "For the last three weeks of the tour, no, she cannot know. If Dad's leftover board appointees were to find out, you'd be stuck in this role until you die."

"Ha-ha." I scowl.

"You know he's right. We *have* to pull this off. Nobody can know. But for three weeks, you'll have way more freedom to come and go, to do business as Horse, to see Virginia even if you can't tell her you're you."

I shake my head. "She'll know. Guaranteed."

"I agree," Horse says.

"She won't," Aiden argues. "If you swapped clothes, I wouldn't be able to tell you apart."

"Oh, Virginia will know," both Horse and I say as one.

The conversation changes to more pressing matters, like ensuring Horse can deliver at least half of my trademark one-liners and that he figures out how to wrinkle his forehead in the right way when he's thinking. Normally, Horse is an eyes-wide-open thinker, while I'm more of a scowler.

"Just imagine someone has kicked you in the balls," Aiden offers.

Horse's expression changes.

"Nailed it!" Aiden says, so loud several diners turn to look at us.

I reach over and drop my fist into Aiden's groin.

He grunts.

Horse barks out a laugh. "You're right. That's Will's resting bi—"

My other fist lands in Horse's lap. He grimaces, grabs my hand, and forces it back into my chest.

"Billionaire, you asshole. Resting billionaire face."

Once we all catch our breath, Horse gets serious.

"Hey, I'm sorry it took so long to do this. I hope it's not too late."

"Why now?" I ask. "What's changed since ... well, any

other speaking season when I've begged you to twin swap with me?"

"I don't know. Virginia said you told her that if you love someone to set them free. And I guess it finally hit me. I need to do this. Because I love you, bro."

I'm grateful we've just been laughing so hard so I can blame the shine of tears on that.

I walk onto the Copenhagen stage to loud applause.

"hej københavn!" I yell. "My favorite city in all of Europe," I say in Danish. I move around the stage far more than normal, in part to calm my nerves and in part to distract the crowd from examining me too closely. Aiden, of course, is right that I've gotten a little squishy—Horse looks trimmer in my suit than I do.

I do my standard introduction patter, words I've spoken more times than Taylor Swift has sung the lyrics of "Shake It Off" at live events. And I'm received with just as much adoration as a platinum-album singer.

Will I miss this? I wonder.

Possibly, but not as much as I miss falling asleep with Virginia wrapped in my arms. This won't get her back, but it's a critical first step. One of many I hope to figure out with her.

After outlining what the room can expect from the seminar, I call Aiden onstage to deliver the first of the ten live coaching sessions we have scattered throughout the day. Aiden—like all Power brothers—can speak a little bit of a lot of European languages. Even though I was groomed from birth for this job, Aiden was born to be a showman. The crowd responds to his smile and his winks. He's softer and more approachable than I am. Having him as the face of our company will absolutely shift the kinds of entrepreneurs we attract. Which, as far as we're all concerned, is a solid nod to our values and is long overdue.

Once the first businessman is seated again, I start the motivational coaching portion of the morning. Aiden and I have delivered this in tandem in five cities now, and we have a pretty decent rhythm. It's not perfect, but we roll with it.

Today we're going to go so far off-script, I'm a little nervous. We each stand with a mic in hand, addressing the crowd, taking turns asking questions, sharing pithy inspirational quotes. There's an amount of jazzing, but for the most part, Aiden delivers the same lines I would, had I been doing this on my own.

My turn to take over and ... my mic goes dead. I talk with enthusiasm, pretending I don't notice until the crowd calls, "We can't hear you." I feign surprise and grab Aiden's mic from his hand.

"My brother will sing to you while I get another mic."

The crowd laughs. Aiden picks up with the exact words I was saying when I toggled the power switch on my mic to the off position. I jog offstage.

"You ready?" Horse and I ask each other, followed by brotherly slaps on the back. I hand the mic to my identical twin. He flips the switch back on and jogs onstage.

I watch for a few minutes, cringing from time to time since Horse isn't delivering the material the way I would. But he is delivering. The audience will never know the difference. Probably. He has four more cities in Europe to practice being me, and then he'll have to convince the harder audiences in North America.

I check my watch. Horse's plane, pilot, and crew are expecting me at the airport in two hours. Well, they're expecting Mr. Colt. I've pulled on a hoodie and ball cap to reduce the odds I'll be recognized and take the stairs to Horse's room.

Now comes the weird part: becoming my much more casual-looking brother. I change into his clothes—except boxers and socks—I would do anything for love, but wearing his underwear? I won't do that.

Looking at my reflection in the wardrobe mirror, I exhale a long breath. I've been relieved of being Will Power for all of ten minutes, and I already feel lighter.

A gentle knock sounds on the door.

"Right on time," I say to the woman who's carrying a discreet black suitcase.

"Did your joke work?" she asks.

"Like a charm, Sarah. Now please, for the love of all that's holy, make me look like myself again."

"Of course, Mr. Colt."

Sarah is the Will Power Industries' staff stylist who makes sure everyone who works for us looks their best. Free haircuts, color, shave—Sarah provides one of the non-monetary perks of being a Power employee. And fooling her that I am Colt is my first acting engagement.

"Did you enjoy your weekend in Copenhagen?" I ask.

"So much!" She beams. "I went to eight bakeries and tried the wienrbrød at every one! I have an entire suitcase filled with the Danish pastries I liked best." Her eyes widen, probably at my reaction, which I suspect looks like horror. "To share with the staff, Mr. Colt! Not all for me. Though, if they froze ..."

I laugh because Colt would laugh.

"Please put me back together."

"I've got a perfect wig and beard right here for you. It will take some trimming and styling, of course, but I'm convinced even you won't know they're not your natural hair."

She's right. Sort of. By the time she secures the hairpiece with some miracle tape that's supposed to last up to six weeks, I find myself staring at my reflection. It's a weird feeling, knowing I could grow this same hairstyle and be able to transform into someone who has an entirely different outlook on life. It's equal parts off-putting and encouraging.

The beard is more of a pain since the spirit gum that holds it in place will have to be reapplied every twelve hours. The upside is that I get to sleep without it while I let my beard grow in to match Mr. Colt's. That should only take five or six days.

The fake fur Sarah glues on is pretty damned perfect. Even up close, it looks like it's growing out of my chin and from my upper lip.

"Back to normal." She smiles.

"Thank you so much. It was disconcerting seeing Will in my reflection. But it was worth it for the joke. Which will stay between us," I add, leveling a serious stare at her.

"Of course, Mr. Colt. A stylist protects her client's secrets as if they were her own."

"I can't imagine a stylist has many client secrets to keep."

Sarah's hand covers her mouth, and she tries to hold in a giggle. "Have you ever heard of a merkin, Mr. Colt?"

I shake my head.

"Well, all I can say is that I have more than"—she counts her fingers—"more than five clients for whom I've made a pubic hair wig."

I cough my surprise and can't help but ask whether this is a service included in our employee benefits package.

She shrugs. "I guess so. I've never asked. I just ... I do what I'm asked. New York Fashion Week in 2018 made them popular. Haute couture shrubberies were all over the catwalk. I mean, on people, not literally on the catwalk. And by shrubbery, I mean—"

I hold up my hand to stop her from talking. Colt may be the fun twin, but I imagine even he would find this conversation a little uncomfortable. Aiden, on the other hand? I'll be asking him if he's one of our hairstylist's secret clients.

Sarah and I travel to the airport together. None of my brother's flight crew appear to suspect I'm anyone other than Mr. Colt. That said, he shares staff with Brian and Aiden, so they're not as dialed in to his quirks when he flies as my team is with mine. This works to my advantage when I sip what I expect to be tonic water, but is more gin than tonic, and react with an uncensored, "What the fuck is this?"

I cover my mistake with an apology, saying it's too early for an alcoholic drink, it being before lunch and all.

This is going to be a long three weeks ...

Today marks the halfway point of Will's trip to Europe. He let me know when he landed in Copenhagen, as he does when he safely arrives in each new city. A text is a tiny thing in the grand scheme of a relationship, but knowing I'm the first person he thinks of, even though he set me free—or I freed myself—makes this freedom from the constraints of his life less sweet.

I miss him more and more every day. And maybe it doesn't help that I have a perpetual reminder of my months with Will in the constant presence of Bruce and Aziz.

As much as I wanted to resist the ceaseless monitoring of my life, it hasn't been so bad. Aziz works the day shifts and accompanies me to work and out for groceries and whatnot. It was even kind of fun having his company when I went plant shopping since he has a serious green thumb and was quite interested in helping me choose the perfect shrubs and flowers for the winter-blooming garden I'm designing for Sophie and Nick in Lily Valley.

And Bruce? He actually chose to work the night shift, which seemed crazy to me until two weeks into having him camped out in my chair while Georgia either worked or they watched TV.

Getting up in the middle of the night to pee is unusual for me, so when I didn't see him in the living room, I might have acted without thinking.

I flung open our outside front door to see if he was in the garden, which set off the alarm to warn us we had an unauthorized entry. I'm not sure how a real kidnapper would have reacted to seeing a butt-naked mountain of a man burst from my sister's bedroom with a pistol in-hand, but I can tell you it sent me diving right back under my duvet.

I'm still shocked that I didn't see the signs of their budding love affair. Clearly, I'm off my game since normally I notice small details and subtle cues in people's behavior without even trying. I'm not myself, and I don't like it.

Georgia's been doing her best to make me feel better, reminding me that we all see what we want to see in difficult situations, and not noticing that she and Bruce had developed feelings for each other is simple self-preservation—I subconsciously didn't want to see her find what I've just lost.

But it doesn't make me feel better. It just makes me want to figure out how to be happy in Will's world.

I look at the clock and do the math. It's 9:13 p.m. in Copenhagen, which means Will is probably winding down, but not asleep yet. I'd promised myself I wouldn't call him until I knew I could have a conversation without crying. Today feels like that day.

Since he's been leaving me voice messages on Whats-App, that's what I use. I hit Call with my video on. The phone rings four times, and I'm about to hang up when he answers.

"Hey. Wow. I'm—wow—surprised you're calling. Happy, of course. How are you?"

Will is sitting on a couch that must be in the middle of a room since I can see open French doors and Aiden pacing behind him.

"Hi, am I catching you at a bad time?" I ask.

"Yeah, no, I mean." Will must follow my eyes since he looks over his shoulder. "Oh, Aiden is trying to memorize the one-liners for tomorrow. There are a couple he keeps mixing together." Will scowls and smiles at the same time.

"You look ... relaxed. I guess having Aiden take on some of the delivery has been working well?"

Will nods but looks toward his lap. He seems distant. I expected this call might be a little awkward, but I get the feeling he doesn't want to talk to me.

"OK, well, I just wanted to say hi and let you know I really love the messages you're leaving and that I'm sorry I haven't called before now, but I didn't want to add to your stress and I figured having me tell you that I miss you wouldn't be particularly helpful, so ..." I gasp in a deep breath. "Sorry. I'm rambling."

"It's nice to hear your voice. I miss you too. Do you think you might want to have dinner when I get home ... in two weeks? I'll have a few days before I have to leave again."

That feels like a brush-off. Like Will is trying to get off the call.

"You seem busy or distracted or something."

"Sorry. I guess I am. Copenhagen is an important city, and we didn't have our patter quite right today. I was off."

"I'll let you go. Call me when you've wrapped up tomorrow and have some time to catch up? I have gossip about my security detail you might find interesting."

Normally, that would have piqued his interest. There's

no way he'd have left that to sit for a day. But Will smiles, a little too large, and says, "Will do."

I'm not sure what the protocol is for telling the man you walked out on that you love him, so I mouth it as little more than a whisper. But Will doesn't see since he's looked away.

"Bye, then," I say.

He looks back. "Bye, then."

The line goes dead, and so do I.

I feel sick. Something is very wrong. Obviously, I waited too long to return Will's calls. He's come to terms with my decision and has moved on.

Thankfully, I'm on my lunch break, inside the building, so I don't have security crawling all over me like a creeping vine. I pull myself together and get back to work, talking to plants who are so much easier to understand than humans.

As it's Monday, I work my way up the highest office floors. Tomorrow I'll start again on the ground level in the afternoon, after visiting Mr. Bernard and his greenhouse in the morning.

At four p.m., I'm ready to call it a day, but I have three more offices to visit—the Power brothers'. All but Will's since he had his plants moved to Colt's for the time he's away. That's where I decide to start.

"Hey, Reshma," I say with as much of a smile as I can muster.

"Hi, Virginia. Did you have a nice weekend? Do anything fun?"

Since my twenty-four-hour protection is supposed to be discreet, I upsell my lockdown lifestyle. "Had a great time bingeing a new true crime series with my sister. You?"

"Celebrated my husband's birthday. Big family event. Still cleaning up." She laughs.

"Hopefully the house-elves finish the job before you get home. Is Colt in?"

"House-elves are in short supply these days." She smiles. "Mr. Colt had an all-day meeting off-site, so you can sing to your babies as loud as you'd like."

I'm surprised by how much my shoulders relax, knowing I'll be alone.

"I'll be done before five so you can lock up. But if I lose track of time, come and get me."

Standing in the middle of Colt's office, I look from his table of greenery over to Will's. Aside from a few pots, the plants are the same, but while Colt's are thriving, Will's look wilted and sad. I'm certain they weren't like that three weeks ago. I wonder if I've done this, if my sorrow has seeped into the soil. Why else would they be looking so woebegone?

"This won't do," I say to the room, then walk to the healthy gathering of greenery.

I poke my finger into each pot on Colt's table, water the few that need it, pinch a couple of dead leaves from the coral bells, and inside ten minutes, I'm done.

"Now, you people," I say to Will's collection, "you have to do better. I am sorry if I've been bumming you out, but this is not acceptable. You are strong and resilient, healthy and happy."

I pick up the hibiscus and hold it so the leaves are directly in front of my face.

"Never forget, when you change your thoughts, you change your world, Hibbi. This world, this small, little world you live in, is better for you being here. You have years of flowers left in you. We need you. Will needs you."

He does. Will *needs* this plant.

But does Will need *me*?

I need Will and his contradictions. Will and his grumpy happiness, his understated passion, his vulnerable overconfidence. I love how safe I feel when he holds me, how comfortable I am taking risks with him, how accepted I feel even though I'm far from perfect.

I love how he knows just what to say when I'm second-guessing myself, tailoring his motivational catchphrases just for me. Sometimes to make me laugh, sometimes to force a spirited discussion, and always to help me see that I'm good enough to be loved by the formidable Will Power.

Maybe that's what these plants are missing—Will's words of encouragement.

"Is that what you need, Hibbi? Do you miss hearing Will spur you on to greater things? To know everything is exactly as it's meant to be?" I shrink a little, not feeling like anything in my life is as it's meant to be anymore. But I don't want the hibiscus to know that. "All right, then."

I think of one of Will's quotes and adjust it slightly for the plant.

"You are a winner. You are making *soil* happen. Nothing will stop you from flowering again. Is that better?"

I smile at the hibiscus, exhale warm breath across its leaves, place it back on the table, and pick up a droopy jade plant.

"Hey, Jade. What's got you down? You need a little pep talk, don't you?" I gently stroke a couple of her fleshy leaves while I think.

"You don't need to be limited by the size of the pot you're planted in. Grow. Show the world you can be more, and your pot will grow to fit your new reality."

I laugh at my adjustment and feel more like myself than I have in days, weeks. Picking up the ponytail palm, I start to dance, swaying side to side so its long, thin leaves move like they're in a gentle breeze.

"You are a powerful life force, unique in the world with your singular combination of roots and stalk and leaves. Let your vitality vibrate, and you will be seen."

I spin around as I say, "Let your energy flow," and see Colt standing in the doorway. I almost drop the plant and quickly turn back to the table and mutter apologies.

I hear him move to his desk and sit. But I don't hear him start up his computer or shuffle papers or make any sound at all. I get the distinct feeling he's looking at me.

I glance over my shoulder and see that he is, in fact, sitting with his elbows on his desk, chin resting on his hands, staring in my direction.

"I'm sorry. I'll be out of your hair in a minute. Just a couple of plants to check and then you can have your space back."

"You don't have to rush on my account," he says. "I'm quite happy to do my work while you do yours."

"OK."

I quietly water a couple of pots, feeling very self-conscious.

Colt breaks the uncomfortable silence. "Tell me one thing. Were you mocking Will's motivational quotes?"

I face Colt but am too embarrassed to look him in the eye. I focus on his right ear. "No. The opposite. I think they might miss him, so I was bringing a bit of Will into their space. I know it sounds weird, but it's scientifically proven that plants experience energy and—" I pause since I realize what I was going to say might be misinterpreted as an insult.

"And my energy is not the same as my brother's," Colt says.

"Exactly." I make eye contact with Colt and feel a jolt, but he immediately turns away. As quickly as it hit, the feeling is gone, replaced by a longing that threatens to bubble up and pollute the positive energy I've finally wrapped around the plants.

"I have to go," I blurt, spinning the trolley and pushing it toward the door. I bump it open with my back and give Colt a wave without looking at him.

I can't get onto the elevator and off this floor fast enough.

My synapses are misfiring. I feel like a genetically modified mushroom in a lightning storm, glowing and dimming, glowing and dimming. The sensation makes me dizzy.

THE BEARD AND THE BEAUTIFUL

Having Virginia within arm's reach and not being able to touch her is worse than being on the other side of the planet. When our eyes connected, I was sure she'd know it was me. Every cell in my body was pulled to dive deep into her gaze. I hated looking away.

I question whether this was a good call, coming home and pretending to be Horse for three weeks. Aside from the risk to our family business's reputation if anyone who dropped $2000 on the seminar found out they weren't paying to see the formidable Will Power—I cringe at the way that moniker comes so easily, even to me—I fear the reward of seeing Virginia is not worth the possible damage of lying right to her face.

I'm not remotely worried about faking it to Mother or Brian or about either of them figuring out the truth since neither has Virginia's keen observational talent. My biggest concern is that I *want* Virginia to recognize me under this wig and fake beard, both of which are uncomfortable as fuck.

I want Virginia to see me. But if she saw me, this flimsy wall keeping us apart would crumble. And if anyone saw us together—her and *Mr. Colt* looking like two people in love —it would be impossible to maintain the ruse.

I open my brother's calendar to see what I have scheduled for the week ahead. No meetings that can't be done remotely, and no work that requires me to be in the office. I lean my head against the high back of Horse's chair and close my eyes only to see Virginia, laughing and calling me toward her with a background of sky. The image of that joy-filled smile when she was standing in the town she loves most triggers tension in my neck, shoulders, and heart. It's a direct contrast to the way I felt when I stood barefoot and bare-assed on that rock outcropping with her.

I wonder if I could recreate the relaxation of those moments on that weekend in Lily Valley without Virginia. How much of the magic is in the place, and how much is with the person who let me see what life could be like if I was anyone other than myself?

What would Horse experience in that same place?

What could I experience *as* Horse?

I mindlessly scratch my cheek at the edge of my itchy fake beard and loosen the spirit gum enough to tug the corner.

"Mr. Colt." Reshma stands at my door with her coat on.

I press my fingers against the fraudulent fur to hide the spot I've worked free. I cannot spend the next five days with this thing on my face. Between the physical itch of my own bristles trying to grow under it and the mental itch of being physically close to Virginia, but entirely out of reach, this office is the last place I want to be.

"Do you need anything from me before I go?"

"Yes, actually. Can you find the name of the Airbnb in Lily Valley where Will and Virginia stayed a few weeks ago?"

Reshma's head drops, and I can see in her expression that she wasn't expecting me to keep her any longer. Too bad. I'm the boss and I need her to be an unwitting accessory to my wrongdoing.

"I didn't know he went away. But ... I can call Virginia and ask her to send you the details. Will that be OK?"

Have Virginia text me? It would be fantastic to have a legitimate reason to be in touch with her. I nod sideways, as if it's a compromise to a better idea.

"That'll work. I'm considering working remotely for the rest of the week, assuming that house is available. If you'd like to do the same, that's fine with me. I'll let you know."

Thirty minutes later, Horse's phone pings on the desk.

VIRGINIA
Sorry about running out earlier. Not
feeling well. Didn't want to infect you.

Too late.

ME
Can I do anything for you?

VIRGINIA
Thanks. I'll be fine. Reshma said you
wanted the place Will and I stayed. It's
called the B'kerson Lodge. 1-800-555-
1212. Owner is Dave.

ME
Thanks. Feel better.

VIRGINIA

Before I rationalize my way out of it, I call the number.

"B'kerson Lodge."

"Hello. I was wondering if I'd be lucky enough to book your lodge for the week."

"What week is that?" he asks.

"I know it's a long shot, but this week. Tomorrow through the weekend, Monday morning."

"Yeah, it's available. Shoulder season between mountain bikers and skiers heading to the hills. How many will be staying?"

Shit. I hadn't thought this through. Myself, one guard, a chef ... and Virginia ... in my dreams.

"Let's say four. It may only be three."

"And how many bedrooms?"

"Three. No. Better make it four. And the master bedroom on the second floor, the one with the window overlooking the ocean. Can we have that one, please?"

"You've been here before. What's your name?"

I squeeze my forehead, a tension headache forming.

"No. My, um, friend stayed recently. She highly recommended it."

"Wonderful. What's her name? I'd like to thank her."

I'm too tired for this, having to think fast about what I can and can't say.

"I'd actually rather she not know that I'm staying. And my name is Colt. Colt *Carter*," I emphasize his middle name, which he uses as his family name when he doesn't have to be a Power. It's a trick my dad used too, so he gave us all middle names that work well as last names.

"So, four bedrooms made up, Tuesday until Monday morning?"

"Mm-hmm."

"Seven nights at four hundred a night. That is—" He pauses, and I do the math in my head faster than he does.

"Twenty-eight hundred dollars. And tax?" I ask.

"Total with taxes is $3136."

"E-transfer OK?"

"Perfect."

He gives me the payment details and tells me the new key code to open the front door. Now to find one of the kitchen staff who's willing to work from Lily Valley for a few days. Security is easy—the company that manages the team will assign someone since Horse only travels with one man. I request a guy who's able to hike a few miles a day with me and who doesn't know Mr. Colt. The last thing I need is to be worrying about things I should know about the guy. And the first thing I'll do is take off this damn beard.

T he drive to Lily Valley, without the hassle of an accident on the highway, is shockingly quick and easy. High-rise door to small-town door in forty-seven minutes. I understand the allure of this village as a bedroom community for city workers.

The winding road is fun to navigate in my high-performance car—at least when the traffic is low. I could see myself doing this commute, maybe not every day, but a couple of times a week.

My security detail, James, is in his own company car, and Derek, the chef, will arrive on his own in time to prep dinner for us. I have a few hours of work to do but want to get a hike in before dark. And since there's no reason for me to stick to office hours, I let James know we'll be hitting the trail thirty minutes after we arrive. He's keen, having heard about this place from some of the guys who were here a month ago.

I carry my duffle bag to the master bedroom, but as soon as I open the door, I feel Virginia's presence and step backwards away from the room.

"James," I call.

"Sir," he appears from the bedroom he's chosen.

"I assume you took the nicest of the remaining rooms."

He nods.

"Swap with me. Take the master."

He nods again, turns back to the bedroom, grabs his bag and pushes past me.

"Thanks," I say.

"Thank you, Sir."

"Meet you at the front door in thirty."

Unlike the casual forest walk with Virginia, I turn this hike into a cardio workout and challenge James, a former soldier who appears to be ten years younger than me, to keep up. He holds his own, and even though I know he could've beaten me to the summit, he stays a few steps behind, as any well-trained security officer would in this environment, protecting my back and watching for what's coming.

"What do you think?" I ask when we reach the flat outcrop that Virginia and I consecrated. Despite being out of breath from the final fifty-yard sprint, the memory of the last time I stood on this spot relaxes my mind.

"Nice view," James says.

We look over the tops of evergreen trees to the ocean. Some of the village houses are visible from this vantage point, including the one I've rented. Virginia had pointed it out.

"James, can you see the flat black roof at the end of the cul-de-sac over there?" I point right.

"Yes, sir."

"Do you believe that where we're standing is a security risk or a security benefit for residents of that house?"

James walks to the edge of the ten-by-ten surface, looks over the cliff, up at the trees adjacent to us, and down to the village.

"Depends what your concern is. A camera could be placed in one of these trees"—he points above our heads—"to record movement at the end of the street near the house. Anyone who broke in would be seen. On the other hand, it's a nice place for a sniper to get a clean shot, though with only one trail out of the forest, and just one road in and out of the village, a virtually impossible place to retreat from without being caught. Unless you had a helicopter."

Blackmail, burglary, and bad press, not bodily harm, are the only risks my family has had to deal with to date—until the kidnapping threat against Virginia. Although no risk is ever zero, worrying about a sniper with a chopper is insignificant, even given my perhaps excessive vigilance when it comes to personal safety.

"While we're here this week, I'd like you to look around and make a note of actions you'd take to ensure the security of that house and the people in it."

"Of course, sir."

"Now, since we know there is no threat between this cliff and the main trail, I want your best race back."

"With pleasure, sir." He smiles as if he's already kicked my ass.

36. Virginia

THE GRASS IS GREENER

The tension between what I need (a life with my feet on actual ground) and what I want (a life with Will) has only gotten worse, to the point where I feel like I have to give up one since this half-measure of a future as nothing more than Will's friend and still spending eight hours a day in a climate-controlled high-rise is killing me.

I have a new understanding of why Will felt so desperate when I met him. It wasn't just the knowledge that every Will Power before him died too young, it's the actual environment he's confined himself to for so many years. Though he doesn't believe it, his soul needs fresh air, sunshine, the risk of a thorn under his skin, and the reward of successfully beating nature, even in a small way.

I expected him to call last night, to let me know he'd safely landed in Italy, but my phone never rang. I debated texting Colt at nine p.m., and decided not to. But at eleven, and still not able to sleep, not knowing if Will was OK, I sent a quick message.

Colt replied immediately, calling Will an asshat for

being so inconsiderate. He assured me Will was fine—for now—and that once he got home, he'd kick his ass for making me worry.

That was sweet. And weird, since Colt and I don't have much of a relationship outside of the times we've spent together with Will.

My phone pings with a text from an unknown number while I'm repotting a prickly pear cactus on the fifth floor of the Power building.

> **WILL**
> Hey, Virginia. It's Will. I put my phone down and someone walked away with it. This is my temporary new number. Sorry I made you worry. Wish you were here. XO

My heart does a happy dance. Over the last few days since Will left Copenhagen, his messages have been clipped. He's stopped signing off with a kiss and a hug. I know it's lame, but those two letters, the x and o, gave me a tiny bit of hope that Will and I might be able to figure out how to make a relationship work. Losing them felt like a decision on his part to not try.

I start to type a reply and stop dead. I'm supposed to report any unusual calls or messages to Aziz or Bruce. A text from an unknown number, claiming to be Will, might be considered unusual. I dial Aziz and leave a non-urgent message for him.

I stare at Will's words, itching to reply, but knowing I shouldn't. I know phone technology is far more advanced than I understand, and replying might tell this Will character exactly where I am. I'm not going to be the idiot girl who runs into the woods to get away from the ax murderer.

I carry on with my job, checking my phone every ten minutes to see if I've missed a message.

Two hours later, it rings.

"Virginia. I was going to call you," Aziz says.

"Oh. Why?" My stomach drops, expecting bad news since in the month Aziz has been protecting me, he's never called.

"The person of interest who was a possible kidnapping threat has been apprehended. The authorities have no reason to believe you're at any more risk than you were prior to this blackmail attempt."

"That's amazing." I lean against the windowed wall, and exhale tension I didn't even realize I was holding. "Who was it? How were they found? Were they serious?"

"I can't answer any of those questions. I was debriefed with only enough information to do my job—and to be confident that I can stop being your personal bodyguard. I imagine if you want details, you'll be able to get them from one of the Powers."

Of course, I'm thrilled to hear this news. But I'm also a bit sad, realizing that in a few days when my contract to care for the plants in the Will Power Industries building expires, I'll have no more reasons to run into Will.

The mixture of relief and grief hit me like a falling oak tree.

Tim-berrrr.

I slide down the wall till I hit the floor. I clench my jaw to keep my emotions from escaping.

"Virginia? You still there?"

"Yup," I squeak out.

"Are you OK?"

"Yup." I hang up, knowing I should call Georgia to let her know, but my fingers text Will.

ME
Have you heard the good news? The
bad guy was caught. You don't need to
worry about me anymore.

WILL
Says who?

ME
Aziz, my security guy, just told me.

WILL
I mean, about worrying about you. I will
always worry about you.

I look up and take in the room. Its bones are the same as every office in this building. Gray concrete interior walls, glass exterior walls facing more concrete and glass, polished concrete floors. A splash of color in a framed print behind a desk, in the upholstery of a chair, on the plant stand.

How do people spend eight hours a day for their entire lives in spaces like this? With windows that don't open, hearing the constant white noise of forced air through ducts in the ceilings, seeing everything in light that doesn't trigger their bodies to produce a single microgram of vitamin D?

When Will was in the space with me, I could look beyond all that's lacking, but without him, I feel like an air plant in a vacuum or maybe seagrass trying to survive in tap water.

Will has adjusted to surviving in this foreign planet environment. But it's not living. He may actually be right about dying before he makes it to forty-four. I know it would kill me.

ME
I worry about you too.

> **WILL**
> When I get back, can I take you to Lily
> Valley again? Just the two of us. Well, us
> and just one guard who keeps his
> distance. And a chef.

The memory of Will trying to whip up pancakes, bacon, and eggs makes me laugh. Any one item I'm sure he could have handled and made delicious. But he didn't consider the cooking time or know what temperature to set the oven to keep the eggs warm while the bacon rendered its fat. And the pancakes? The first one is always a tester you expect to throw away, but by the time Will passed the test stage, we only had two small pancakes left, some very crispy bacon, and scrambled eggs that were so dry, they cracked like toast.

> **ME**
> Sounds perfect.

> **WILL**
> If you can envision it, you have the
> power to make it so.

I know Will is being playful with his motivational quote, but its irony thrusts me back into reality. I can easily envision a perfect life, but I don't have the Power to make it so. I'd need Will beside me, and a weekend a month in Lily Valley wouldn't be enough to keep me from losing my mind, spending so much time in this thirty-two-story crypt.

> **ME**
> It's late there. I should let you sleep.
> Buona Fortuna tomorrow. Not that the
> formidable Will Power needs good luck.

WILL
You'd be surprised. Can't wait to see
you. xo

ME
Night, Will. xox

I'm suddenly exhausted. It's midafternoon, but it feels like the right time to call it a day.

First, I head to Human Resources. Over the last four months, I've gotten to know the names of all the receptionists who sit outside the elevator doors on each floor. I've even given them each their own plant, custom chosen to match their personalities, to have at their desk. Most accepted my gift. Some argued they couldn't because they'd inadvertently kill it (they got one, anyway). And some outright refused, saying they didn't like plants.

The woman at the HR front desk is one of those. From day one, we did not hit it off. No surprise. Saying you hate plants is like saying you hate joy or life.

"Hello, Willow." I always chuckle inside about the irony of her name.

"Virginia." She emphasizes the second half of my name, making her voice high on the *yuh*, like I'm a question.

"Who do I talk to about my contract?"

"Is it a short-term with an end date, one that has rolling renewal, or a permanent contract?"

"Renewal type."

"Your contract is being managed by ..." Willow types quickly, then looks up. "Maurice Szostak. He's here, and I'm pretty sure he's available. Would you like to speak to him?"

"Please."

"Office 17. Knock before you enter, of course."

"Of course." Does she think I'm an idiot?

Office 17 is a tricky one on virtually every floor since it gets no direct light, being blocked by another high-rise. Mr. Szostak was one of the people who believed he was guilty of criminally negligent herbicide since he'd never been able to keep a plant alive in his office. Now he has several thriving beauties.

I knock lightly, and he calls for me to come in.

"Virginia! Nice to see you so soon. Do your thing."

"I'm actually here to ask about my contract."

"Oh. Well then, please have a seat." He points to the chair facing him. "Remind me of your company's name."

"The Other Side of the Fence."

"Right." He chuckles. "The grass is always greener. Clever." He taps some keys. "All right, I've got your signed contract here. What are you wondering about?"

"What do I need to do to prevent it from renewing? Or better yet, to break it early?"

"She did what?"

"I'm just the messenger." Horse sighs. He hates drama.

Having to carry my phone, take my calls, and react as I would to whatever new catastrophe has arisen is stressing him out. "I don't think I can be a credible go-between with HR on this, Will. I think you need to let all the relevant staff know you were careless and lost your cell. Give them your burner number for the next couple of weeks."

"You're a clever asshole," I say. "That way, I get to deal with all your work and all the bullshit coming at me. Two-for-one deal."

"Or, we could ..." Horse pauses, and I know exactly where he's heading.

I finish his thought. "Or we could swap back to our normal selves."

"Have you noticed how much of a prima donna Aiden is? If he becomes the new Come Into Power speaker, the hotels are going to beg for your second coming."

"Whatever. And no, I don't want to swap back. I have

things I still want to do under the radar. You really are a lucky asshole. It's like nobody cares where you go, what you do."

Horse grunts. "Yup. Real lucky." He doesn't sound convinced.

"Things are going OK, other than Aiden's penchant for mollycoddling? No complaints?"

"Don't worry about us. Focus on figuring out what's going on with Virginia. Do not fuck this up, Will. You'll never meet—"

"I know. Jesus. I just wish I could tell her I'm here—"

"Will—"

"She wouldn't tell a soul. I trust her."

"You know what? Forget it. I am coming home. Pack your damn suitcase. If you tell Virginia that you're you and anyone—*an-y-one*—sees you two together, we're dead."

"We can keep it professional in public," I say.

"Will, if I *ever* looked at Virginia the way you look at her—not that I could or would—but if I did, security cameras a block away would catch the chemistry. I'd be labeled the biggest asshole brother on the planet. Do not do that to me, Will. Not all press is good press."

He's right, of course.

I hate it, but I have two choices: swap places and finish the European dates myself, or keep pretending I'm Mr. Colt. Since I'm committed to giving this life with my feet on the ground a fair shot, the decision is simple.

"Fine. I'll use your phone to let staff know that your dumbass brother lost his and can be reached at the new number."

"Don't make me look like I'm gloating too hard about your boneheadedness," Horse jokes. "And so we're clear, from the minute I hang up, the only messages I'll be replying to on your phone will be from you. All others I'll ignore and delete. And don't forget to fix the thing with Virginia."

"As if," I scoff. "Would have slipped my mind. Horse? Thanks for everything. I'm lucky to have you as my doppelgänger. I love you, bro."

"Don't get weird. Save that for Virginia. I gotta go. Aiden's ordering room service like a fucking rock star—and not in a good way. God help us ... once he's famous, we're going to have to make sure he's on the road three hundred and sixty days a year."

I take a deep breath and look out the window. At trees. And a yard that I can see has so much potential. I've never looked at a field of grass and seen more than an opportunity to build. But if this yard was put in Virginia's care, I can imagine it would become nothing less than a real-life, Snow White's forest, complete with dancing squirrels and singing rabbits and birds with hearts for eyes.

It's only been a few days since I gave up being a famous face and assumed the life of a low-profile billionaire. The contrast is shocking. I can walk around Lily Valley with James and people treat us like we're just two outsiders renting the big house at the end of the cul-de-sac at the top of the hill. It gives me a chance to get a feel for the little village.

It's friendly, quiet, and apparently quite safe. Strangers talk about leaving their cars unlocked. And I've been told about some strange community pet-sharing co-op where neighbors freely borrow each other's dogs to walk, when the owners aren't home. That's what makes James and I stand out most, I think—we're two people strolling around the village *without* a dog. With no sidewalks, everyone—people, kids, dogs, cats, raccoons—use the roads like it's Mardi Gras every day. Road hockey nets sit right in the middle of the street, and drivers patiently wait for them to be pulled aside to pass.

It's like I've dropped into a 1950s family TV show—but with a scent track of marijuana. So. Much. Pot.

There's little I miss about the city and lots I've begun to appreciate about living with my feet on the ground, as Virginia would say. Even without her sweet voice reading to me, or my arms wrapped around her in bed, I fall asleep more easily and stay that way longer than in the city. It's like there's more oxygen in the air; my breaths are deeper and slower. And even though I'm constantly switching between my work and Horse's, my phone and his, I'm not as stressed as I expected to be.

Virginia always said that being in nature alleviates tension as well as, or better than, many pharmaceuticals. She insists that taking breaks with trees and grass and plants fuels creativity, and I—a lifetime skeptic—have started to believe it's true.

Despite the extra work and my irritation about not being able to invite Virginia up to share this space with me, I am happy. My face feels different, like smiling might be easier than scowling if I were to stay here long enough. It makes impersonating Mr. Colt easier, that's for sure, except my only audience is a security guard and a chef, neither of whom has ever worked with him.

My phone rings and pulls me out my mini vacation staring into the backyard, back into the temporary office on the second floor of this house that I'm seriously considering buying.

I put Horse's phone on the left side of the desk and

mine on the right to keep track of who I'm supposed to be when I answer. I have to be on the ball, since the two phones look identical. I thought it would be easier not having to learn new navigation, but keeping them straight has proven a challenge.

"Colt here," I answer, holding the phone to my left ear.

One of the board members wants a report on some minutiae about the Power Broker Program. I'm sure the four nonfamily members were helpful when Dad worked with them, and I appreciated their experience when I was still green. But for the last decade, they've just been pains in our asses, holding on to the old ways of thinking and doing.

I tell him I'll get the info to him, making a note for Horse to deal with this when he returns from overseas.

I hang up, and the phone on my right rings. Now that the VPs and directors all have the new number, I'm doing my job, too, even though they know I'm in Europe and less available to troubleshoot their shit. I'm mid-sentence when Colt's phone rings.

I check the caller ID and want to take the call. I hang up on my VP.

"Colt here."

Then my phone rings.

"Will speaking."

Then Horse's.

"Colt here."

Mine again.

"Will speaking."

After a solid thirty minutes of back-and-forth between being myself and my brother, I'm mentally exhausted. Twin-swapping at sixteen for prom was way easier than this.

One phone rings. Caller ID says it's Virginia. My shoulders relax, just seeing her name.

"Hey, how's my favorite plant whisperer?"

"Um, I'm good? How are you?"

"Honestly, I'm disappointed. I'm sad and even a bit angry that you didn't talk to me before you tried to cancel your contract." I try to keep my voice neutral, professional.

Silence.

"Virginia, are you there?"

"Why are you angry? And why would I talk to you first?"

The way my heart rate spikes, I know my tone will be neither neutral nor professional when I answer.

"Are you serious? You didn't think I might like to help solve whatever the problem is that has you quitting a job I thought you loved? One you're damn good at? One that's making hundreds of people happier and healthier in their offices?"

"I'm sorry. I truly am. But it's too hard being in the building. And seeing you earlier this week made me realize that it's going to be impossible to function once Will gets back. I can't do it. Can't be that close to him and not be with him."

My gut drops. I pull my phone from my face and tap the screen. *Shit, shit, shit.* She'd called Colt. I'm supposed to be Colt.

"Why did you call Virginia?"

"Because Reshma said you were working off-site all week, and I need to talk to you." She sighs and inhales a long breath. "But really, because I'm a coward."

I clench my jaw so hard it throbs. I want to argue that she's brave beyond belief, but Horse can't say what I'm thinking. So I wait.

"Will asked me to go away with him, back to Lily Valley for a weekend when he gets home. But I suppose you know that, since you booked it, right?"

"I, um ..." Right. Reshma asked her the name of this place for Horse. "Yeah, sorry if the surprise was spoiled."

"He already asked me so, it's all good. And I said yes, but ..." Virginia pauses and the "but" hangs like an axe over my neck.

"I'm sure that made him happier than you can imagine." I hear the frustration in my voice and force a fake smile so the next words I say sound more authentically Horse.

"I can't do it, Colt. I can't pretend that a weekend away will be enough. I can't live in Will's world, and he can't live in mine, and there's no middle ground here. I have to tear off the world's most painful Band-Aid." Virginia inhales a ragged breath. "But I can't do it. I need your help. Please."

Muting my phone, I yell, "Fuuuuuck!" and punch the wood desk. A shock of pain shoots through my knuckles and up my arm. I hit it again.

"Colt? Are you there?"

I take three fast breaths, knowing they aren't nearly as calming as they need to be.

"Colt?"

"Give him a chance to make it work. You haven't given him a fucking chance, Virginia."

"But—"

"You think he's just sitting around, accepting that there's no compromise to be found, no solution to this? Is that what you think? That he's just given up?"

"No, but—"

"But *you're* giving up. Your solution is to walk away?"

I wait, but she doesn't answer. "You know, for some reason, I thought you loved him."

"I do," she whispers.

"Funny fucking way to show it," I mutter.

"I'm sorry. I shouldn't have called you. I thought ... Never mind."

"You're right. You shouldn't have called me. You should have called Will. What do you expect me to do?"

I can hear she's weeping, and my anger softens. "Why *didn't* you call him?"

"Because Will ... Will makes me believe anything is possible. Even the impossible. He thinks we can be friends. See each other at work and that everything will be OK. But it won't be for me. It won't be enough."

Virginia lets the silence sit between us. As Colt, I don't have a response. I can't have one.

She continues. "So, I hoped you'd tell him I'm sorry. And maybe once he's done all his traveling, maybe by then, my heart will have healed itself enough to talk to him. But right now, I just can't. I can't."

"I am sorry you're hurting, Virginia. Truly, I am. But I'm not telling him."

I hear a raspy intake of breath.

"And Virginia. In case you forgot, tomorrow's his birthday. I know he's looking forward to a call from you."

It's a miracle that I make it to the end of the week without having a full-blown meltdown. Yesterday was Will's forty-second birthday and I just couldn't bear to call him. By mid-day I felt so guilty I texted him a lame emoji with a cake and "hope you had a fun birthday."

No number of potted, high-rise plants will make this better. I need to get out of the city, to dig my bare hands into the ground, as cold as it's going to be.

Sophie and Nick are happy for me to come up, offering me my regular bed—the top bunk in their son, Leo's room.

Even though Aziz no longer has to shadow my every move, I'd promised he could work with me to plant the winter flowers he helped choose for Nick and Sophie's garden. Sophie gives me the name of the economy bed-and-breakfast she recommends in Lily Valley, and I let Aziz know they have a room available for Saturday night. He offers to drive me and the plants up in the morning. Wins all the way around.

Normally I work alone, but having Aziz to chat with while we're digging and planting is a pleasant distraction from the conversations I've been having with myself since talking to Colt two days ago.

He texted a couple of hours after our uncomfortable exchange to apologize for being so harsh. And he asked what I planned to do. I told him I'd wait for Will to call me so I could tell him directly why I gave up the contract. Colt agreed that was a good idea. Of course, Will hasn't called, which has left me on edge, feeling like I'm keeping a not-so-secret secret from him.

After an amazing dinner of shepherd's pie, made with Sophie's dad's Quebecois recipe, Nick offers to take us down to the firehall to shoot pool. Aziz is quick to accept, but I stay back to gossip with Sophie since we've had no quiet girl time in months.

I sit on the floor with Leo and his wooden trains. He chatters in a language that sounds more Muppet than any taught in schools.

"Frenglish? Franglais?" I laugh.

"Actually, I think he's speaking canine. I am one hundred percent convinced those two communicate tele-pathically. How else to explain that Max knows exactly when to skulk into the kitchen when I'm not looking and steal food from Leo's hand? People say cats are sneaky. They've obviously never had to deal with the antics of a toddler and a former service dog."

"You seem really happy," I say, pushing a Thomas the Tank Engine boxcar back toward a tiny hand.

"Happier than I ever could've imagined possible." Sophie smiles and then grimaces. "I'm sorry. Not what you want to hear right now."

"No. I mean, of *course,* I want to hear that. After the crap you went through with your stupid family, you deserve all the happy."

"Yeah, well, so do you."

"I know." I nod my agreement because I believe we all, every one of us, have a right to be happy.

"So, why aren't you?"

"Who says I'm not?"

Sophie forces a burst of air from between her lips that's so loud, Max jumps and Leo's little face contorts into a grimace.

After the split second of silence, Max barks, Leo winds up like a fire engine siren, and Sophie and I burst out laughing. She picks up her small human and cuddles him onto her lap. He pulls at her sweater and she gives him her nipple.

"That easy, eh?"

"Until he turns two. Then we'll have eighteen to twenty years of not so easy, and then, assuming he's straight, some other woman's breast will calm him."

I hug myself. An overwhelming desire to be held in Will's arms, the way Sophie is cradling Leo, makes me sigh in sadness.

"You two are great together. Why are you so sure you can't work it out?" she asks.

I shake my head and bite my lower lip. Shrug. "City mouse and country mouse."

"Mice don't drive Lincoln Aviators. There are options."

"I canceled my contract with his company. I've done the paperwork, at least."

"Did Will let you cancel it?"

"No. It's not his call. The contract is with the company, not him personally. He doesn't have a say," I reply, perhaps a little defensively.

"You know, when I met Nick, he was all, 'I'm never going to live in a small town.'" Sophie deepens her voice, and Leo looks up with amused eyes. "But a few months here and ..."

"That's because of you. You are a much better draw than anything the city could ever offer that man. He is darned lucky you put up with his crap while he figured that out."

"He put up with his fair share of crap from me, too."

"Well, it's not like I have any better alternative to offer Will. 'Hey, you want to move into my low-rent, two-bedroom apartment with my sister and give up your elevator commute and your on-call chefs and anything you could ever want delivered to your door within ten minutes of you thinking about it?' Not going to happen. He's a billionaire, Sophie. With a capital B."

I attach all the little trains together and push them around the figure-eight track. "Will is on his track and mine is ... I don't know. I don't even have a track."

Sophie rolls her eyes. "Pity is not a good look on you, Virginia."

I stick out my tongue. "Fine. I just don't see how we can get ourselves on the same track."

"Because?"

"Because," I say, pointing at the train, "infinitely wealthy," and then at myself, "barely getting by."

"Huh. I thought you said the problem was that he wants to live in his city high-rise and you need to live closer to the ground. So the truth is that you're still not accepting you're worthy of all the things your dumbass dad said were too good for you." She stares down at me from her chair.

"No!"

"Yes," she says in little more than a whisper. "You should talk to Nick."

"Why?"

"He changed his name when he was in his early twenties, since his father wouldn't accept his blue-collar life. He gave up everything to follow his heart. Have you even asked Will what he'd give up? Have you made a list of the things your are willing to let go of for once-in-a-lifetime love?"

"Argh! I hate that you're so young *and* so smart."

"I'm putting this guy to bed, and I'll be crashing soon. Go shoot pool with my man. See if he can give you some insight into the male mind."

I walk the half mile down the hill to the firehall. There are a few vehicles in the lot and both trucks are in their bays. I glance up at the second floor and see at least six men moving around.

Including ... I squint and tilt my head to get a better angle.

One that looks like ... no, that's impossible. Sophie would have told me.

Blood pounds in my ears. Colt is here. In Lily Valley. In my safe space. At the firehall. With my friends. Why? And why didn't he tell me when I talked to him two days ago?

I push into the meeting room on the ground floor, storm to the stairs that lead to the pool room, take the steps two at a time, and throw open the door with fire burning in my core.

Music is playing, the larger-than-life television is on, and three guys are staring at the pool table, arguing. I might as well be invisible. My eyes are glued to the back of Colt's head.

Aziz is the first to notice me. "Hey, Virginia! You made it."

Colt turns. Our eyes meet. His mouth drops open.

In what is probably a nanosecond but feels like a long minute, we stare into each other's eyes. My anger turns to elation and then to fury as I realize that the hair does not make the man.

"William Wallace Power, tell me why you're here, pretending to be Colt, or both of you will pay a price far greater than you can afford. I'm not talking dollars—I'm talking *flesh*."

TICKLING THE PINK

"Um, I, um, eh, ahh ..."

I have never before in my life stuttered. Until this moment.

I imagine I sound like a deep-voiced toddler trying to answer why my face is covered in the cake I was told not to touch.

Virginia's hands are on her hips. Her nostrils flare, eyes unblinking. And then she inhales so deeply, she looks like she's trying to double in size. I prepare for the hurricane of expletives, but as she releases her breath, her expression softens, and she smiles.

"It's really you." I read her lips since I can't hear her over the music.

I nod, and she crosses the floor in three long strides and literally jumps into my arms. I bury my face in her hair and whisper, "I've missed you more than you can imagine."

She snuggles closer, holds me tighter. I feel her heartbeat against my chest. I push aside her wild curls and run my thumb over her lips. She opens her mouth, grabs my index finger with her teeth, and runs her tongue across the tip. My body lights up. As much as I want to respond, I am not one for public foreplay.

When I look up, I see seven pairs of eyes giving us their full attention. Before I willingly give Virginia my flesh, I've got some explaining to do.

Virginia drops to her feet and turns to face the firefighters and Aziz.

Nick is the first to speak. Or try to. He points at us. Tilts his head left. Then right. Opens his mouth. Closes it. Grimaces. Throws his hands up and finally says, "Each to his own, Bro. I'm not judging."

"No, it's not like that," Virginia is quick to correct.

I squeeze her hand, then drop it. When she makes eye contact, I shake my head as subtly as possible and whisper, "Let me explain."

She nods almost imperceptibly. But I notice.

"I'm not sure what you think you see, but as trained professionals who understand the importance of client confidentiality, I'm requesting you treat this, whatever it is you *think* you just saw, whoever it is you *think* I am, the same way you'd treat a medical response to a well-known person." I look around the room and make direct eye contact with each of the men I've been lying to about my identity.

"No crime has been committed, but reputations could be put at risk if my presence here was to be found out. Can I have your assurance that what you *believe* just happened was, perhaps, a drunken hallucination?"

"Dude, what happens in the firehall, stays in the firehall, right guys?"

Nick nods. The other firefighters agree.

And Aziz, though he looks utterly confused, says,

"Power secrets go to the grave, sir." Adding after a pause, "Mr. Colt."

"Thank you. James, please stay and enjoy the evening. I'd appreciate at least two hours alone with Virginia before you return to the house."

My security detail nods his understanding and without another word, I walk toward the door. Virginia is right behind me. She tries to kiss me in the stairwell, but I shake my head. "Not here." But once we're in the empty meeting room on the first floor, I take her in my arms and we kiss like nobody's watching.

"As much as I want to throw you over my shoulder and carry you back to the house, I need you to pretend I'm Colt while we're in public. I'll explain it all once we're home."

Virginia moans. "It's a fifteen-minute walk. Not even holding hands? I don't think I can do that, Will. "

"You don't know how happy that makes me. But this is a really critical 'short-term pain for long-term gain' situation."

Turns out Virginia is a damn fast power walker. We make it up the mile-long hill from the firehall to the house at the edge of the community in under ten minutes. She's breathing hard, but not as heavily as I plan to make her pant.

"Shower and then I'll explain everything," I say, opening the door.

She stops at the entryway and puts her hands on her hips.

"No," she says.

"No?"

"No," she repeats.

My heart drops into my gut and my abdominal muscles twist until I feel like I might have to dial 9-1-1.

"Virginia," I plead.

"A five-minute shower, one hour and forty-five minutes of love making. And then we can talk." She steps through the doorway. "But I already understand."

My stomach releases my heart and it bounces back into my chest so hard it forces all the air from my lungs. I exhale a month's worth of tension.

Virginia grabs my hand and pulls me upstairs. She tries to enter the master bedroom, but when I block her, she looks panicked.

"Seriously, Will, I forgive whatever lie you told. You don't have to explain."

I laugh, relief rolling over me in waves. "It's not that. I gave this room to James. I couldn't bear being in it without you. We're down the hall."

The shower takes much longer than five minutes, but that's okay because as soon as our clothes are off and our bodies are pressed together, Virginia could have been reciting the news from Podunk, USA and I'd still have been in my version of heaven.

I soap and wash every inch of her body, never taking my eyes off her curves and her freckles, her small scars from misadventures of youth and the spot that I know when my tongue touches just right will make Virginia squirm.

"All clean," I say, feeling some regret at having to stop this focused attention.

"My turn."

Virginia does me. And then, with just one word, she undoes me.

"Mine," she whispers against my ear.

I shut off the water and step out of the shower first,

wrapping her in a towel and drying her. "Don't move a muscle," I order, "because you're mine, and tonight I am going to make damn sure you know it all the way to the core of your being."

Virginia shivers. "I love it when you own my core."

I slap her ass. "Bed."

She pauses and stares at me. Then she holds her hands horizontally, as if to frame the top and bottom of my face.

"It's too weird. The hair, the beard. Can you take them off?" she asks.

I shake my head. "The hair requires some magic super-power *un*glue. And the beard? It's actually mine. But I am not willing to shave right now because my beard has a deep desire to rub itself against your inner thighs and it will not hear of missing that opportunity."

I lift the foot of the duvet and tug Virginia's legs. She slides toward me and I drop to the floor, putting the crooks of her knees over my shoulders. With her calves on my back, she pulls us closer, so the heat of my breath pushes back to me from the warmth of her sex.

I press the tip of my nose just above her clit and my lips against her soft skin. Her hips arch forward in invitation. But I want to spend as much time here as she'll allow, which means taking it slowly, not getting greedy. I tilt my head so my chin touches her inner thigh. She squirms and squeals.

"It's ticklish!"

I press my mouth hard against her and growl while my tongue starts to explore her soft curves and sexy crevices. When I lick her opening, she responds with a moan followed by a flow of fluid that tells me, weird, ticklish beard or not, Virginia is present. She is comfortable and feeling safe, and that is all I need to stop holding back.

I spread her wide with my fingers and lap in long, flat-tongued strokes. I can feel the shape of her change and her lips get fuller as her blood seeks my attention.

"Will," she stutters.

I look up her body. She's squeezing her breasts and pinching her nipples. Her eyes are closed and her mouth is open.

"Fu-uck." I had planned to spend an hour here, between her legs, but this is an invitation I can't turn down. First, I have to make her come.

I insert two fingers and pulse them the way I've learned drives her wild while my tongue vibrates on her clit. Her contracting inner muscles and how she's pressing her hips as close to my face as she possibly can tell me she's silently pleading for me to finish the job.

Within a second of feeling her lose all control, Virginia rolls away, pulling my fingers out and my tongue off of her shaking body.

I feel like we're good.

I hope we're good.

I need to know we're good.

"Virginia ..." I slide into the bed beside her.

She presses herself to me, so our hearts are touching.

"You came back. For me."

"I came back. For us."

40. *Will*

A FAKE FLOWER IN FULL BLOOM

The next day, I negotiate renewing the rental with the owner and also pick up the cost to upgrade a VRBO for the people that Virginia and I displace by staying in this house that she loves and where I feel comfortable enough to relax. We lie low, out of the public eye, for weeks.

Derek, the chef, agrees to stay as long as his partner can join us. Aziz asks to be assigned to day coverage in Lily Valley, which I'm thrilled about since I can't spend as much time on the hiking trails as Virginia would like, being in the midst of reworking the Power Industries business plan.

Everyone is happy, but no one is as happy as I am.

Virginia and I establish a routine that fuels and fulfills both our needs. We let the sunlight wake us, which means we're sleeping until eight a.m., unheard of for me. It feels decadent but also sensible, since Virginia has helped me understand seasonal energy cycles. As the days shorten, so does my workday, but my productivity has remained equal, if not better.

"It's because you've stopped fighting nature," she says.

That may be, but I'm also sleeping a solid seven hours without waking. The threat of nightmares is a distant memory.

We wake, spend thirty minutes fueling our physical touch tanks—otherwise known as having full-contact sex— eat a healthy, gourmet breakfast, and then work for a few hours until lunch is served at one.

We all have dinner together—James, Aziz, Derek and his partner, Jim, join us like some modern upstairs/downstairs amalgamation.

Since Virginia has asked everyone in the house to respect a digital sunset by eight p.m., our evenings are filled with board games, card games, and so much laughter, I don't miss my abs workout bench at all.

By ten thirty, we're in bed. Virginia and I take turns reading to each other. I don't remember being read to as a child, but Mom insists she did and that it was my favorite time of day. I don't doubt it since nothing beats the quiet, focused attention.

As for work, Virginia has hired a new contract employee to take on her role in my building and needs to be in the city once a week to visit Mr. Bernard and his greenhouse. I arrange my in-person meetings on the same day so we commute in together, drop her off in the British Properties (so nobody from the office sees "Mr. Colt" with Will's woman), and then Aziz meets her there and brings her back to Lily Valley when her work is done.

At least, until three days ago, last Thursday, and the Vancouver delivery of the Come Into Power seminar, which I led with Aiden and some appearances from Horse.

The tour has wrapped up without one request for a refund. A first since I've never gone an entire season without pissing off at least one person. Even better, Horse and Aiden's combined energy on stage has increased our applications into the executive coaching program by ten percent—and when you're dealing in hundreds of millions of dollars, those small percentages make a big impact on the bottom line.

The nonfamily board members are happy, and that makes me happy since, even though we came clean and admitted the ruse we'd played on over 50,000 paying clients, I've got everyone's unanimous blessing to retire as the face of the company.

Virginia's been front row-center in the seminar all weekend, encouraging me with her unfaltering support and smile. And today, in the last coaching session, I have a surprise I've been dying to tell her about.

Horse and Aiden finish their motivational cheerleading to loud applause from 1300 entrepreneurs. I jog onstage and high-five my brothers.

"Give it up for Fire Power, a.k.a. Aiden," I yell.

Cheers rise and a woman's voice carries over the crowd. "I love you, Aiden!"

Aiden blows kisses toward the audience.

"And for Colt, who we all know and love as Horse Power!"

The applause increases. My brothers bow and step off the stage. The cacophony quiets.

"For anyone who's ever been to a Come Into Power seminar before, you know that this delivery was different from previous years."

A chorus of voices, overlapping one another, fills the air: "It was amazing!" "Best ever!" "I want more!"

"What you might not know is that this is my last time onstage." I hold up my hand to stop the chatter so I can continue. "That means this will be my very last public coaching session. The person who is called up next will be part of Power family history."

A dozen or more men stand, ready to storm the stage.

"Thank you for your enthusiasm." I laugh. "But it has been my commitment to ensure the final coachee I bring up is always a female entrepreneur. And today will be no different." I hold up a finger. "Except for one thing. Today I know exactly who I'm calling on."

Now a dozen women press their chests forward and lift their chins, virtually vibrating in their seats. Virginia turns to look into the crowd. When she turns back, she's laughing and gives me a thumbs-up.

When I point at her and say, "Let's make history together," her expression changes from delight to "Oh, no you don't!"

She crosses her arms in front of her green, plant-patterned dress and shakes her loose curls to say no. She looks as wild and gorgeous as the first day we met. Her reaction doesn't surprise me, so I'm prepared. I wave offstage.

Savannah, Horse, and Aiden walk on, holding sad specimens of potted plants.

"Virginia Beach, founder and owner of The Other Side of the Fence, will you please come to the stage and tell me what this hotel has been doing wrong with these plants?"

She bites her bottom lip and shakes her head, but her eyes are laughing as she stands and crosses to the stairs as my brothers and Savi place the plants behind me. My brothers leave.

"Almost ten months ago, I called this entrepreneur to the stage as my last coaching victim of the seminar. She truly was a victim since I gave her the gears in a way I'd never challenged a coachee before. Am I exaggerating?"

Savannah hands Virginia a mic and walks off.

"You really were an asshole," Virginia says, prompting great laughter.

"I was. It's true." I squeeze her hand, then let it go and face the crowd. "And do you know why I was such a jerk? Because in the few minutes she was onstage with me, Virginia 'Rainforest' Beach triggered an inner knowing that I'd been ignoring my entire adult life. She touched me, literally and figuratively, and my world collapsed.

"I humiliated her on stage, in front of a thousand people, because I was shit scared of what I felt in those three or four minutes with her. I didn't want to see what her passion for her tiny business, a business caring for people by caring for their plants, was forcing me to look at."

I turn to face Virginia. Her eyes are glassy, so I hand her the hanky from my pocket.

"And then what happened?" I ask her.

She looks at me like a deer in headlights. "Really?"

I nod.

"Will, Mr. Power, covered my beautiful dress in the jacket he was wearing. I wore it home and found a golden ticket to his executive coaching program in a secret pocket, and ..." She pauses, her eyes are wide; I pick up the story.

"And she bluffed her way in, folks! She stepped up and owned her potential, claimed her place, accepted the opportunity that was put in her hand. Had she earned it by regular methods? No. Did she prove she deserved it? Yes, she did, one hundred percent.

"Virginia, what fueled your confidence to step into that space?"

"Um ... I figured I had nothing to lose by taking the risk."

"Yes, and,"—I look out to address the crowd directly— "if you're not convinced that affirmations work, try repeating this one every time you face a situation that makes you question whether you'll succeed."

I look back at Virginia. She gets it. She pulls the mic to her mouth and looks out at the crowd.

"You all know this one. Ready?" Virginia pauses, then raises her fist and says, "I am a winner."

She holds the mic toward the audience, and a thousand people repeat the phrase.

"I am making shit happen!" Her enthusiasm and belief in that statement are contagious.

The echo from the auditorium is twice as loud.

"Nothing will stop me from success."

The roar of people yelling these words is accompanied by clapping and foot stomping.

Not at all what I was expecting or shooting for, but I know this enthusiasm will drive more applications to the coaching program, which will keep the board happy, which is great since I'm about to go even farther off-script.

I raise my arms above my head, and the crowd settles.

"Virginia, Ms. Beach, mentioned a 'golden ticket.' For those of you not familiar with Willy Wonka, that is her charming way of referring to my gold business card."

Laughter and applause.

I take off my jacket and nod to Virginia to turn around so I can help put it on her.

"Does she look better in my suit?"

The unanimous consensus from the crowd is no, she does not.

"Power Family Industries, formerly Will Power & Bros., was founded by my great-grandfather over sixty years ago. My father passed on the leadership to me and my three brothers. And we've been growing this enterprise for over twenty years, following the same market model that was created in the 1950s, when society deemed the best jobs for women were in the home, supporting her husband."

I turn from the crowd and address Virginia. "As a successful entrepreneur who had a goal of doubling your business income to live a more comfortable life, how well did our coaching program do? You can tell the truth."

"It was amazing at first. I was able to achieve that goal within three months and was really happy."

"And then?"

"And then my coach insisted my business had the potential to grow to twenty times its size. But I didn't want to be that big. I didn't want to lose contact with the part of the work I love most, getting my hands dirty with my clients' plants."

"So ..."

"I quit the program."

Gasps, followed by a few men who call out they'll gladly fill her spot.

"People, our executive coaching program has a ninety-eight percent success rate. You set a goal that your coach supports, and you will achieve it. The two percent who didn't hit their targets all have one thing in common: the business targets they were aiming at weren't theirs. They'd been coerced to shoot higher, but that's not what the entrepreneur wanted.

"And all of those previously considered failures were female entrepreneurs. Virginia Beach, founder of The Other Side of the Fence, taught me, the *formidable* Will Power, that my world view was in great need of broadening."

I signal offstage to let Aiden and Horse know that they're up. They jog out and move in beside me.

"I'm leaving you in the highly capable hands of my

brothers to wrap this up and let you know how to join either our traditional Power Broker coaching program or the beta delivery of our brand new Holistic Power program, designed for entrepreneurs who prioritize life balance over bank balance."

The crowd is quiet at first. I hear voices repeating "life balance over bank balance" and then one rises above the rest. "Where do I sign up?"

Aiden answers without missing a beat. "Anyone who wants more info about the new program can meet me in the bar once we're done, and I'll give you all the details."

I take Virginia's hand and lead her offstage to the green room.

"Why didn't you warn me that you were going to call me onstage?"

"Honestly, I didn't know I was going to until an hour ago. It was a spontaneous decision. When I thought about inviting up any other woman with you sitting right in front of me, I couldn't do it."

"You took a big risk telling everyone that I snuck into your program and then dropped out."

I shrug. "Maybe. It's only business."

"How do you feel, knowing that's the last time you'll have to stand onstage?"

"I feel good. But there's something I feel even better about. Check the secret pocket in the jacket."

Virginia squints at me.

"The gold business card pocket?"

"In this case, I think *golden ticket* is appropriate, because I feel like I won the lottery when I chose you from the crowd."

She pulls out a gold business card. On quick glance, it looks like the same card she used to get into the coaching program. She looks confused and then flips it over and reads it out loud.

"Will Wallace ... VP of Miscellaneous Stuff ... Lily Valley."

She looks up at me with her mouth open. Speechless, apparently.

I pull a similar card from my pants pocket. It's gold with green foil text. I hand it to her. She doesn't read it out loud, so I do.

"Virginia Beach, The Other Side of the Fence, Lily Valley."

"I don't understand."

"I bought the house," I say with a nod.

"The house?"

"The house in the town that's your favorite place on earth."

"You're moving to Lily Valley full-time? For real?"

"*We're* moving to Lily Valley full-time. For real—if that fits into your business development plan."

"We're staying in Lily Valley," she repeats as a tentative statement. "We're staying in Lily Valley!" she squeals, jumping into my arms. "I love you, I love you, I love you!"

It's been twenty-seven days since Will told me he'd bought the house in Lily Valley. And for the last twenty-five, we've been living back at the condo while carpenters did their carpentry thing to turn a nice five-year-old monster house into a home fit for a billionaire.

I've been back to our soon-to-be new home twice with measuring tapes and color swatches and an interior designer at my side.

I cannot express how much joy I got choosing furniture with Will. Our couch, our bed, the patio swing and fire table. The rugs and artwork and paint colors for the walls. And it was like a fantasy come true having Derek-the-chef work with me to design the renovated kitchen and then shop for all the appliances he'd buy for his own dream cook space.

I feel like I was told to create a vision board of my perfect home and then a fairy godmother waved her magic wand over it to bring it to life. Only my fairy godmother came in the form of a grumpy, workaholic, fatalist billionaire.

But the twist is that I have a magic wand, too. And now the forehead crease between Will's eyes is less obvious because the laugh crinkles beside his eyes are getting deeper by the day. It makes me love him more and more.

We pull into our driveway—just the thought that this house has my name on the property tax bill makes me giddy —and even the cold December rain isn't dampening the tingle that's running through all my nerves.

"Are you as excited as I am?" I bounce in my seat.

Will turns off the ignition and looks from me to the house and back again. "You know, I am."

I lean over the middle console and kiss him.

"Welcome home," he says. "Now, let's go christen every room so your energy is all we can feel from now on."

Everything has already been moved in—our clothes, food, everything—so we step out of our new Tesla (since becoming commuters was a good excuse to buy a new car, Will said) and Will nudges me to punch in the code to open the front door.

"No key!" I squeal like a crazy fool.

Will laughs and kisses my head.

"What? I'm allowed to appreciate the small things!"

"Hold your squeals for the big surprise."

I rub my hand down the front of his pants, just below his belt.

"That's not the surprise I was thinking about, but you could persuade me to show you that one first."

We step into the newly renovated entry. The floors have been sanded and are now a honey color of hardwood with a polish that shines. I pull my palm from Will's promise and cover my face as I look around the living room. The walls are a warm, sea foam green that brings the spirit of the forest into the house.

"Do you love it? I love it so much. It's ... I can't believe how great it looks. For the first time in my life, I feel like I'm in a house that fits me."

Will wraps his arms around my body and pulls me against him. Against his ...

"Oh. Oh my." I press my bum against the growing bulge. "Shall we try out the new couch, see if—"

Before I finish my sentence, Will grabs the hem of my hoodie and in one fluid motion, pulls it over my head, only to find a T-shirt. And then a tank top.

He growls.

"What? I was cold." I laugh.

I push my hands under his T-shirt, over his chest and feel the heat radiating off his body. My man pushes himself away and holds me at arm's length. His eyes bore into mine with an intensity that makes me shiver. "Cold?"

I shake my head. "I'm only *half*-naked."

"That won't do." Will pulls me toward him and scoops me into a cradle hold. I assume he's going to carry me upstairs to the bedroom, but he walks past the stairs toward the back of the house.

"Where are you taking me?"

"To your surprise."

We pass the kitchen, which I can only glance at. We pass the guest bedroom and the laundry room and he carries me down the hall to the door that opens to the private back-yard. I squirm and try to get out of his grip.

"It's too cold, Will. Don't open the door," I beg.

He holds me tighter. "You'll survive."

"My nipples will break off. How will you explain that at the hospital?"

"Trust me. I would never put your nipples at risk. Close your eyes."

"Fine." I relax again and let him open the door without struggling. But the cold, wet December air I was expecting doesn't hit me. I sneak a peek with one squinty eye and see a glass roof overhead. "Will, what is this?" Both eyes are wide open now.

He drops me to my feet and I feel heat. The ground isn't dirt or wet grass, it's polished concrete and it's warm. We're in an enclosed tunnel that connects to—

"A greenhouse? You built me an entire greenhouse?" I squeal and rush into a large room that's made entirely of glass and metal, stand at the entrance and look around in awe. Will has brought in several dozen plants that sit on chrome potting tables. I listen and look for the source of the sound that registers. "Is there ... is there a fountain in here?"

He takes my hand and leads me around a collection of plants and potted trees to the far side of the room where a five foot tall sculpture of a bonsai tree stands. Water cascades from each individual cluster of leaves.

"Will ..." I can barely breathe.

"It's made of copper and bronze," he says.

"It's the most beautiful thing I've ever seen."

He takes my hand and leads me to a small plaque on a wood stand. I read in a whisper, "Let this fountain be a testament to the power of love that endures beyond all obstacles."

Will raises his eyebrows, as if to ask, "Do you like it?"

I pull his face to mine and our lips crash together. He takes control of the kiss. His hands are everywhere at once, pulling me close, tugging at my jeans, trying to undo my bra. Electricity sparks. I press my hand against the bulge in Will's pants and try to unzip him.

He takes my hand, presses a kiss to my palm. "Not here. I have one more surprise."

"Please, Will. I want to make love here. This is paradise."

"I'm not arguing that or suggesting we leave." He takes my hand and leads us to a folding privacy screen. He folds back one panel. Then a second.

A wood table, covered in baby evergreen branches and moss, fills the space. A pile of wool blankets and what look like hemp pillows are stacked on a small shelf to the right of the table.

"I made sure the builders didn't pour concrete in this area. Look." He points at the floor. "It's the same rock that makes up the whole mountain. It's from the property. It's granite—"

"Shut up you beautiful man, and make love to me."

Will pauses. "Virginia, I've never been happier than I am right now. And that's saying something since the last year with you has been the best of my life. I can't imagine a future—hell, I don't want to even imagine a day without you and your wild hair and hippie earth magic and calming energy wrapped around me."

The Disneyland-worthy fireworks that ignite in my abdomen are anything but calm. My heart dances and that voice of doom that I thought I'd always have with me—the one that whispered I'd never be good enough for a man like Will—it shakes its little head, sighs, and floats away.

SAVED BY DAYLIGHT SAVINGS

Six months later

It's been a little over a year since I stood in this hallway with Virginia, looking at the wall of the Power men photos.

"Last time I was standing here," she says, "I was so overwhelmed by everything, your mom's orchid and having just spent the night with you, that I didn't register that there are no pictures of your mom here. Seems … wrong."

"There used to be, when we were kids—before Horse, Brian, Aiden and I needed so much room," I laugh.

"It's not funny, Will. It's sad."

I take her hand and push open Mother's bedroom door. "She's never shown you the room she calls her study, has she?"

Virginia shakes her head.

"It was a closet when Dad was alive and Mom needed a thousand pairs of shoes for all the events they attended. But a couple of years after he died, she got rid of all his clothes and most of hers, too."

I push open what should be a walk-in closet door. The lights come on automatically and I lead Virginia inside.

The room is easily twenty feet long and ten feet wide. The clothes portion is limited to a small section right near the entrance. But beyond that, the space has been transformed into a museum and gallery of the love and life my parents shared for not nearly as many years as they deserved to have together.

The walls are covered in non-studio photos taken on family holidays. Mom and Dad are never together in the early ones, but once Horse and I were old enough to get cameras of our own at about age six, that's when badly composed shots of their love start appearing.

Virginia points to random photos and I do my best to remember where we were when they were taken. She sniffles, then drops my hand to wipe her eyes.

"What's wrong?" I ask, confused at why she'd be sad.

"Nothing. I'm just moved." She points to the gold brocade fainting loveseat beside a small table with a reading lamp. "She comes here to read?"

"And talk to Dad."

Virginia looks up at me, eyes glassy. "Do you ever come in here to remember old times? Or, you know, talk to your dad?"

I exhale a hard puff of air. How to say this without sounding defeatist?

"When I was in my twenties, I would. Less in my thirties. And honestly, this is the first time I've stepped foot in here since I turned forty."

"Because?"

I point around the room, but keep my eyes focused on the discreet urn Mother has placed atop a small bookshelf. "When I was younger, in my twenties, I saw my future on these walls. I always thought I'd have what they had one day. But in my thirties, seeing how losing Dad crushed Mom's spirit, I came less ... once I started to look as old as Dad does in his last pictures ..." I hope she doesn't need me to finish the sentence.

"Will." Virginia steps into my line of sight, takes my face in her hands, and makes intense eye contact. "There is no reason to believe you won't have photos on the wall in your mother's hallway for another forty-three years or more."

"Mm," I grunt.

"Will."

"What?"

I lead Virginia out of my mother's sanctuary, back to the public and posed photos, and point with two index fingers to mine and Colt's birth certificates. She looks up and nods.

"It was predestined. I know you don't like to hear it or want to believe it, but unless you have the power to change those, Virginia, I know it's not logical, but I just can't simply turn off a belief I've had for more than half my life."

"But you have been changing it, little by little, day by day, since we moved to the most perfect place on earth."

She is right. I have become less fatalistic. I don't expect to be dead in a year anymore. But I also have no reason to believe I'll still be driving her crazy in all the best ways in forty, thirty or even ten years. That's just not William Power's fate.

Virginia has been staring at the wall and bursts out a loud, "Will!" Her eyes are wide and she looks like she's seen a ghost in the birth certificates. "Will take them down. Take them down!"

Virginia grabs the two frames from my hands and virtually runs back to the living room where Mother and my brothers are eating birthday cake to celebrate Aiden's thirty-eighth birthday.

"What's going on?" Aiden sidles up beside her.

I close in on her other side so I can see what she's looking at.

"Shh." Virginia waves us away, then pulls her phone from a pocket in her vulva flower dress. She taps the keyboard quickly and pulls up a search result for the day and year Horse and I were born.

She taps each frame right over our times of birth, then waves her phone in my face. Virginia starts to laugh. She's laughing with her head flung back and with a joy like she's standing in a summer rain after a drought.

"Virginia!" Mother snaps. "Settle down. What's so funny?"

It takes her several breaths, but she manages to collect herself. "I'm sorry. It's actually not funny." She bites her lip, clearly trying not to laugh.

"Maureen, do you remember anything unusual about the day Will and Colt were born?"

"Virginia, get to the point."

She waves her phone at my mother. "They were born on the first day after Daylight Savings Time ended. I mean, one of them was."

"Okay," Mother says.

Horse, Brian and Aiden have all pulled out their phones and are busy tapping.

Brian pushes me out of the way and looks at the both certificates. "Holy shit," he mutters.

"Right?" Virginia replies, breaking into laughter again.

"What?!" Aiden, Horse and I all yell.

Virginia taps my birth certificate. "It says you were born at 1:30 AM. And that Colt was born at 1:52 AM PST."

"Yeah, twenty-two minutes after me," I say, confused.

"No, bro," Brian says. "Yours doesn't say PST. That means Colt was born ..." His lips move silently. "Colt was born thirty-eight minutes *before* you!"

"Right?" Virginia repeats. "Am I right?"

"I think you're right," Brian says. "Holy shit. Holy shit."

Then there's silence and the penny drops. "I was never supposed to be Will Power." I point at Horse. "You're the fucking rightful Will Power. You sneaky baby bastard!"

"William Wallace Power!" Mother chastises.

"Not it!" I point at Horse, then I start to laugh with Virginia.

"Wait a minute," Horse says, getting up in my face. "You stole my job? You stole all that fame from me? I should have been the one getting all the applause?" He gives me a hard, but friendly, punch in the chest. "You're the sneaky baby bastard."

"Colt Carter Power, enough!"

"I have no idea why you're yelling at me," Horse says. "My name is Will."

The party takes an unexpected turn and I join everyone in drinking champagne. Virginia and I decide to spend the night in the city, something we don't do often but makes sense given how much we've both had to drink.

Virginia is already in bed when I collapse beside her.

"How are you feeling?" she asks.

"A little tipsy, but not so much that I can't perform." I roll up on an elbow and move to straddle her.

She gives me a gentle nudge. "That's not what I mean. Emotionally, how does it feel to know you were *never* the one who was *supposedly* cursed? That you don't have a predetermined expiry date. And you never did."

I scrub my beard—the one I've let grow since becoming a mountain man in Lily Valley.

"Do you feel different?" she asks.

"I don't have an expiry date," I repeat. "I don't know yet. It's strange to even consider. And maybe kind of maddening, too, that I spent all those years worrying about something that was never mine to worry about."

"I don't think that's quite accurate. When I met you, you actually did have lots to worry about, Will. You really were living like a man who was doing everything in his power to be dead by forty-four."

"Yeah, I guess that's true. And as fucking amazing as the last year has been, and how well I sleep now, I've still been carrying around this, I don't know, weight that it could all come crashing down any day."

"Do you think now you might be able to put that weight down?" she asks.

"I'd like to. That's for damn sure."

"I have an idea that might help."

"Sex?" I waggle my eyebrows.

"If sex hasn't worked for the last ..." Virginia scrunches her nose, the way she does when she's thinking, "six hundred or so times, I wouldn't put my money on it."

I give her my best pout.

"Not saying I'm not willing to try," she says, "but I was wondering if maybe now you'd be ready to get a puppy? Make a commitment to picking up dog poop for the next fifteen years ..."

I roll onto my back and can't help but laugh. "It's as if you've learned nothing from your stint in the Power Broker

Program or having listened to sixteen thousand episodes of The Will Power Hour. Your sales pitch sucks."

We lay in silence and I realize that I do feel different. More hopeful. Lighter. I have a conversation in my head with Virginia. She asks, "What would you do if you knew you had another forty-four years to live?" And my answer is as clear as the flawless diamond that's currently being set in a custom-made engagement ring.

"What kind of puppy?" I ask.

Thanks for reading The Billionaire's Shrubbery. If you're not quite ready to say goodbye to Will and Virginia, I have a treat for you—a bonus epilogue that's only available to people like you, who've read to the end of this story!

Geni.us/Shrubbery-bonus

And, or, read Nick and Sophie's story in their rivals to lovers, small town firefighter romance, *First In: Cheeky With the Fire Chief.*

Geni.us/FirstIn

About the Author

Danika Bloom is a *USA Today* bestselling author who always wanted to be the mom in The Partridge Family or The Brady Bunch, but since she only had one child, she lives out her mom-of-many fantasies in her rom-com series about bands of brothers. *

Danika lives in a tiny village in British Columbia, Canada with her plant whispering husband who never tires of complaining that she spends too much time in her office and should go for more walks.

Visit DanikaBloom.com/books to check out all of Danika's steamy rom-coms and quirky contemporary romance titles. Or use your phone's camera to scan the code below and be taken there like magic:

* **EDITOR'S NOTE:** *Danika, that's kind of creepy ... moms writing steamy rom-com about their sons ... you might want to rethink this bio.*